I0557962

Murder Ignited

Penrose and Pyke Mysteries, Book 6

Rose Pascoe

Published by Flax Bay Books, 2024

Copyright

MURDER IGNITED

ISBN: 978-1991181398 (Softcover POD)
978-1991181381 (Epub)
Publisher: Flax Bay Books, New Zealand

Cover design: Rose Pascoe
Cover images from Shutterstock, Adobe Stock and Unsplash

Contents

Missing Bride

Charlie Pyke slid his watch from the pocket of his new waistcoat. Eleven o'clock on the morning of Saturday, the twenty-first of January, 1893. The beginning of a new life.

Behind him, a gentle murmur of conversation rose and fell in a sea of Sunday-best clothes and familiar smiles, in pews filled to squeezing point. The minister stood ready, radiating serenity. The organist kept an eye on the door, poised to play as soon as the bride appeared.

Charlie's best man checked the rings in his waistcoat pocket for the fifth time. Alistair Stewart had been his commanding officer and mentor, but now he was Charlie's business partner in their private investigation agency. Slim, faultlessly dressed, with the calm confidence of a gentleman in his club, former Detective Inspector Stewart had fooled any number of criminals into thinking he was no threat. In contrast, Charlie's groomsman would never be mistaken for anything other than a policeman. Detective Sergeant Declan Kelly stood at ease, feet apart, hands at sides, biceps at the ready, eyes scanning the crowd for threats from force of habit.

Charlie stared straight ahead, hoping that the snakes writhing in his belly did not show on his face. Deep down, he knew his bride, Grace Penrose, would be here soon. Nothing would stop them getting married, short of kidnapping. The snakes formed a knot. Grace would *not* be kidnapped, he told himself. Their lives might be besieged by murder and mayhem, but *not* today.

He began counting off the seconds to distract himself. Charlie did not relish being the centre of attention. As a private detective, he preferred to be an inconspicuous presence – to the extent that a six-feet tall, broad-shouldered, quarter-Chinese man could be inconspicuous. Last year's feature in the Dunedin Ladies' Journal hadn't helped. He craved anonymity, but teetered on the tightrope between recognition and infamy.

Charlie's count reached three hundred. Grace was now over five minutes late. It felt like five hours. Alistair had warned him that a little tardiness was normal for a bride, but Grace was rarely late when it mattered. The door of the church opened, just a crack. Thank heavens. The organist struck the first notes. Charlie's heart thundered as he turned to see his bride.

A middle-aged, grey-haired woman slid through the narrow gap into the church, obviously hoping nobody would notice her. Everybody noticed – Charlie most of all. The music shuddered to a halt. Miss Newland mouthed "sorry," and slid into a non-existent gap on the nearest pew. As the woman in charge of the day-to-day running of the local women's refuge, Lavender House, no doubt Miss Newland had a good reason for being a little late.

The communal surge of excitement ebbed away. Charlie resumed his count, but lost track when he reached the high eight-hundreds, almost fifteen minutes after the wedding ceremony had been due to start. By then, even Declan and Alistair were shuffling their feet. The minister's lips moved as he whispered a silent prayer. The low murmur in the church had risen to chattering level. Charlie had the awful feeling that people were glancing his way with that very particular expression of embarrassed sympathy he loathed. He kept his eyes averted.

Charlie's heart told him only the direst of catastrophes would stop Grace from walking down the aisle. Perhaps she had torn her gown in her haste to get to the church, or her great-aunt, Anne Macmillan, had had another fall? Anne, the director of Lavender House, was in her seventies and increasingly frail of body, but as sharp as ever of mind and tongue. Grace's other attendants were Charlie's Aunt Lily and Grace's best friend, Molly Ravenwood. A crusader in her seventies, a tiny middle-aged half-Chinese healer, and an eight-month pregnant woman. Grace Penrose was never conventional in her choices.

The door slammed open so forcefully it crashed against the wall, sending reverberations around the church.

A young man stood in the doorway, his cap askew. "Lavender House is on fire!"

Able-bodied men leapt to their feet and rushed from the church. The wooden buildings of Dunedin could burn to the ground in less than an hour, taking their neighbours with them. Older guests dipped their heads in fervent prayer, their memories etched with the horror of the catastrophic 1879 fire in the Octagon as if it was yesterday.

Charlie stripped off his black morning coat, not wanting to damage a new garment. As he followed the exodus, two thoughts crossed his mind. First, please let all the women staying in the refuge be safe. And second, would this be the only wedding in memory where neither the bride nor the groom were there?

Abandoned Gown

Grace Penrose tried not to look at her abandoned wedding gown, draped over a chair in her room at Anne Macmillan's house. Her gaze slipped sideways to the mantelpiece clock. Five minutes to eleven o'clock. She was going to be late. Very late. Grace hated being late for important events. Being late to her own wedding counted as excruciating torture.

She cursed herself for falling into the trap of believing her wedding would be perfect. And so it had seemed, until now. The families had arrived safely and showed every sign of forming a bond of friendship, as well as kinship. Grace's tearaway brothers had behaved perfectly (under threat of being shipped to a remote speck of rock in the icy southern ocean). Even the morning had dawned brightly after days of rain.

And now the clock ticked relentlessly towards the hour and her abandoned gown mocked her. Grace imagined her beloved Charlie Pyke waiting at the altar, growing increasingly alarmed. He would be worrying she had been kidnapped, or, worse still, worrying she had decided not to marry him.

Molly moaned. Grace switched her focus back to her best friend. In all the time Grace had known Molly, her friend had always been cheerful and strong. Now, she was hunched on a bed, rivulets of sweat streaming down her pallid skin, staring at Grace with terror in her eyes. A wedding could be delayed, but a first baby determined to arrive early could not. Grace held Molly's hand and murmured for her friend to breathe. Molly muttered an oath, which was most out of character. Grace didn't blame her. Another contraction came and went with a drawn-out wail from the patient.

Grace's great-aunt examined Molly with practiced hands. Anne Macmillan had delivered more babies than most qualified doctors would see in two lifetimes. Grace had seen her fair share too, even though she still had another two years before she completed her training at the Otago Medical School.

Anne checked her watch as Molly had another contraction. "Five minutes that time." Like Grace, Anne had stripped off her finery in favour of a smock. Births and white satin gowns did not mix.

Five more agonising minutes passed. The mantlepiece clock downstairs chimed eleven times, with a deep, ominous dong. As the last dong reverberated, the door slammed open and footsteps thundered up the stairs.

"Molly, where are you?"

"In here, Rory," Grace called, with a surge of relief.

Grace had sent her other attendant, Lily Stewart, to get Molly's husband, Doctor Rory Ravenwood. Grace desperately wanted to send Lily to tell Charlie what was happening, but she conceded the priority must go to the father of the baby ruining Grace's wedding day.

Rory rushed to his wife's side, taking over Molly's hand from Grace. He wasn't foolish enough to ask how Molly was feeling, when her face was slick with perspiration and tight with pain. Instead, he wiped her forehead with a cool cloth. "Won't be long now, my darling. How far along is she, Anne?"

Anne looked up from her watch. "Molly's contractions were down to four minutes apart, but they're back to six minutes now. We may have a false labour on our hands."

Grace glanced at the clock again. Even if she dressed straight away, she'd be appallingly late.

Rory saw the direction of her glance. "Grace, we're so sorry to have ruined your wedding day. Lily caught me just as I was leaving for the church. She dropped me here and said she was going to tell Charlie what has happened. Lily will come back to pick you up as soon as she can."

Grace blew out a puff of pent-up breath. Thank heavens Charlie wouldn't be worrying for too much longer. "Babies take precedence, Rory. Charlie will understand." Grace prayed it was true. Her heart ached for the thought of him, standing in front of all their friends and family as the minutes ticked by, feeling abandoned. She scrubbed her hands in the basin of water on the washstand.

"I'll take over here, Anne," Rory said. "while you help our lovely bride back into that beautiful gown."

"Seven and a half minutes apart that time," Anne said, snapping her pocket watch closed. "Your baby has decided a wedding takes precedence, after all."

By the time Anne had helped Grace into her wedding gown and seen to her hair, Molly had regained her normal colour. "Will you ever forgive me, my dear Grace?"

Grace didn't answer. She stood by the window, watching her father and mother get out of the hired landau. Lily was not with them. Her heart contracted. Her father was supposed to be waiting at the church, ready to walk her down the aisle.

Doctor George Penrose knocked before entering. "Lily said Molly is in labour. I've come to assist Rory if he needs it."

"The baby has taken pity on me, Father. We have an aisle to walk down." The stricken expression on her father's face caused Grace's heart to contract again. "What's happened?"

"A fire at Lavender House," her mother said, with all the nonchalance of a person reporting a minor annoyance of no consequence. Three decades of marriage to a doctor and six boisterous children had left Mrs Louisa Penrose with the ability to remain calm and competent in any crisis. "You're not to worry, Grace. We will wait here until the blaze is out. After that, the wedding will proceed as planned." Mrs Penrose gave a mirthless little laugh. "Better late than never, I suppose."

Grace was more like her father than her mother. Slim and dark-haired, with the energy of coiled springs – she and her father both remained calm in a crisis only when busy. She tugged at her veil. "Where's Charlie? Please don't tell me that idiot almost-husband of mine has dashed off to be a hero again?"

Mrs Penrose crossed the room to save the delicate veil from being ripped. "Rest easy, Grace. There are dozens of able bodies eager to help put out the fire. Alistair Stewart will stop Charlie from doing anything stupid on his wedding day. That's what a best man is for."

Grace snorted. "If there is one person more likely to put Charlie Pyke in harm's way than me, it's Alistair Stewart. Get me out of this gown, Mama. I want to be there if Charlie needs medical help."

Her mother touched three fingers to Grace's cheek softly, a gesture that had soothed her tempestuous daughter over the past twenty-three years, from broken toys, to grazed knees, to faithless boys. Grace forced herself to stand still while her mother undid the dozens of tiny buttons down the back of her wedding gown. An hour ago, the gown had seemed the most perfect garment in the world. Now it was a straitjacket, tormenting her frazzled patience.

"Be reasonable, Grace." Her father, this time, using the same soothing tone his wife had used. "A fair proportion of the doctors in Dunedin are at your wedding. Lily stayed to help too. This is one day your medical skills are not needed."

"If the fire spreads quickly, there may be more injuries than doctors to tend them," Grace replied. "We can use the church hall as a temporary shelter."

Grace knew her great-aunt's heart would be breaking at the thought of Lavender House in flames. Anne had established the free medical clinic and refuge decades ago. It was her pride and joy, and her legacy. Grace was on the verge of suggesting her mother stay here with Anne, but Anne had already shaken herself out of her initial state of shock. Anne shot Grace an all too familiar "don't you dare get in my way" glare, before grabbing her medical bag and heading for the door. The thump-thump of her walking stick on the floor brooked no opposition.

11

In the end, they all went. Molly insisted she would be fine sitting in the church hall, while Rory, who was the medical director at Lavender House, tended to the injured with Grace and her father and Anne. Mrs Penrose carefully wrapped the wedding gown in a sheet, ever the optimist, and joined them to help look after the displaced women and children.

Inferno

Charlie smelled the fire before he reached the corner of Maitland Street. Lavender House backed onto the town belt, a wide strip of grass and trees circling the city of Dunedin. One rogue spark and the fire could spread for miles around the city. Yesterday, Charlie had been praying for the unseasonal barrage of rain to stop. Today, he thanked the rain gods for leaving the ground so sodden.

Behind him, the church bells tolled, calling the community to action. Ahead, the siren in the street-side fire alarm box still blared. As Charlie rounded the corner, he saw smoke billowing from the rear of Lavender House, but no flames leaping from the roof, as yet. Hordes of locals, driven by fear, were already working together to douse the fire in the crucial minutes before control became impossible.

A bucket brigade passed water over the row of lavender bushes and herbs to the front door. Two teams of muscled men from the local volunteer fire brigade worked the pumps, pumping water into the hoses snaking up to two men on ladders, who directed the jets of water at the flames through the second storey windows. A throng of young lads and lasses hauled buckets of water from nearby houses to damp down any sparks in the vegetation. Thanks to the quick actions of the local community, the structure appeared largely intact so far, although the volume of smoke surely indicated a level of destruction that would bring tears to Anne Macmillan's eyes.

On the outskirts, a growing crowd gathered, slack-jawed.

Beyond them, a group of men clapped and jeered. One tried to start up a chant, "Burn the witches! Burn the witches!" The other men did not join in, but nor did they stop his vile rant. Protesters regularly gathered outside Lavender House to yell abuse at those who sought refuge within. Men whose beaten wives had run away. Men who distrusted any place that kept them out. Men not used to losing control of their womenfolk, whom they saw as their property.

A tall, broad figure with flaming red hair directed the firefighters in a voice loud enough to wake the dead. Mr Campbell, foreman at the local carriage-works and captain of the local volunteer fire brigade. The perfect man for a crisis. He had saved Grace from an attacker once, to Charlie's eternal gratitude.

As the protesters continued to chant, Campbell bellowed a name and jerked a finger. A bull-sized man left his spot on the pump and ran across the road. The chanting man took one look at the charging colossus and swinging fist, and took to his heels. The avenger was back at the water pump thirty seconds later.

Charlie's groomsman, Detective Sergeant Declan Kelly, veered to the side and collared the protester. A policeman to the bone marrow, he pulled out a notebook and started taking a statement. Declan yelled to a newly arrived constable and directed him to take names of witnesses, starting with the protesters. A wise move, in Charlie's opinion. The protesters had become increasingly aggressive in recent times. Arson would be a leap beyond their normal activities, but it wasn't impossible. As a quick means to shut down the women's refuge, a destructive fire could not be faulted.

Charlie diverted his attention to Miss Newland, who was herding a group of wide-eyed women and sobbing children away from Lavender House. One of the local doctors followed them. Doctor Harvey, Charlie recalled, on seeing his elderly face. Harvey barked a question at Miss Newland, who indicated one of the women.

Doctor Harvey pointed at Charlie. "Bucket of cool water, quick as you can."

Charlie ran to the bucket line and commandeered a heavy enamel basin. In the few seconds he was absent, Harvey had the woman's sleeves rolled up and his own cravat off, ready to use as a cloth to bathe the patient's burns.

"Does she need to be taken to hospital, Doctor Harvey?" Charlie wanted to help, but he was also determined to be sensible. The local folks had the situation under control, so there was no need to barge in and risk making a widow of Grace. Not that she would be a widow, as they had failed to exchange vows. Charlie pushed that thought aside.

The doctor shook his head. "Minor scorching. Cold water will do the trick for starters."

"The church ladies are setting up the hall to take minor injuries and anyone needing respite." Charlie ruffled the hair of a soot-smudged child. "There's a feast waiting for you from an abandoned wedding. Before you go, Miss Newland, can you confirm that everyone from Lavender House is accounted for?"

Miss Newland dashed a tear from her red eyes. "I'm not sure. It's difficult to tell in the chaos. A woman was brought in just before the wedding, which was why I was late. She's not out here with the other Lavender House women, but she was drunk, so she may have wandered off."

A prickle of foreboding raised the hairs on Charlie's arms. "How do you know she is not inside?"

Miss Newland gestured at the young woman with the burn, who also had a black eye fading to purple. "Kathleen raised the alarm and checked all the rooms. She found the drunk woman's room locked, the key gone, and no answer when she banged on the door. I cannot even recall the woman's name, I was in such a hurry to get to the church. I'll never forgive myself if she didn't get out."

"What room number was she in?"

Miss Newland glanced up at the building, fear ravaging her usual imperturbable façade. "Number four, where those flames are coming from."

A hand came down on Charlie's shoulder. "Don't you dare even think of going up there, Pyke." Alistair Stewart's Scottish accent always became more pronounced in a crisis. "Grace would string me up by the sporran if I let any harm come to you today."

"Yes, Uncle Alistair." Since Alistair Stewart had married Charlie's Aunt Lily, this was a legitimate form of address, but only used when Alistair worried unnecessarily about his protégé.

"Good. Have you seen my wife?"

Charlie pointed out Lily Stewart, who was kneeling on the pavement, tending to a bucket brigade casualty. Smoke inhalation, by the dazed look on his face. Charlie had been in a fire before. He knew how quickly smoke could suck the oxygen out of the air, adding to the disorienting effects of a smoke-filled room. His father had saved him last time. Charlie never again wanted to experience that feeling of his brain shutting down, unable to find a way out when he knew the door was only a few paces away.

A ruckus behind him drew Charlie's attention. A woman, with two crying children clinging to her, was refusing to go with Miss Newland and the other women.

Miss Newland beckoned him over. "Mr Pyke, Mrs Coster's son is missing."

The woman looked up at him with desperate eyes. "Have you seen a boy in blue dungarees and a plaid shirt? Six years old, blond hair? Fred Coster's his name. I thought he was outside playing with the other children, but I can't find him."

"I'll find him, don't you worry. Go to the church hall and I'll bring him to you."

Charlie spotted his parents and some of the other wedding guests. He ran over. "We need to find a missing boy. Fred Coster, aged six, blond, blue dungarees, plaid shirt. He could be hiding in the trees behind the house or in the neighbouring gardens." Charlie crossed his fingers and prayed the lad wasn't inside. "Pa, can you alert the bucket brigade and the man in charge, Mr Campbell? I'm going to check around the other side of the house."

Sergeant Thomas Pyke didn't waste time with words. He was off before Charlie finished his sentence.

Charlie sprinted to the far end of Lavender House, where fewer people were gathered. He called Fred's name several times, poked through the hedge between the two properties, and called again. He was about to go into the next garden when a flash of movement from above caught his eye. A small face, topped with an explosion of blond hair, pressed up against the upstairs window. Charlie caught a glimpse of terror before the face disappeared again.

"Stay there, Fred," Charlie yelled. "I'm coming."

Mr Campbell was at the front door by the time Charlie reached it, with Thomas Pyke beside him. Charlie leaned in close to be heard over the noise. "The boy is at the far end of the house on the second storey. I know where to find him."

"Wait," Charlie's father said. He ran over to a woman huddled within a thick woollen blanket and ripped it from around her with the most cursory of apologies. Thomas flung the blanket over Charlie, while Mr Campbell ordered his men to dump two buckets of water over Charlie's head.

"We'll bring one of the ladders around," Mr Campbell said. "Throw the boy out the window if you have to. We'll get another blanket and men to catch him. You too, if necessary. Don't stay inside any longer than you have to."

Charlie's father gripped his arm. "Be careful, Charlie. I'll get that ladder as quickly as I can."

The last thing Charlie heard before he plunged into Lavender House was his mother's scream. He hoped Grace hadn't made a late arrival on the scene.

Smoke filled his lungs as soon as Charlie stepped through the door. Downstairs, the curtains, furniture, walls and ceiling were all black with soot, although the ground floor structure of Lavender House appeared to be remarkably intact, thanks to the determined efforts of the bucket brigade. They had soaked the entire space from floor to ceiling in water, creating a swirling, choking mix of steam and smoke. Wet blankets hung from a cluster of chairs, where embers must have caught and been doused.

A line of buckets passed Charlie as he went up the stairs. For each bucket, a man came back down, minimising the time any one man spent near the heat of the blaze. At the top of the stairs, the heat hit him as a physical blow. A coughing figure emerged from the nearest smoking room with a bucket.

An arm shot out as Charlie moved aside to let the man pass. "It's not safe beyond here. We're keeping the spread of flames at bay in the nearby rooms, while the hoses do their work at the heart of the fire."

Charlie pushed past. "There's a young boy trapped at the end of the building."

The arm retreated. Another bucket of water sloshed onto him before he had time to draw the blanket over his head. "God be with you," a smoke-roughened voice said in his ear.

"Don't come looking if I don't come back," Charlie replied. "We'll go out through the window."

Charlie bent low, but smoke filled the upstairs corridor from floor to ceiling. He took a gulp of air and held his breath, before charging towards the far room. Five paces in, he realised he had underestimated the fire. Black smoke streamed around the edges of a door halfway along the corridor, making it all but impossible to see where he was going. Water gushed under the bottom of the door from the fire hose at the window.

Despite the quick actions of the fire crew, the heat was intense. Charlie paused, but there was no going back. He made a run for it, half-blinded by smoke and steam. Right at the peak intensity of the heat, he stumbled over a mop and bucket. Charlie fell sideways, his head colliding with searing metal on the door. Charlie had time to register the number four before his upper arm burst through the thin shell of charred timber. In an instant, heat scorched through his shirtsleeve, where the blanket had fallen away.

Charlie jerked away from the pain, falling to his knees and gasping for what little air remained at floor level. The smell of fresh floor polish mingled with smoke, ash, and a dash of blessed

18

air. He stumbled to his feet and ran on, towards the last door, his alertness seeping away in a swirl of oxygen-sucking smoke.

The door knob on the last room was hot to the touch. Charlie opened it with a corner of the blanket and burst into the room. Fred Coster lay curled on the floor under the window. Even across a smoke-filled room, Charlie could see that the boy was hurt and dazed. Fred barely reacted to his forcible entry into the room.

Charlie darted towards the boy, babbling a hoarse stream of reassuring words in between coughs and gulps of air. "Fred. I'm Charlie. Let's get you out of here." He heaved up the window, which was swollen and stiff with age. "I can see why you couldn't get this open, Fred, especially with those burnt hands of yours. I'm going to pick you up now and wrap you in this blanket."

Charlie's father appeared around the corner of the house with a long ladder. Mr Campbell held the far end. Together, they heaved the ladder up against the wall. The fire brigade captain reached the top in the time it took Charlie to wrap Fred in the blanket. Charlie passed the boy through the window into safe hands. Taking deep gulps of fresh air, he followed them down the ladder as soon as they reached the bottom. He'd never been happier to reach solid ground, even if his eyes and throat and arm stung like the devil.

Thomas Pyke wrapped his son's good arm around his shoulders and helped him to a waiting cart, on which Lily was already kneeling, dunking the boy's hands in cool water. Two men held the horse's head as its nostrils flared in fear and its hooves skittered on the road, trying to get away from the terrifying smell of smoke.

Thomas Pyke picked up his son – no mean feat, given Charlie's bulk – and placed him beside the boy in the cart. "Take them to the hospital, quick as you can. Charlie, your mother and I will be right behind you."

"Grace?" Charlie croaked, but the surrounding clamour drowned out the question.

"Sip this." Lily put a bottle to his lips and tipped bitter liquid down his throat. "Sip, Charlie, don't gulp. And don't try to speak."

Charlie obliged, gratefully. In the absence of his intended bride, he hoped the medicine would take away more than the pain of his burnt arm. Beside him, Aunt Lily alternated her attentions between the boy and Charlie. The soothing relief of cool water on his burn became his single point of focus as his mind drifted.

Refuge

Grace arrived over thirty minutes late to find the church almost deserted.

Miss Prudence Beechworth, the daughter of family friends, rose from a pew. "Grace, at last. We've all been so worried. Mrs Stewart said Molly went into labour."

"A false labour, as it turned out." Grace glanced around, hoping that Charlie would miraculously appear. "I hope Lily Stewart was able to tell Charlie why I was late. I feel dreadful for keeping my poor fiancé waiting."

"I expect she will have told him by now," Prudence said. "Mr Pyke and the other men had already left to fight the fire when she arrived. Mrs Stewart asked if I would wait here for you while she went to help the injured."

Prudence took her to the church hall, where the wedding breakfast had transformed into a bizarre mix of ashen fire refugees and wedding guests in their finery. Charlie and the other members of the wedding party were nowhere to be seen.

Grace spotted the lady who helped to run Lavender House. "Miss Newland, thank goodness you are all right. Are there any injuries?"

Miss Newland, who was comforting a pair of crying children, looked at Grace with an ominous expression of compassion. "A child had to be rescued." This set off a fresh round of howls from the children. "There now, my loves, Fred will be fine. A brave man went in to rescue your brother. We'll have word back from the hospital soon, I promise."

Grace's heart sunk to her pelvis at the words, "brave man" and "hospital". Alistair Stewart pushed his way through the crowd to

Grace's side. Her heart sank past her ankles when Alistair put his arms around her. "Charlie?"

Alistair tightened his embrace. "Nothing but a wee burn and a touch of smoke in the lungs, Grace. Charlie was only taken to the hospital because the boy he rescued was badly burned. Charlie's parents and Lily are with him. Knowing our Charlie, he'll be demanding the doctors release him immediately, so he can get back here to be with you. You've nothing to worry about."

Grace stepped out of his arms and gave Alistair a look that she hoped conveyed her scepticism. A ruined wedding, a hospitalised bridegroom, and an injured child – not to mention Lavender House in flames – were not what she would call "nothing to worry about".

"Everyone is alive, I mean." Alistair, for once in his life, appeared not to know what to do next. He filled the awkward silence with news. "Lavender House is badly damaged, but still standing, thanks to a quick response from the local community. The city fire brigade has arrived with their steam-powered pump, so the fire will be out soon, although it will take a while to damp down the embers."

Grace closed her eyes and took long, slow breaths. She was glad the boy had been rescued, of course she was, but why did it have to be Charlie, on his wedding day?

Alistair read her thoughts. "I tried to stop him, Grace. But Charlie was the one who spotted the missing boy. He knew the way ..." Alistair must have decided he had said enough, because he opted for distraction. He waved feebly at the tables, where the much-depleted wedding feast was laid out. "Can I, er, get you a plate? Tea? Brandy?"

Mrs Brown – Anne Macmillan's housekeeper-cook – had created a delicious feast, with the help of a large group of friends and family. Dear, kind Mrs Brown adored Charlie, and had great respect for his prodigious appetite. Grace was glad to see the food being enjoyed by those in need, as well as invited guests, but hunger was the furthest thing from her mind.

Grace ached to go to the hospital, but she had to help here if needed. Ash-covered wedding guests steadily trickled into the church hall, but none of them appeared to be injured. She scanned the room, seeing Rory tending to his wife, Molly, who was tucking into a plate of finger sandwiches with apparent relish. Anne and Miss Newland had the Lavender House refugees in one corner, covered in blankets and sipping mugs of tea. They appeared uninjured, but shocked.

Grace's parents hurried across the hall to her. Doctor Penrose reached her first and caught her up in a tight embrace. "We've heard Charlie is fine. He'll be back here before you know it."

"Why don't you greet your wedding guests, Grace?" Mrs Penrose's cheery tone made it sound as if nothing out of the ordinary had happened. "I've sent your brother to the hospital. Mrs Brown has kept food aside for the celebration and wine for the wedding toasts. Your lovely minister says he'll be able to marry you, as long as Charlie is here within the hour. Your gown is in the room at the rear of the hall, all ready for you."

Grace blinked back a tear at the rush of welcome news. Not least her mother's remarkable ability to adapt her carefully orchestrated wedding plan and come up smiling. She hugged her mother close, wishing she didn't live to so far away. Suddenly, Grace was overwhelmed with the desire to have Charlie at her side, saying "I do". She yearned to drink toasts, to indulge in Mrs Brown's creations, to dance and laugh.

To please her mother, and to keep herself occupied, Grace circulated amongst their guests, explaining about the baby-induced delay and thanking everyone for coming to the most unusual wedding of the decade. Half an hour later, Grace was kissing the last of the soot-smudged cheeks when a cheer went up. Charlie Pyke stood by the door, surrounded by a crowd of excited guests. He smiled as well-wishers clapped him on the back of his borrowed coat. When a burly fellow punched him on the left arm, Grace saw Charlie turn that peculiar shade of sickly white that often preceded a faint.

Grace rushed to his left side and fended off the crowd. "Away with you. Let my man through."

A woman's voice rose above the clamour. "Let the poor lass get her hands on her husband. Ye cannae blame her, for her man's a hero."

"Not my husband yet," Grace replied. "I'll have to drag him to the altar first."

The crowd laughed and cheered, but they also parted. Grace pushed Charlie forward, steering clear of his arm. Alistair took the other side, with Charlie's rescued morning coat draped over his arm.

Doctor Penrose stepped in behind them. "Would the wedding guests return to the church, please? We'll get the bride ready and be with you shortly."

Grace led Charlie to a small room at the back of the hall, filled with bench seats and folded trestle tables. She sat him down and eased off the borrowed coat over a thickly bandaged arm. His sleeve had been ripped off, but still showed burn marks on the tattered edges. As for his grey trousers and waistcoat, it would take a month of Sundays and a miracle to get the black marks off.

Charlie clutched her hand. "Grace, you're here. Lily said Molly's baby came early."

"Of course I'm here, Charlie." Grace stepped aside to allow more light on his face. His voice sounded woozy, matching his uncharacteristically droopy eyelids. "How bad is it, Charlie? Burns can be utter agony. You looked as if you were about to faint."

"It's nothing to worry about, my darling. Not now you are here. The nurse gave me something for the pain." Charlie's words may have been light-hearted (or, more likely, light-headed), but his brow was wet with sweat and red from the scorching heat of the fire. Even his thick black eyebrows looked odd, curled up and singed at the ends.

Grace considered her would-be husband dubiously. "Are you of sufficiently sound mind and body to get married?"

"There's not a man on earth who could stop me from marrying you, Grace Penrose. Right now, before a plague of locusts descends upon us." Charlie squeezed her hand. "Sorry, Grace. I must look a mess. I tried to clean off the worst of the soot at the hospital."

"Charlie, my love, there is no need to apologise. I don't care what you look like, as long as you are sufficiently conscious to say 'I do' at the appropriate moment." Grace beckoned over the cluster of family who were hovering at a respectful distance in the doorway. "Alistair, can you get the groom to the altar without further heroics? Mother, can you help me into my wedding gown? Brothers, can you help tidy the hall for the reception? We've got a marriage to celebrate!"

Grace's brothers let out whoops. The rest of the wedding party went about their tasks with the efficiency of seasoned military campaigners. Charlie's parents and Alistair swooped in to prepare the groom and take him to the church, while Lily, Anne, and Grace's mother transformed the bride into a vision of white satin and lace.

Within a remarkably short space of time – the minister having noted Charlie's condition and cut to the chase of exchanging vows – Grace emerged from the church on the arm of her husband as a newly married woman, and flung her bouquet to the heavens. Prudence Beechworth used her superior height to nab it, to the obvious delight of the man who was courting her, the police surgeon, James Cranston-Hartfield.

"How does it feel to be Mrs Penrose Pyke, at last?" Charlie whispered.

"I feel like the most fortunate woman in the world, marrying the hero of the hour."

Mrs Penrose Pyke. How odd it sounded, and yet how right. Charlie had surprised Grace by offering to let her keep her own name. He knew she had been looking forward to carrying on a family tradition by becoming the third Doctor Penrose. He even said it didn't seem odd to him, as Chinese women could keep their own name when they married. Grace had been grateful for his thoughtfulness and tempted by the argument, but in the end had decided she wanted to have the same surname as him. Charlie had come up with the perfect compromise. They would do as some wealthy folks did and keep both names. Or, as he had put it, it would be useful to have a second surname as an alias for his detective work.

Grace stretched on tiptoes so she could whisper in the ear of her legally wedded spouse. "Welcome to matrimony, Detective Pyke, or Mr Penrose, or whoever you are."

"Today, I am Charlie Penrose Pyke," he whispered back, "and I am all yours."

Grace subdued a sudden desire to throw her husband into the landau and escape. "Our guests have come from far and wide to help us celebrate. I will have to share you for a few hours yet, more's the pity. I'm not looking forward to all the teasing the unexpected events of the day will heap upon us, but I am looking forward to dancing with my husband for the first time."

Grace was right. Few of the guests passed on their congratulations without making a jest about the happy couple's inability to do something as simple as being in the same place at the same time to exchange vows, without being drawn into medical dramas and daring rescues. Charlie laughed along with them, but Grace couldn't fail to notice that her husband winced every time one of his well-wishers slapped him on the arm or bumped into his left side.

But joy filled the air (along with a lingering odour of burning wood) and the speeches brought tears to the eyes of even the most hardened of policemen and serious of surgeons amongst the crowd. Even Detective Inspector Wallace, whose smile – a mere twitch of the lips – rarely made an appearance, was seen laughing and wiping his eyes.

Doctor George Penrose extolled Charlie's virtues and remembered to thank all the important people during his speech – Anne Macmillan for giving first Grace and now Charlie a home,

26

Lily Stewart for making Grace's beautiful wedding gown, Jasmine Pyke for arranging the flowers, Mrs Brown and her team for the wedding breakfast, his wife for arranging the wedding, and Alistair Stewart for giving Charlie a new life as a policeman and private detective. Charlie's father, Sergeant Thomas Pyke, was similarly complimentary to Grace and her family.

Alistair's speech as best man recalled walking into a police station three years ago to find Grace haranguing a corrupt policeman, while Constable Charlie Pyke tried to keep out of her way. "One of the best days of my life," Alistair declared. "Not only did I gain an exceptional, if rather raw, Detective Constable, but I gained the superb medical skills and investigative talents of Miss Penrose. And now, of course, I have been blessed with a business partner, a wife and a new family, too."

Grace's face ached from smiling, until she noticed that Charlie's smile had become fixed against a background of sickly, pallid skin. With impressive sleight of hand, Charlie's glass dropped below the lip of the table. He added a glug from a medicine bottle hidden in his pocket, while laughing at one of Alistair's jokes. When another toast was called, Charlie drank the contents to the last drop.

She longed to drag him away and strip off his bandage, so she could see just how bad his burn was. Fortunately, they had cleared their schedules to spend time together over the next few days. Charlie would need the time to rest and heal. Grace had imagined spending an unusual amount of time in bed, but this was not exactly what she had had in mind.

When the best man sat down, Grace leaned over to kiss him on the cheek and whisper in his ear. "Lovely speech, thank you, Alistair. Charlie's arm is giving him pain. Do you think we could move on to the first dance? After that, I think it would be best for us to leave."

When the music started, Charlie had to use the table as a prop to get to his feet. Grace took his arm and smiled into his eyes. He leaned on her, his eyes unfocussed. From afar, Grace hoped they presented a perfect picture of blissful newlyweds clinging to each other in devotion.

She drew his head down to hers. "Holy smoke, Charlie, what on earth is in that medicine bottle and how much have you had?"

Fortunately, some deep part of his brain took over for the dance. They twirled slowly around the room, their bodies close. Charlie breathed words of love into her ear, albeit in a rather slurred and disjointed way. Lovely as the dance was, Grace greeted the final notes with relief.

Grace's mother hurried towards them with a knife as long as a sword in her hand. For an instant, Grace stared in horror at the weapon, before realising it was time to cut the wedding cake. She shook her head at her foolishness. What kind of young bride saw a long knife and immediately thought "murder weapon"? As she clutched Charlie's worryingly limp hand and sliced through the beautiful layers of stiff white icing and red fondant roses, Grace vowed to spend less time chasing murderers and more on joyful activities.

Once the cake was cut, Alistair gave them a few minutes to thank their guests, before announcing that the time had come to see the newlyweds to their carriage. Mr and Mrs Penrose Pyke departed to a cacophony of cheers and ribald comments.

The Morning After

Charlie woke up with wool for a tongue and a gong clanging in his brain. He didn't recall coming home. Indeed, he recalled little after dancing with Grace. Sunlight streamed through the windows, taunting his eyes. The short hand on the mantelpiece clock crept towards ten o'clock with painfully loud ticks. With the mental agility of a geriatric tortoise, it occurred to him that he was on the sofa in the drawing room, not in bed with his new wife. He would never live it down if word got out that he had failed in his matrimonial duties on his wedding night.

When Charlie pushed himself upright, he had no trouble recalling that his arm had been injured. Pity he hadn't remembered before putting his weight on it.

Grace appeared in the doorway. "I gather from the shocking oath you have just uttered that my new husband has finally awakened from his drug-induced stupor. I had to prod you occasionally during the night to make sure you were still alive. I must say, dearest, this is not the start to our married life that I have long dreamed of."

Charlie couldn't meet her eye, but he took hope from her tone, which was teasing rather than cross. "Have pity on a wounded hero, wife."

"I can do better than pity." Grace put a tray down in front of him, laden with a glass, pot, cup, covered plate, and medical kit. "Don't worry, Charlie, nobody but me will ever know. The idiot doctor at the hospital should never have given you such a powerful painkiller without strict instructions about the correct dose."

The heady aroma of fresh coffee hit Charlie square in the nostrils. He took the cup and tossed it back. "A nurse insisted I take it when I told her I was leaving the hospital, whether or not she wanted me to. I told her I didn't want to take laudanum, because I didn't want to feel sleepy. She gave me something else, supposedly so mild it's used in children's cough syrup. She did tell me to take only half a spoonful when the pain got too much."

"Half a teaspoon, Charlie, not half a soup ladle. You wouldn't believe what they put in those patent medicines for children. If it's not opium-laced laudanum, it's probably morphine, which is derived from opium. Opium is bad enough, but morphine is highly addictive and lethal in sufficient quantity. Giving it to innocent children and naïve detectives is nothing short of criminal. Medical professionals have been lobbying the government to regulate the use of all opiates, but their demands fall on deaf ears."

Charlie swilled the water until his mouth no longer tasted like the hind end of a sheep, before glugging down the rest of the glass. By the time he had a second cup of coffee in his hands, he felt almost human again. Stupid, but human.

He finally had the courage to look up. Grace's eyes twinkled with suppressed laughter. Her dark hair spilled around her face, falling to the white satin of her dress. "Grace, why are you still in your wedding gown?"

Grace twirled to show him the row of tiny buttons down the back. "Three women got me into the gown and I had nobody to help me out of it. It took all my remaining strength to get you up the path and into the house."

His last remaining vestige of self-respect crumpled. "I'm sorry, Grace. What a disaster."

"Not a disaster at all, my love. You saved a boy's life, we got married, and nobody was murdered. I call that a good day, for us."

"And that's why I love you." Charlie still couldn't believe his good fortune in finding a wife who could laugh off events from which other women would run shrieking. "Come here, my goddess, so I can take off that beautiful gown and make amends to you."

30

Charlie got to his feet and swept his wife into his arms. Fortunately, Grace was slender enough that he could carry most of her weight with one arm, especially when her arms were around his neck, as they were now. She rained kisses down his face and neck, which was deliciously distracting. Nevertheless, he made it up to their bedroom without tripping on the stairs.

Grace slid her feet to the floor. "Charlie, is that a '4' scorched under your hairline?"

"I fell against a numbered door. The smoke was so thick in the corridor, it was impossible to see. Or breathe."

"My hero." Grace's nimble fingers undid his waistcoat and shirt and tossed them aside. She smiled as she ran her fingers over his chest and shoulders, coming to rest over the bandage on his arm. "I need to check your burn before I allow you to risk further pain."

Charlie removed her hand and spun her around to tackle the buttons holding her captive. "Forget the burn, Grace. When people aren't bashing me on the arm, I can hardly feel it." A slight stretching of the truth, but yesterday's lancing pain had died away to a dull throb. The top button slipped through his fingers again. "Darn it, what fool makes buttons this tiny and slippery? It'll take me a week to get your wedding gown off."

"Snip the buttons off, Charlie. Lily is going to remake the gown into an evening dress anyway." Grace wriggled out of his grip and went to the dressing table by the window for her scissors.

The delicate threads holding the buttons fell away one-by-one until the gown dropped to the floor. Charlie took a moment to enjoy the silky softness of his wife's skin before his fingers reached for the laces of her corset.

Grace's muscles tensed. "Oh no! My family is coming up the path. I'd forgotten my brothers have to return to Wellington today." She pulled him away from the window and apologised with an all too brief kiss. "We'd better make haste."

Before he could protest, she'd scooped up her wedding gown, placed it over a chair, and slipped a simple dress over her head. Grace was at the head of the stairs, as outwardly in control as ever, when the bell at the front door rang for the second time.

Charlie closed his eyes and counted to ten, before stooping to open the trunk filled with his belongings, which were still packed after being transferred from his former lodgings. A familiar tingling at the base of his spine gave him a shiver of foreboding. He would have ignored it, but he had come to trust the sensation as a reliable warning of trouble afoot.

He descended the stairs to sounds of laughter from the drawing room. His brother-in-law, Jake Penrose, was making merry at the expense of his sister, inevitably. Charlie paused at the door to flatten his rumpled hair.

"Trust Grace to put a birth above her own wedding," Jake said. "I would have loved to have been there to see your face, sister dearest, when you arrived at an empty church."

"Jake, that's enough," Mrs Penrose said. "I didn't see you dashing into a burning building to save a boy's life. What a terrible pity Charlie couldn't save that poor woman as well. Burning must be a horrible way to die."

Charlie's heart constricted. A woman died?

Doctor Penrose added his voice of reason. "Nobody knew the woman was still in her room. Alistair said it was a miracle Charlie reached the boy. The woman must have perished in the fire long before anyone had a chance to save her. A dreadful tragedy, and nobody's fault, assuming the fire was an accident."

"I talked to one of the firemen," Grace's oldest brother, George, said. "The fire started upstairs, not in the kitchen. On a warm summer's day, the fire was unlikely to have been started by a dropped candle or a spark from a fireplace. Detective Sergeant Kelly thinks a protester lost his head and started the blaze. He had to arrest one of the scoundrels for chanting, 'burn the witches.'"

"Disgraceful," Mrs Penrose said. "Where's that darling husband of yours, Grace? Is the poor man too badly injured to come down and give his mother-in-law a hug?"

Jake laughed. "Or too exhausted."

Charlie summoned his heartiest smile and entered the room. "Morning, everyone. My arm is perfectly fine today, thank you, Mrs Penrose. I trust our quiet little wedding wasn't too dull for you."

"Charlie!" Mrs Penrose enveloped him in an embrace, avoiding his arm. "My favourite son-in-law. We wouldn't have disturbed you, only the boys have to go back to Wellington today."

"We've brought presents," Peter said.

His twin, Paul, rummaged in his bag, scattering clothes out as he hunted for the parcel. "Aha, here it. Open it."

Grace unwrapped the present, a copy of *Mrs Beeton's Book of Household Management*. She swung the heavy tome at her twin brothers' heads, giving them time to duck. "Very amusing, you little devils. I suppose I could use some help on domestic matters."

"It's not for you, Grace. It's for Charlie. He's going to need it with you for a wife." Peter and Paul collapsed in giggles on the floor.

Charlie nudged the nearest twin with the tip of his boot. "I'll have you know, your sister cooked me an excellent breakfast this morning." He hoped they wouldn't notice the abandoned tray, with its untouched plate, on the side table. "But, thank you, boys. I could certainly use a few tips."

"This might be more to your taste, Charlie." George passed over a heavy box.

Grace and Charlie ripped off the wrapping together. George, who ran a business importing scientific instruments, was always to be trusted on the matter of presents. "A microscope," Grace squealed.

"You shouldn't have," Charlie added, as he gently pulled the instrument from its box. "I've longed for one of these. Thank you, George."

"I can't top that," Jake said, handing over two gifts. "This one is from Martha and me, the other is from Luke, who sends his regrets from the depths of some tropical island whose name I cannot recall."

Grace opened Luke's present first. It was wrapped in strong brown paper and covered in postage marks from a faraway land. A family Bible. Jake's present was a music box. "Very amusing, Jake. I've always longed for a music box, as well you know. Will you all stay for tea?"

"We must be going, Grace," her mother said. "We'll see the boys off at the station. After that, your father and I have promised to help Anne with the Lavender House refugees. Anne's gentleman friend, Mr Drummond, has kindly offered his house as a temporary medical centre and refuge, while a replacement is found for Lavender House."

After an extended round of hugs and handshakes, peace once again descended on Charlie and Grace's new home. Grace closed the door on the world and took Charlie's hand. "You overheard, didn't you? My mother was not implying you were at fault. Quite the opposite. She commended your bravery for going into the burning building to rescue the boy."

"Miss Newland told me the missing woman had been put in room four, Grace." Charlie fingered the faint '4' branded into his skin. "I was right outside her door, as she lay inside, dying in agony. I might have been able to save her."

"You know that's not true, Charlie. The smoke and heat nearly overcame you, long after the fire started. She must have been dead before you arrived."

"Logically, perhaps. But isn't there a chance she was still alive?"

"Not a sparrow's chance in a hurricane, my love, and I am going to prove it to you, to set your mind at ease." Grace dragged him back to the drawing room, where her medical kit still sat amongst the wedding presents. She pushed her amused spouse down on the sofa and pulled his shirt over his head. "First, I'm going to check your burn, and then we are going to visit the police surgeon to find out how quickly the poor woman died. After that, we will visit Lavender House to pay our respects."

"And later?" Charlie asked, as expert fingers skimmed his upper arm, unwinding the bandage.

Her fingers trailed across his chest. "And later, once we have set your mind at rest, we are going to lock the door, draw the curtains, and not let anyone else in for at least a day."

Charlie caught her wandering hand, bringing it to his lips. "Make it a week and you've got a deal."

Post-Mortem

Grace had assisted the police surgeon during many an autopsy, but never when the victim had died in a fire. While the smell was not as bad as a corpse found in an advanced state of decay, the stench of burnt flesh was not for the fainthearted. She glanced at Charlie, whose face betrayed a combination of nausea and horror. Grace closed her eyes for a moment, shutting out the blackened remains on the mortuary slab, trying to picture the woman as she might have been while alive. An impossible task, of course, since she knew nothing of the woman, but the ritual lent a touch of humanity to a grim task.

Doctor James Cranston-Hartfield didn't even glance up at their arrival. "Is this your idea of a honeymoon, Grace? After the excitement of your wedding, I thought the mortuary would be the last place you'd want to be."

Grace put on a surgical apron before approaching the corpse. "And good morning to you, Jamie. Charlie had to pass the victim's door while he was rescuing a boy from the fire. It would give him peace of mind to know she was already dead."

The police surgeon looked up from his work. "Rather you than me, Charlie. Fires are unpredictable beasts, spreading fast and flaring up, catching people unawares. However, I can set your mind at ease in this case. The victim was drunk when she arrived at Lavender House. The fire started shortly after her arrival and the poor woman was dead before she could rise from her bed."

Charlie took a step closer. "How do you know? Her body appears contorted, as if she was trying to move."

"Intense heat causes the muscles to contract, hence the contorted limbs. I examined the scene. From the presentation of her remains – lying in the middle of the bed, supine – we can be sure she did not even wake up, let alone attempt to escape. Her body is badly charred, although the deeper organs are still discernible, thanks to the rapid arrival of the fire brigade. The layers of burned fabric on top of the body indicate she was fully clothed and covered in a woollen blanket, which is an excellent fire retardant."

"Strange that she didn't scream or react in any way," Charlie said. "Surely even a drunk would have awakened when the fire reached her, unless she was completely comatose?"

"Asphyxiation." Grace studied the blacked remains, a silent witness for a woman who could no longer speak for herself. "The smoke and lack of air could have killed her before the flames reached her room."

"In fact, the scene examination indicates the fire started in her room," the police surgeon said. "In the circumstances, I am doing a full autopsy to determine her cause of death. Would you like to stay, or should I send a messenger to you with the results?"

"I'll stay," Grace said. "Charlie?"

"I like to watch you work."

Cranston-Hartfield shook his head, but he had known Grace and Charlie long enough that he was not surprised by their choice. He took up his instruments and began his work, with Grace recording his observations.

After a few minutes, the police surgeon paused. "That's odd. No sign of ash or sooty mucous or other contaminants in the victim's trachea or bronchial tubes."

"If she didn't inhale any smoke or fire debris ..." Grace began.

"She was dead before the fire started," the police surgeon finished. "Which explains why she was lying on the bed, not having made an attempt to flee."

"Acute alcohol poisoning? Heart failure?"

"Probably not the former, Grace. The police report said the woman was significantly intoxicated, but not so much that she was comatose, or even close to it. Miss Newland, who is an experienced and sensible woman, would never have left her alone if she was at risk. Let's have a look at the victim's heart."

Grace resisted the urge to lean closer. Jamie Cranston-Hartfield knew what he was doing. She was so focussed on the snick of the blade as it sliced into the blackened chest, she jumped when he grunted again.

"What do you make of this, Grace?" the police surgeon asked. "Go carefully. It's a delicate one."

Grace probed the shrunken remains of the heart. "Is that a puncture wound?"

Charlie took a step forward to look over Grace's shoulder. "A knife wound?"

"Not a knife. A long, thin puncture wound. I've never seen anything like it, except when Sally Morely got a hat pin through the side of her palm when she was jousting with her little brother."

"Could she have been so drunk, she fell onto a hat pin?" Charlie sounded sceptical, and rightly so.

"I'm not saying it was a hat pin. She would have had to be extraordinarily unlucky to have been skewered by a hat pin accidentally, precisely through the heart."

James Cranston-Hartfield lifted the heart. "It goes all the way through. How long is a hat pin?"

"A few inches at most," Grace replied. "This wound is narrow and round, but wider than the average hat pin. A meat skewer, perhaps?"

"I'm not sure the precise details of the murder weapon are the critical issue at this point," Charlie said.

"Murder?" Grace had that sinking feeling in her intestines again. She had wanted the victim to have died in the fire before Charlie passed her door to ease his mind. She definitely didn't want to dangle a murder investigation in front of her dedicated detective husband. Grace's intestines twisted into another loop as Charlie continued in the authoritative monotone he reserved for police matters.

"How else do you explain a dead body laid out on a bed? If she stumbled onto a sharp object, she would have been found on the floor. The victim must have been stabbed deliberately, with clinical precision, through the heart. Either the killer murdered her in her sleep, or he laid her out on the bed after the stabbing to make it look like a natural death. He even covered her afterward to make it appear as if she was asleep. A mistake, since the day was too warm to need a woollen blanket."

"Setting the fire to cover his tracks," the police surgeon said. "If the volunteer fire brigade hadn't been so close by and quick to act, the victim's body would be nothing but ash and bone. Despicable, to risk so many other lives, but also a clever way to cover up a murder."

"Clever, maybe," Charlie said, "but I will see the fiend swing for this."

Grace noted the jut of her husband's jaw and said a fond farewell to her honeymoon. Charlie was right. Lavender House should have been a sanctuary. They owed it to Anne Macmillan, and all the women of Dunedin, to ensure this killer was removed from the streets forever.

The police surgeon bent down to resume his examination. "I'll send a messenger to Detective Inspector Wallace, although I hate to disturb him on a Sunday, especially after last night."

"The fire, you mean?"

"No, Grace. The wedding. Wallace got together with his old comrades in arms last night after you left. By the time I left the festivities, DI Wallace, former DI Stewart, and Sergeant Pyke were slugging back whisky and reminiscing. Wallace will be as cheerful as a grizzly bear with a sore head this morning."

Grace and Charlie arrived at Lavender House shortly after noon. Tears sprang to Grace's eyes at the sight of the building, built with love and charity, and now roped off and deserted. The frontage appeared largely intact, but the rear was badly charred, especially on the upper floor.

A constable circulated through the crowd of sombre onlookers, taking statements from anyone who had witnessed the fire. He recognised Charlie. "Detective Sergeant Kelly is inside, Mr Pyke. The building has been deemed safe to enter for the investigation team, but take care. Some of the timberwork is damaged and may be unstable. The lady can wait outside."

The lady wished to do no such thing, but she refrained from telling him so. Grace hitched up her skirt and followed Charlie through the front door. The constable guarding the entrance took one look at her expression and stepped aside.

Grace tried to shut out the sight and smell of destruction, but seeing her beloved Lavender House in such a state caused a stabbing pain in her guts. Charlie reached for her hand.

"Declan? Are you here?" Charlie called.

Declan's voice drifted down from above. "Upstairs. Mind how you go, Charlie. There's no telling how badly the structure has been weakened by the fire."

Detective Sergeant Declan Kelly met them at the top of the stairs, his expression grim. "It's a right old mess, isn't it? Looks like it was an accident, though. We found the remains of a candlestick next to a brandy bottle on the floor of the room where the fire started. A woman was brought in drunk. I'm not sure if you've heard that she died. Not a thing anyone could do to save her."

"We've just come from the autopsy," Charlie said. "She died before the fire started. The victim was stabbed through the heart."

Declan Kelly perked up at this news. "Was she now? Apologies for my unseemly enthusiasm. Wallace promised me I could lead the next murder investigation, now that I'm a detective sergeant, as long as the victim wasn't anyone so high in society as to merit Wallace's personal attention."

"Do you know anything about the victim, Declan?" Grace asked.

"I've sent for Miss Newland, who was the only person to have had contact with the woman. She ought to be here soon. I hate to expose her to the damage, but I thought she might notice anything out of place or unusual. Maybe you should have a look instead, Grace, as you have worked here for years."

Grace looked down the blackened corridor leading to the victim's room. Even now the fire was extinguished, the destruction sent a shiver up her spinal column. The thought of Charlie running down the corridor when it was burning, to get to the trapped boy ... Not a thought she cared to dwell on. Charlie's fingers had gone to his bandaged arm, as if the burn was itching again. She took his hand in hers and squeezed.

"Lead on, Declan," Charlie said, showing no trace of tension in his tone.

Grace noted the number '4' on the remains of the open door. An exact match for the mark on Charlie's head, just as the hole in the door matched his shoulder. The door had been forced open, judging by the fresh splinters around the lock. "The door was locked?"

Declan pointed to a charred remnant of furniture. "We found a blackened key on what must have been a dresser. The room was locked from the inside with the key removed. That's part of the reason we thought the victim's death was an accident. My first thought was that a protester threw an incendiary device into the room, but you can see that there isn't much broken glass inside the room. The window glass shattered in the fire, with the glass mostly falling outside. There is no doubt the fire started inside this room."

"The window was closed when you found it?" Charlie asked. "Locked?"

"The firemen found it closed, but not locked. The second storey windows have no locks, due to the height and difficulty of access from the narrow rear of the building. There's no way of climbing up without a long ladder."

Charlie moved slowly across to the window, testing the floorboards to see if they could take his weight and examining the scene as he went. Grace looked around the room from the doorway. The room was narrow and furnished only with the most basic of furniture. A narrow bed, a dresser, and a small bedside table, now in ruins. The remains of the twisted candlestick and broken brandy bottle lay alongside the bed.

Charlie crouched down beside the bottle. "Brandy would be perfect for starting a fire. I doubt Miss Newland would have allowed the victim to bring alcohol onto the premises. The killer could have brought it with him. The question is, how did he get into a locked room? And why? I take it no ladder was found outside?"

Declan shook his head. "The fire brigade brought their own two ladders. Mr Campbell, the volunteer fire captain, keeps the fire equipment at his carriage-works, just down the road. He is also a volunteer at Lavender House, part of a group of local men who see to the maintenance. Thus, there is no ladder kept on the premises. None of the neighbours had a ladder long enough to assist the fire fighting."

Charlie's hand went to the stubble on his chin. "A locked room, with no access through the window. And Lavender House itself locked up and inaccessible to the killer. Even if he got in, he would have been seen by the women present. Lavender House is always busy."

"It's a puzzle, right enough," Declan agreed.

"You are assuming the killer was a man," Grace said.

Charlie shot her a proud look. "A fair point, Grace. But even if the killer was a woman who had access to Lavender House, she would have needed a key to lock the door, as the room key is still inside. Do you know where she might have gotten a key?"

They went downstairs to Anne's office, where the spare keys were kept. The room was a mess of damp ash, but the otherwise intact. Grace used her own key to open the top drawer. "No keys missing. Anne Macmillan, Miss Newland and Doctor Ravenwood have master keys, but they carry them on their person at all times. There is no way a stranger, or even a regular visitor, could have come into Anne's office without being seen."

"We need to talk to Miss Newland."

As if summoned by Charlie's words, a tentative "hello" drifted down the corridor.

Grace made haste for the front door, with Charlie and Declan close behind. None of them wanted Miss Newland to see the full extent of the devastation if it could be avoided. Truth be told, Grace was glad to leave the blackened depths of the building. She offered the loyal administrator of Lavender House a handkerchief and ushered her down the road towards the church hall, where a restorative cup of tea might be administered. Grace could do with a cup herself, after the rapid series of highs and lows of the past twenty-four hours.

The church hall bustled with friends tidying up after the wedding and ladies sorting through the charity boxes for clothes for the refugees. Grace was reminded that she was neglecting her own duties. She ought to be home, sending notes of gratitude to all those who made their wedding day special. Instead, she dispensed a series of hugs and thanks, accepted an offer of tea, and retreated into the back room.

Miss Newland settled into the chair offered by Charlie. Her hands shook as she sipped the tea, but her expression remained resolute. "Your message said a body was found in room four, Detective Sergeant Kelly. A terrible shock. I had hoped Mrs Seaton escaped the fire. Kathleen, who was in the room next door, banged on the door and got no reply. She said she checked the door, finding it locked and the key gone. Naturally Kathleen assumed Mrs Seaton had left." Miss Newland's thin face pinched still thinner as she held back tears. "I should have checked when we couldn't see Mrs Seaton outside. She was drunk, you see. I thought she must have sobered up enough to leave before the fire started."

Grace took Miss Newland's hand. "You and Kathleen did a wonderful job of getting everyone else to safety. It would have been foolhardy to go back into a burning building. The medical evidence showed Mrs Seaton died rapidly."

Grace had enough experience of police investigations to know not to share the dreadful news that the victim had been murdered. She caught Declan's eye. He nodded, so she continued. "Miss Newland, perhaps we could start at the beginning. That is, Mrs Seaton's arrival at Lavender House."

Miss Newland dashed a tear from her eye and sat up straighter. "A young lady brought her in. I assumed the lady was a good Samaritan, who had found a drunk woman in the street and knew where she could find refuge for the poor soul. But, now I think about it, the lady was very solicitous. Mrs Seaton appeared to be in service. Probably a cook, from her garments. Perhaps the young lady was her mistress?"

"Was Mrs Seaton sober enough to supply an address?"

"She told me her name, but nothing else. I don't like to pry when women first arrive, as the circumstances are often deeply distressing for the women who seek refuge with us. We give them shelter and build their trust before asking about their troubles." Miss Newland rifled through her bag. "However, the lady who brought her in gave me her calling card."

Grace read the card, but the woman's name – Miss Henrietta Tucker – meant nothing to her.

Declan took the card. "Thank you, Miss Newland. This should make tracing Mrs Seaton easier. Do you know if she had a bottle of brandy with her?"

"We have a policy of inspecting the bags of all newcomers, Sergeant. Mrs Seaton had nothing with her except a change of clothes and a knitting bag." Miss Newland paused. "Come to think of it, the knitting bag belonged to Miss Tucker, the lady who brought her in. I did not search Mrs Seaton's person. Alcoholics can be quite cunning about how they conceal their vice, but there are limits to how intrusive we can be. The woman's need for care is more important than her reason for seeking refuge."

Charlie stiffened in the chair next to Grace. "A knitting bag? With knitting needles?"

"Yes, Mr Pyke."

Miss Newland and Declan appeared puzzled by his interest, but Grace realised exactly why Charlie had asked. Long, thin and round, a knitting needle might not be a common murder weapon, but it fit the wound in this case.

"How did this Miss Tucker act with the victim … Mrs Seaton?" Charlie asked.

"Miss Tucker did not say much, but she was gentle and kind. She helped me to get Mrs Seaton up the stairs into the room. I was vexed that I was running late for the wedding, so we did no more than take off the woman's boots and coat. Miss Tucker settled her on the bed and closed the curtains. We left her to sleep it off. She was in one of our rear rooms, facing the town belt, so the noise of the protesters wouldn't disturb her. It's nice and dark when the curtains are drawn, the sun being on the other side of the building."

"So dark that Mrs Seaton might have lit a candle when she woke up?" Declan asked.

Miss Newland's cup rattled in its saucer. "Oh, is that how the fire started? A candle? I suppose she might have lit one. Mrs Seaton would have been getting on for fifty years old. If she'd done a lot of needlework in her time, her eyesight might well have been poor. I should have taken the candlestick away, but I was in such a hurry."

"Merely establishing the facts, Miss Newland. There is no fault implied on your side. How disabled by alcohol was she?"

"She was reeling and unsteady, but conscious and in no danger. I had no concern that she might have been so afflicted that she would choke on her own vomit or anything of that nature." Miss Newland blushed. "Please excuse my directness, Sergeant

Kelly. You will appreciate we deal with all sorts at Lavender House."

Declan nodded. "I understand, Miss Newland. Indeed, I admire the staff of Lavender House for their good work under trying circumstances."

"Was Miss Tucker left alone with Mrs Seaton at any point?" Charlie asked.

"Only for a few minutes, while I went to get a jug of water. I stopped to get a basin too, in case she felt sick. When I came back up, Mrs Seaton was already asleep. We crept out and left her to sleep it off."

"Locking the door behind you?" Charlie asked.

"No, Mr Pyke. I left the door closed but unlocked. Mrs Seaton must have locked the door after we left, as the woman next door found the door locked when the fire broke out."

"We found the key on the dresser," Declan said. "Never a good idea to take the key out of the lock, in case of fire. Too easy to panic and forget where the key was left."

Grace glanced at Charlie, who appeared calm, but she knew he was quivering with excitement on the inside. He had the look of an English Pointer dog, standing stock still at the scent of game, but alert from head to paw.

Charlie glanced at Declan, whose case it was. When Declan didn't speak, Charlie asked the next question. "Miss Newland, did you or anyone else hear any sound from within the room once you had closed the door? Or see anyone who ought not to have been inside Lavender House?"

"I didn't, but I was running very late by then, as you know, Mr Pyke. I saw Miss Tucker out and locked the door to Lavender House behind me. I had given instructions for nobody to be let in, except in an emergency." Miss Newland wiped away a tear. "I ought not to have left my post. Lavender House is my life – and now look at it."

46

Grace touched her hand to Miss Newland's cheek. "Lavender House is not the building, Miss Newland, it's the people and the service they provide to women in need. Mr Drummond's house will be a fine substitute until the structure can be rebuilt."

When Miss Newland faltered on the edge of fresh tears, Grace decided it was time to end the interview. "If you have no more questions, gentlemen, I suggest I take Miss Newland back to Mr Drummond's house. They cannot manage without her for long." Grace helped Miss Newland up. "We can take the donated clothes with us. I'm sure our refugees would welcome fresh garments. I'd wager that Mrs Brown is whipping up a batch of scones for afternoon tea as we speak. I'm looking forward to meeting the lad who was saved from the fire."

Henrietta Tucker

Charlie watched with mixed emotions as Grace escorted Miss Newland away. He wanted nothing more than to be alone with his wife of twenty-four hours, but Declan did not yet have all the facts he needed to investigate the murder of Mrs Seaton. Grace turned to wave at the door, and then she was gone. Charlie resisted the urge to run after her, instead explaining to Declan why he had asked about knitting needles, in view of the long, thin puncture mark through the victim's heart.

Declan rocked back on his chair, his solid build causing the legs to creak alarmingly. "Blimey, that's a new one on me. Stabbed with a knitting needle? I can see that Miss Tucker had the opportunity, but it was one heck of a risk. Miss Newland could have come back into the room and insisted on checking the victim again."

"Miss Newland had made it clear she was in a hurry. It would be daring, I grant you, but not impossible."

"But why, Charlie? Miss Tucker could have killed Mrs Seaton in a secluded grove of trees in the town belt or in a quiet alley. Why risk escorting the victim to Lavender House, a place closed to all but a few? Why show her face and leave a calling card?"

Charlie knew his friend was right. It made little sense. But neither did a murder in a locked room. And that was another gaping hole in his theory. Dead women do not lock doors, so how was the room locked from the inside after Miss Newland and Henrietta Tucker left? Miss Newland had been in a hurry to get to the wedding. Might she have locked the door behind her without thinking? Charlie's head throbbed in synchrony with his arm. All he could do was shrug.

Declan was looking at him as if sizing him up for a shroud. "Go home, Charlie. I've seen healthier complexions on corpses. I'm big enough and ugly enough to interview Miss Henrietta Tucker on my own."

A tempting offer, but Grace would be busy at Mr Drummond's house for a while and this case was turning into an itch Charlie felt compelled to scratch. "Declan, my friend, I know I can leave the investigation in your capable hands, but the mystery of a murder in a locked room will give me sleepless nights. Do you mind if I join your visit to the Tucker residence? I promise to leave the interviewing to you."

Declan rose from the creaking chair, his usual sunny self again. "Always glad to have your intimidating presence at an interview. Miss Tucker would have to be a tough nut not to crack under that pressure. Come on then. Their house is only about twenty minutes' walk away if we go through the town belt and down Eglinton Road. Fifteen minutes if you stop pining for your wife and let those long legs of yours loose. You'll be back in time for scones and tea."

The Tucker residence was in a side-street off Eglinton Road, towards the lower end, where the sea views were scarcer and the houses more workaday. The house struck Charlie as unusual even before they'd stepped across the threshold. Two pairs of scuffed men's work boots had been cast off in the front porch. Along the side of the house, he glimpsed sturdy workmen's clothes flapping in the breeze on a clothesline. However, the house was no workers' cottage. Charlie estimated at least three or four bedrooms upstairs. Flower vases and pretty lace curtains graced the downstairs windows.

The lace curtains in the front room twitched as they approached.

A sombre-faced woman answered the door, wearing the plain, dark dress of a housekeeper. "The family is in mourning and will not be seeing visitors today."

Did the family know of the death already? Miss Newland had described the two women who arrived at Lavender House as a young lady and a drunken woman of the serving classes. Perhaps Miss Newland had been mistaken about the status of the victim. Or perhaps the dead woman was a respected servant of long standing.

Declan put his hand out to stop the door closing in his face. "We must speak to Miss Henrietta Tucker. I am Detective Sergeant Kelly of the Dunedin police."

The housekeeper looked him up and down. She allowed a moment to pass to show him his place. "Please remain where you are, Sergeant. I will see if Mrs Tucker is willing to let her daughter talk to you."

The housekeeper retreated. Declan rolled his eyes and stepped into the entrance hall. Charlie could hear the reluctance in the low murmur of voices within the front room, but the housekeeper returned and showed them in.

"Detective Sergeant Kelly, ma'am," the housekeeper announced.

Charlie noted the housekeeper's deference to the lady of the house, who perched on her armchair like a queen on her throne. Her heavy black mourning gown emphasised the pallor of her narrow face. She must have been sweltering in the summer heat. A man – presumably her husband – stood beside her, as big and surly as a bull in a pen. He made his wife, who was of average height and tending toward gaunt, look delicate and feminine.

The lady of the house flicked her eyes in Charlie's direction, but Kelly offered no name for his associate. Her nostrils pinched at this lack of courtesy. "What do you want, Sergeant Kelly? As you can see, your visit is by no means convenient."

The man beside her put a protective arm around her shoulders. He thrust out a broad jaw and growled, "Come back tomorrow. Can't you see we are in mourning?"

"I apologise for the untimely interruption, but I come on a matter of urgency." Declan pulled a battered notebook out of his pocket. "May I ask your name, sir?"

"Mr Jack Tucker. This is my wife, Mrs Ariadne Tucker. What do you want?"

"I wish to speak to Miss Henrietta Tucker."

A young woman in the corner of the room jerked her head up, revealing red eyes in a face whose features derived more from her father than her mother. On her, the square jaw and solid body took on a look of competence, rather than her father's belligerence. Her hands were busy knitting a navy-blue scarf with fine wool. Her fingers move so quickly and so independently of her other actions that they seemed a separate, disembodied entity.

Charlie had imagined Henrietta Tucker as an older Samaritan, helping a fellow woman in need. This young lady was probably in her mid-twenties. She looked strong and capable, but perhaps not capable of murder.

The father rose to his feet, inserting his bulk in front of his daughter. "Why do you want to speak to my daughter? Surely you need not bother the citizens of Dunedin on the Lord's day." Jack Tucker's voice rumbled out of his broad chest like water over gravel, and was followed by a deep-seated cough.

Declan didn't so much as twitch. "I understand your daughter accompanied a woman by the name of Mrs Seaton to a women's refuge yesterday morning."

Mr Tucker's jaw relaxed. He resumed his seat, letting out another hacking cough. He must have been handsome once, but time had etched deep lines around his red-veined eyes and untrusting mouth. "What's the old biddy done then? Thrown a tizzy and broken the crockery?"

51

Miss Henrietta Tucker was quick to the defence. "Father! Mrs Seaton was not herself. The grief unhinged her, poor dear. Mrs Seaton was dreadfully upset yesterday, Detective Sergeant Kelly. I accompanied her to Lavender House, which is a medical clinic and refuge for women."

"Your kindness was appreciated, I'm sure, Miss Tucker." Declan's Irish accent lent a gentle croon to his words, lulling the unwary with its sympathy. "You had the good sense to give your calling card to Miss Newland at Lavender House. We have no other information on the woman, hence the visit to you today."

Henrietta's concern sharpened, no doubt realising that a Detective Sergeant would not be inquiring after Mrs Seaton out of politeness. She dropped a stitch, but knitted on, regardless. "Is Mrs Seaton … unwell?"

"I regret to inform you that Mrs Seaton passed away yesterday."

"Oh, how dreadful." The scarf and needles fell through her fingers to the floor. "I ought not to have left her, but she did not seem ill, just a little … out of sorts."

Her mother blew air from her narrow nostrils. "Out of sorts, indeed. The truth is, Mrs Seaton got shamefully drunk yesterday morning. She could hardly walk. I expect she fell down the stairs, did she?"

"More likely drunk herself to death out of guilt," her husband mumbled.

Before Declan could inquire why Mrs Seaton might feel such fatal guilt, Mrs Tucker interrupted. "I hope you don't expect us to see to the funeral arrangements. We have enough to do preparing for my dear departed brother's funeral."

Henrietta Tucker's handkerchief dropped from her eyes. "Mother! Mrs Seaton served Uncle Arthur for decades. I will not have her left to a pauper's grave. I feel dreadful. I should have stayed with her, but there was so much to attend to after my uncle's death. Laying out his body in his favourite clothes, dealing with the undertaker, talking to the vicar. If only I'd stayed and tended to the living instead, but I thought Mrs Seaton would sleep off her condition."

Her mother rose to her daughter's defence. "Henrietta is not to blame. She would never have left her if the woman was ill. My daughter is a trained nurse, Sergeant Kelly. The cook was drunk, and that's an end to it."

Charlie noted that Mrs Tucker showed no embarrassment at leaving her daughter to attend to both the drunken cook and all the funeral arrangements for Mrs Tucker's dear departed brother.

Henrietta showed no sign of resentment, only sorrow. "Poor Mrs Seaton. Clifford said that Lavender House was the perfect place for her to recover, otherwise I would never have taken her there."

Declan lifted his pencil from his notebook. "Clifford?"

The daughter blushed. "Doctor Clifford Johnstone. I work for him as a nurse. He was also my uncle's doctor, which meant he was with us when Mrs Seaton ... had her turn. Lavender House seemed the best option. Doctor Johnstone will be mortified if Lavender House failed in their duty to protect her. The doctor is such a considerate gentleman."

"Don't you worry, Henrietta," her mother said. "I expect Mrs Seaton discharged herself from the refuge and met her end elsewhere. Your doctor has nothing to feel guilty for."

Two young men entered the room. The larger and rougher of the two said, "What's all this, Hen? Did I hear you say Uncle Arthur's cook died at Lavender House? Blimey, did the poor old sot burn to death?"

The speaker was another chip off the Tucker block in appearance and had the same blunt way of speaking as his father. The younger man was slighter and favoured his mother's side of the family – not just in looks, but in his neater attire and greater air of refinement.

Declan had been sitting back, watching the family paint a picture of their characters. Now he clamped a steely look on the larger of the young men. "And you are?"

"Bert Tucker." Bert jerked a thumb at the younger man beside him. "My brother, Sid. And who are you to be barging into our house asking questions?"

"Detective Sergeant Kelly of the Dunedin police. Mr Charles Pyke is also a detective."

Charlie thought the moment had come to assert himself. "Mr Tucker. I don't believe Detective Sergeant Kelly mentioned that Mrs Seaton's death occurred during a fire. How did you know?"

Bert Tucker's jaw tightened, his scowl intensified by the dark bristles of his careless shave. "Someone at the tavern mentioned the fire at Lavender House."

Charlie had the strong sense that Bert had been about to say more and stopped himself. Drinkers at a tavern might well include the type of fellow who protests against places offering refuge to beaten wives. He would save that discussion for later. Declan would save it for later, Charlie corrected. There was no need for Charlie to be drawn into the investigation any further.

"We are all very upset, Sergeant," Mrs Tucker said. "Grief has frayed our tempers. I must ask you to respect a family in mourning and leave us be. Henrietta has offered to see to Mrs Seaton's funeral arrangements. Isn't that enough?"

Declan bowed his head. "Much obliged, Miss Tucker. We just need a few more details. And again, our apologies for intruding at this difficult time."

Charlie remained standing by the window. "One more question, Mr Tucker. Mr Jack Tucker, I mean. Why did you say Mrs Seaton felt guilty?"

"What?"

"You said, 'More likely drunk herself to death out of guilt.' What did you mean by that?"

Mr Tucker glared at him. "I meant nothing by it."

His wife cut in again. Charlie thought she might make a habit of it.

"My brother, Mr Arthur Glanville, passed away the day before yesterday." Mrs Tucker's gaze slid to the portrait in pride of place above the mantelpiece. "Mrs Seaton was his cook. After many decades of serving him, she was deeply upset at his passing. We had no notion that she ever let a drop of the demon drink past her lips. Arthur's untimely death must have unhinged the poor woman."

Charlie had noticed the portrait, which showed a man with a rifle big enough to shoot an elephant. His boot rested on the neck of a dead tiger. The man had the same narrow face and thin nose as Mrs Tucker. "Is this your brother, Arthur Glanville, Mrs Tucker?"

"Oh no. That is my father, Horatio Glanville. Our father, I mean. Arthur and I were children when this portrait was painted. Our father was a man whose great courage was widely admired."

Charlie caught the momentary tightening of Declan's facial muscles. Was it the name, Horatio Glanville, or repulsion at the man's obvious pride in besting a noble beast? Charlie wondered how much bravery it took to shoot a tiger from a distance, presumably with a band of servants, gun-bearers, and beaters at his beck and call. "I still don't understand why the cook would feel guilt at his passing."

Sid Tucker spoke for the first time. "Mrs Seaton was upset out of remorse, Constable. She cooked the meal that killed my uncle."

"Sid, that is cruel," Henrietta said. "It was a dreadful accident. Mrs Seaton was not to know that the shellfish were off. Uncle Arthur always said she was the best cook in Dunedin. She was devoted to him. I have never once seen her take a drop of alcohol before this."

Sid rubbed his hand over a perfectly smooth jaw. Unlike his coarse brother, Sid must have had an expert barber or valet. He waved a hand in vague apology. "I did not mean to sound cruel, sister, or to imply any fault on the cook's part. I simply spoke the truth. Mrs Seaton cooked the meal that killed Uncle Arthur. A tragic accident."

Declan's jiggling knee told Charlie it was time to leave, but he still had questions he thought should be asked. So much for his promise to leave it to the police.

"I don't see what Mrs Seaton's tragic death in a fire has to do with us," Mrs Tucker said.

"Detective Sergeant Kelly will want to know her next of kin, Mama," Henrietta said.

"Well, really, we are hardly likely to know the personal circumstances of my brother's domestic servants."

Henrietta ignored her mother. "Mrs Seaton worked for my grandfather as a kitchen maid when he and his family first arrived in New Zealand from Calcutta over three decades ago. When Uncle Arthur set up his own household, Mrs Seaton went with him as his cook. As far as I know, she has no family. She never married. The 'Mrs' was a nod to propriety, as there was no lady of the house. My uncle was a bachelor."

"I'll need to speak to the other members of Mr Glanville's household, Mrs Tucker," Declan said.

"Oh, very well." Mrs Tucker waved at Henrietta, who went to a writing desk in the corner and wrote the address.

"Miss Tucker," Charlie said, "Did you take Mrs Seaton to her room at Lavender House?"

"Yes. The lady who received us was in a hurry, so we didn't stay long. I don't recall her name, but she said she was late for a wedding. We took Mrs Seaton upstairs to the room the lady indicated. We helped her out of her coat and boots and put her to bed before we left."

"Did you notice if the window was closed and the curtains drawn?"

"The window was closed. I drew the curtains myself, Detective Pyke. I thought the darkness might ease her recovery. The lady brought a jug of water and a basin for Mrs Seaton."

Henrietta had an air of a competent nurse about her, tempered with a slight edge of distaste. "Mrs Seaton had imbibed rather a lot of brandy, I'm sorry to say."

"Did she have the bottle of brandy with her?"

"Not that I am aware of." Henrietta pursed her lips. "I suppose she may have tucked it under her clothes. It would have been inappropriate to search her person. We left her to sleep it off in peace. I confess I was tempted to join her, but there was much to do after to my uncle's untimely death."

Charlie could detect no hint of anxiety in Henrietta's voice, although the questions must have sparked her suspicions. He wished all witnesses could be as helpful as Miss Tucker. "Can you recall if you left the door locked? Or whether there were candles in the room?"

"I couldn't say. Is that how the fire started? She awoke and lit a candle?"

Charlie let his silence reply for him. He did not want the family to know at this stage of the inquiry that the death was anything other than a tragic accident. Not that it was his problem. The newly promoted Detective Sergeant Kelly would investigate in his usual thorough way. Charlie had thoughts of a much more pleasant nature on his mind and was relieved when Declan brought the interview to a close.

Declan strode away from the Tucker house as if his coat-tails were on fire.

Charlie jogged after his friend. "Where are you off to in such an almighty hurry, Declan?"

"I'm off to stop Arthur Glanville's body from being tampered with. Could you send a message to the police surgeon to meet me there? We'll need a post-mortem."

"Two deaths in one household within two days does sound suspicious," Charlie agreed, "especially as we know Mrs Seaton's death was murder. But what was it about hearing the Glanville name that set that old bloodhound instinct sniffing?"

Declan slowed down for Charlie to catch up. "Horatio Glanville was no dashing war hero, fit to bear Horatio Nelson's name. He was part of the East India Company before he came to New Zealand. Three decades ago, Miss Tucker said, which means after the Indian Mutiny, when the British were finally beginning to rein in the powers of the company. The Dunedin police have kept a close eye on Horatio Glanville ever since, but he has evaded our best efforts to convict him of any offence. Friends in high places, no doubt."

"What is his game, Declan? Apart from slaughtering tigers."

"All we know is that Horatio arrived a very wealthy man from his time in India. He added to his wealth here by establishing an importing business. We believe he was the main importer of opium into Dunedin. With Chinese miners arriving for the gold rush, he began supplying opium for smoking as well as medicinal purposes. Not illegal, of course, but the government keeps a close eye on the opium trade, as you know. His family might consider Horatio Glanville a hero, but I viewed him as a peddler of misery."

"I know the Chinese community is campaigning to stop the importation and sale of opium. My Aunt Lily is one of those trying to make their voices heard."

"I agree with them, Charlie. Drugs like opium rob users of their lives and livelihoods. DI Wallace and other senior policemen have made submissions opposing the trade, but the real change will come when opium smoking spreads into wider society. We've heard rumours of that happening already. I doubt opium smoking will be legal much longer."

"You don't need to convince me, Declan. I grew up in the goldfields, with a Chinese grandfather and a policeman father. I could tell you stories that would curdle your stomach contents."

They walked on in silence up a steep stretch of the road. Charlie went over the family connections in his mind. "The man who died was Arthur Glanville, Horatio Glanville's son and Mrs Ariadne Tucker's brother. Was he in the opium trade too?"

"We thought Arthur Glanville took no part in the family business. In fact, Horatio Glanville sold the business before he died last year to a man called Clive Jardine, who is as shadowy as a wisp of opium smoke. DI Wallace doesn't like having such phantoms on his beat."

"No wonder you are jumping at the opportunity to investigate Glanville's death, Declan."

"Too right. This may be our excuse to dig into the Glanville family finances at long last. But not you Charlie. You have other priorities."

Charlie glanced up, noting the sun sinking towards the hilltop. The afternoon was drawing to a close, and he was eager to get home to his bride. On the other hand, he knew Grace abhorred the drug trade too.

They reached the point where their paths diverged. Charlie grasped his friend's hand. "Good luck to you, Declan. If I can help in any way, please ask. Grace and Lily and Alistair too. They'd walk across hot coals to help you take down the opium trade."

Declan grinned. "Hot coals, eh? Perhaps not the best choice of words in the circumstances, but I'll bear it in mind. We're short of men, as always. I'll be lucky to get a single constable to help with this investigation."

Before Declan could get carried away with recruitment, Charlie cut in. "But you're right, old friend. Right now, I want nothing more than to be at home with my new wife."

Declan slapped his friend on the back. "Don't blame you. Make the most of it before you're knee deep in nippers. I've got one down with croup and another teething. My missus and I feel as if we haven't slept in a month."

Half an hour later, Charlie burst through the door of their High Street home, finding only silence, a bowl of Mrs Brown's famous hotpot, and a scribbled note from his wife.

When he recovered from the blow of her absence, he settled down to the much-needed meal and rounded out the evening browsing *Mrs Beeton's Book of Household Management*. From the latter, he learned a great deal about the hitherto unknown art of running a household. The rules of appropriate conduct had Charlie enumerating the many, many times he had unwittingly been at fault by the standards of polite society. Not that Grace was any better. Her activities this evening, for example, were far from the recommended evening entertainments for ladies of the household – "Light or fancy needlework, varied by an occasional game of chess or backgammon."

He wasn't sure if Grace would throw Mrs Beeton out the window or keep the book for its amusement value, but he looked forward to hearing her thoughts upon the matter when she finally made it home.

Temporary Sanctuary

Grace and Miss Newland arrived at Mr Drummond's house with arms full of clothes for the women and children evacuated from Lavender House. Although little more than a day had passed since the fire, the temporary refuge was already functioning in a fairly orderly fashion.

Fortunately, Kenneth Drummond owned one of the larger homes off the upper end of High Street. Even so, the serene, spacious home Grace knew well was now more like a boarding school on the first day of term. Donated goods lined the hall. Children's feet thundered across the floorboards upstairs, despite their mother's admonitions. Pots rattled in the kitchen. Grace sniffed, identifying the delicious aroma of Mrs Brown's mouthwatering hotpot, reminding her she hadn't eaten for hours.

Grace heard the doctor calling for his next patient and realised it was her father. When she went to investigate, she found Anne Macmillan directing the patients who had found their way to the temporary medical clinic, which had been set up in the largest of the downstairs rooms. Anne appeared to be in a particularly cheery mood, Grace thought. Indeed, her elderly great-aunt – feared by many, respected by all – was actually humming a merry tune. Most uncharacteristic. Grace looked a little closer, noting the bloom of pink on her great-aunt's cheeks. Nothing like a crisis to add a little sparkle to a tough old campaigner like Anne Macmillan.

"You seem to be enjoying your temporary home, Auntie," Grace said over the top of the pile of clothes.

Her great aunt's head jerked towards her, the pink cheeks deepening to red. Anne pushed herself up with her walking stick. "Mrs Grace Penrose Pyke, what the dickens are you doing here? Not bored with your new husband already, I hope."

"Husband? Oh, goodness me, I must have put him down somewhere and quite forgotten about him. Where do you want these clothes, Auntie?"

Grace waited for Miss Newland to move through to the next room. She bent close to Anne's ear. "Charlie felt guilty he hadn't rescued the woman who died in the fire yesterday. I made the mistake of taking him to the autopsy to prove he could not have saved her. Keep it to yourself, but Mrs Seaton was murdered before the fire was lit. I'm here to see if I can find any witnesses."

Anne's arthritic hand went to her heart. "A murder? Inside my own sanctuary? Are you sure?" Anne waved the question away. "Of course you are sure. What can I do to help, Grace?"

"Keep your ears open. Lavender House is a busy place. Somebody must have seen or heard the killer."

"Consider it done. You and Charlie shouldn't be investigating, of course, but I am grateful. A murder on my watch cuts me to the bone." Anne paused as Miss Newland wandered back, still with an armful of clothes. "Grace, dear, could you take those clothes upstairs to your mother? Everyone has been so wonderful at helping in a crisis."

They found Mrs Penrose in a small upstairs sitting room with the refugees from Lavender House. Mr Drummond's house was bursting at the seams. Grace wondered where Anne was staying, since all the guest rooms were full. Could Anne's suspiciously good humour have a more romantic explanation? Kenneth Drummond had been pursuing Anne for months, if not years. It would be ironic indeed, if Anne had enjoyed a more intimate night than the newlyweds. Grace sighed and pushed the idea aside as one she didn't wish to pursue.

Instead, Grace sorted through the clothes until she found a dark green dress suited to Kathleen's fair complexion. She took it over to the young woman in the corner, whose hunched body exuded grief. Kathleen looked up at her approach, her fading black eye half-hidden under a curtain of ginger hair.

"Kathleen, isn't it? I'm Grace. We met when you arrived at Lavender House. Why don't we find somewhere private to try this pretty dress on?"

Kathleen fingered the soft velvet dress, which must have been donated by a wealthy benefactor. "Oh, that's lovely." She showed Grace to her room, which she was sharing with another woman.

Grace helped her into the dress, pulling the laces tight to adjust it to Kathleen's gaunt body. "There now, doesn't that look marvellous? A stitch here and there is all it needs."

Kathleen twirled in front of the looking glass to examine the new outfit from all angles. "It's too good for the likes of me, but it looks lovely."

"A perfect dress for a heroine. I heard you did a fine job of raising the alarm yesterday and getting the other women and children out of Lavender House."

Kathleen sank onto the bed. "I made a terrible mistake, Grace. A woman died in the fire and it was my fault. I thought she had left, because I hammered on her door and heard nothing. Her door was locked and the key was gone."

Grace put an arm around her. "You did exactly the right thing, Kathleen. The woman didn't answer you because she had already died. There was nothing you could have done to help her. If she had been alive, your bravery would have saved her for sure."

"Is that true, Grace? Did the demon drink kill her? She was a bit the worse for wear when she arrived, but didn't have the look of a hardened drinker. Poor woman. Reckon life must have dealt her a wicked blow to get drunk like that."

"That's what we'd like to find out, Kathleen. Could you tell me everything you remember about her arrival and what happened next? Every little detail, no matter how trivial it seemed at the time. Your room was right next door, wasn't it?"

Kathleen's account matched Miss Newland's description of Mrs Seaton's arrival at Lavender House, except in one crucial detail. After Miss Newland and the other lady left, Kathleen heard

Mrs Seaton get up and lock the door. The sound was unmistakable, because Mrs Seaton knocked into the wall and dresser on the way to the door, and fumbled with the key in the lock.

"And after Mrs Seaton locked the door?" Grace leaned closer, eager to hear her answer.

"She went back to bed," Kathleen said. "Between the squeaking bed springs and her snoring fit to rock the foundations, I decided it was time to go downstairs and do my daily chores. When I came back upstairs with a mop and bucket about ten minutes later, I smelled the smoke and ran to bang on the door to her room. When there was no answer and no sound of snoring, I went to raise the alarm."

Grace praised Kathleen's actions again and left the young woman feeling less guilty. Kathleen hurried away to show the other women her new dress, leaving Grace even more flummoxed than before. Kathleen was adamant Mrs Seaton had locked the door herself after Miss Newland and Miss Tucker left her. And the door was still locked when Kathleen raised the alarm after the fire started. Therefore, Henrietta Tucker was not the killer, unless she and her knitting needles had found their way back into room four of Lavender House through two locked doors, and out again, unseen.

Grace made her way downstairs. Kenneth Drummond, the distinguished retired barrister who owned the house, was in the entrance hall, carrying a grinning boy with his hands wrapped in bandages. Two excited children bounced around them, swinging on their mother's arms. The triumphant return of the boy rescued from the fire, Grace concluded.

Mr Drummond held the lad out of reach of his enthusiastic siblings. "Children, I know you are thrilled to see your brother, but you must be careful. His burns will take a while to heal."

Grace followed the procession through to where her father had set up a consulting area behind a pair of gorgeous Chinese lacquered screens. Mr Drummond put Fred Coster on the bed behind the screens, while Miss Newland took charge of the other children.

Doctor Penrose unwrapped the bandages and declared himself satisfied with what he saw. "If you are careful, young Fred, you'll be able to use those hands again in a few weeks. In the meantime, you'll have to be patient and let everyone here help you. Now then, would you like to meet the wife of the man who rescued you? My daughter, Mrs Penrose Pyke."

The boy nodded, but was too shy to speak.

"Hello, Fred," Grace said. "My husband will be delighted to hear you are out of hospital already. He will come to see you as soon as he can. He's busy being a detective today."

Fred's eyes widened. Mrs Coster spoke for him. "My Fred would love to meet Mr Pyke, the famous detective. I am ever so grateful to your husband for going into that fire and rescuing my wee lad. On his wedding day too. Whoever heard of such a thing?"

Grace refrained from mentioning that Charlie's wedding-day heroics did not surprise her. "Would you like to help us, Fred? Mr Pyke is investigating how the fire started. I bet a young lad like you is good at noticing what's going on."

Fred nodded again, more eagerly this time.

"The fire started in room four," Grace prompted.

"Where the old lush was," Fred said.

Mrs Coster blushed a bright red, but Grace ploughed on. "You're right, Fred, she'd had a lot to drink. Did you see her arrive?"

Fred nodded. "I hid in the end room in case she started laying out with her fists. I didn't come out again until Miss Newland and the other lady left."

Grace studiously avoided looking at the poor lad's mother. Most of the women who came to Lavender House were escaping abusive husbands. Grace hated to think of innocent children growing up associating alcohol with flying fists. "Did you see Kathleen, the woman in the room next door?"

"She went downstairs a bit after the other ladies."

"What about after Kathleen went downstairs, Fred? Did you see anyone or hear anything?"

Fred glanced at his mother, who nodded for him to go on. "The drunk woman had a man in with her." The boy's voice quavered with the outrage children feel when someone else gets away with breaking the rules. "Grown-up men aren't allowed."

Grace's pulse quickened, but she forced herself to remain calm. Fred was only about six years old. Young children could be good observers, but they could also have active imaginations. He sounded certain, but she had to be sure, especially as he must have had only a fleeting impression as he passed the room. "Are you sure there was someone else in the room, Fred? Sometimes people who drink too much talk to themselves."

"It wasn't the drunk woman. She sounded different."

"I don't doubt you heard someone, Fred, but I wonder if it could it have been a woman with a deep voice. Or are you sure it was a man?"

Fred considered the question. "I thought it might be Mrs Macmillan at first, before the person spoke. But it sounded like a man to me. I think he was trying to wake her up to ask a question. He said a rude word."

"Why did you think it was Mrs Macmillan?"

Fred shrugged. Grace would have let it go, but the point was crucial. Perhaps if the boy saw and heard Mrs Macmillan again, his memory would be triggered. "Father, can you ask Auntie Anne to come in, please?"

Anne hadn't hobbled beyond the doorway before Fred perked up. "Tap, tap, tap, like Mrs Macmillan's walking stick. A bit like that, anyway. I'm not sure really, but the sound reminded me of her."

Grace took a moment to think. What would she do if she was a curious six-year-old boy who overheard something amiss?

"You've given Mr Pyke a very important clue, Fred. What a pity you didn't look through the keyhole."

The expression on poor little Fred's face reminded Grace of the time her teacher caught her dissecting a dead bird she had found on the road. Guilt, laced with fear of the consequences. She patted his hand. "I know looking through a keyhole would be wrong normally, but not when there is a man where he shouldn't be, in a woman's room in a women-only refuge. You would be right to look, so you could tell an adult."

"I didn't see nothing much, Mrs Pyke," Fred whispered. "The man – the person – was near the head of the bed, which is beside the door. And the keyhole was ever so small. But I did see a black glove holding something white."

"White like the colour of my shirt?" Grace asked. "Or silver perhaps, like the candlestick on that table over there?"

"Neither. More like cream you get on top of milk."

"Can you describe the object?"

Fred pressed his lips together until his face crumpled in thought. "I only saw a little bit of it. It was hard, not soft like cloth. A handle or a stick or something, maybe."

Mrs Penrose had been watching on with interest. Now, she opened her bag and took out two pairs of black gloves, handing a pair to her husband. Dr Penrose caught on quickly. He took two sheets of paper and rolled them, one loose and one tight.

Mrs Penrose put on her own black glove and held it out to Fred, fisted around the thinner roll of paper. "About this size? Or thicker, like the one Doctor Penrose is holding?"

Fred immediately pointed to Doctor Penrose's wider roll of paper. "The glove was more like the doctor's in size too."

Grace took out a knitting needle from her mother's bag, which held the beginnings of a baby's jacket for Molly. "Could the cream-coloured object have been as thin as this, Fred?"

Fred shook his head emphatically, causing his blond locks to fly.

Anne held out her walking stick. Fred took it by the straight bottom end, rather than the hooked top, and passed it to Doctor Penrose to hold. "About that size, I think. But hard and knobbly, not round. And pale, not dark." He drew a circle in the air, close around the fist. "That's all I saw. I really couldn't tell what the person was holding. I'm sorry."

Grace could see that Fred was trying his hardest to help, but not succumbing to the temptation to make up details when he reached the limits of what he saw. "You have wonderful observation skills, Fred. Mr Pyke will be most impressed. Can you tell me what happened after that?"

Fred's face crumpled. "I got a fright when I saw the person so close to the door. I thought he might hear me. So I crept down the hall to our room to tell my mama. Except she wasn't there. I hid behind the bed. Then there was smoke and a bell ringing. Mama said always run away from a fire, but I couldn't, because the only way out was past it. I waited for someone to come to get me, but the smoke only got worse. Then I remembered the woman in the room. I tried the door handle, but it was so hot it burned my hands. There was so much smoke, I couldn't breathe. I didn't know what to do, so I ran to the room at the far end of the hall, but I couldn't get the window open." His steadily rising tone reached a wail. "It seemed like ages until Mr Pyke came for me."

"You were very brave, Fred," Grace said.

Mrs Coster took her son in her arms and hugged his tears away. Grace whispered an apology for upsetting the lad and left them together. The information she'd gained would be invaluable for hunting the killer, but the price Fred had paid left her feeling wretched.

Mrs Penrose took one look at her daughter's expression and wrapped her in a warm embrace. Mrs Brown came out from the kitchen and added to her recovery by pressing a steaming dish of hotpot into Grace's hands for their dinner. Grace thanked her effusively. The comforting aroma left her longing to be home with

Charlie, sharing a meal, exchanging vital evidence, and retiring to bed early.

Anne stopped her as Grace opened the front door. "I know you're longing to get home, Grace, but we've just received an urgent message to say Molly is in labour. Unfortunately, Rory is out on a patient call and I'm busy here. Hopefully, Rory will be back soon."

The tantalising smell of hotpot drifted away with the breeze. "I'll see to Molly. You send a message to her husband, if you know where Rory went. I'll go via our house to leave a note for Charlie."

Twelve hours later, Grace finally returned home. Above her, stars twinkled in a velvet sky, their light blurred by her exhaustion. Molly's labour hadn't been easy. Grace couldn't desert her best friend even when her husband returned, especially not when Molly's face was pinched white with fear and pain. Grace's hand still throbbed where Molly had clutched it.

Charlie lay asleep on the sofa, still wearing yesterday's clothes. On the table beside him lay the note Grace had scribbled in haste late yesterday afternoon. "Molly in labour. Rory on a call. Hope to be home soon." She'd signed the note: "Your loving wife. PS. Eat all of Mrs B's hotpot. I may be late."

Little wisps of singed hair edged Charlie's jet-black eyebrows, making him look both vulnerable and irresistible. He lay awkwardly on one side, his bandaged arm resting on a cushion. With a rush of joy, she realised this sight would greet her every morning for the rest of her life, hopefully without the injuries. Grace didn't bother wondering why he wasn't in bed. She had felt the same last night. Their first foray into the marital bed ought to be together – as soon as they could find a chance to be in the same place for long enough.

Grace was trying to decide whether to wake him when fatigue overwhelmed her.

When she woke up again, a ribbon of sunlight bordered the heavy curtains in the drawing room. Green eyes flecked with gold observed her, with a trace of rueful amusement dancing at the edges.

Charlie held out his good arm. "Alone at last, my love."

Grace moved into the warmth of his embrace, making sure she didn't touch his burn. "I'm so very sorry, Charlie. Molly went into labour and Rory was out with a patient. Firstborn children have a habit of taking their time."

Strong hands stroked the tension from her shoulders. Charlie freed her hair from its clasps. "Are Molly and the baby well?"

"One perfect baby girl and one blissfully happy mother. I won't bother you with the gory details. Molly suffered minor bleeding and is exhausted, but she will soon forget that, or so the experts say."

"You must be exhausted too."

Grace closed her eyes as Charlie's fingers ran through her hair. "All I want to do is sink into bed."

Charlie kissed her on the cheek and rose from the sofa. "You get settled in bed while I make you a cup of tea. I'll leave you alone for a few hours to recover."

"Come back here, husband." Grace grabbed his hand and pulled him down beside her. "I said I wanted to sink into bed. I didn't mention anything about wanting to be alone."

Charlie breathed in short, ragged breaths against her neck as his good arm went around her. "This time, nothing is going to disturb us. I'll lock the doors, shutter the windows, set the tiger traps, and be right back."

"I applaud the sentiment, Charlie, but there aren't any tigers in New Zealand."

"Knowing my luck, one will have escaped from the circus." Charlie was already heading for the door.

Grace heard the deadbolt being shot, and then he was back, looking delectable with his braces dangling and his hair sticking

70

up. Before they could ascend the stairs like civilised human beings, they were tearing at each other's clothes and flinging items in all directions.

The bell at the front door rang.

Charlie's hand froze on her thigh. "Ignore it."

Grace glanced at the curtains to ensure they were drawn. The bell rang again, a longer peal this time. "What if it's urgent, Charlie? Molly might be suffering post-partum haemorrhaging."

"She's married to a doctor, Grace. More likely, your brothers have decided to stay and torment us." But Charlie sighed and tucked his shirt in, while Grace smoothed his rumpled hair. "If this is one of your brother Jake's pranks, he'll live to regret it."

Grace hurried to straighten her clothes and sweep her long hair into a knot. Her uneasiness rose another notch when she heard an unfamiliar voice at the door. As she retrieved her stockings from the flower vase on the side table and stuffed them under a cushion, two sets of footsteps came down the hallway.

An overpowering sense of foreboding had her regretting the decision to answer the door.

An Untimely Visitor

Charlie had opened the door cautiously, hoping for a messenger who would be on his way in seconds, but fearing the worst. A stranger stood on the doorstep, hat in hands and head bowed politely. A stranger so unexpected, Charlie was lost for words. He was a slight man of advanced middle age, with dark skin, sharp features, and black hair peppered with grey. The ancient tweed coat he wore over a grey waistcoat seemed far too bland for its exotic occupant.

"I have come to ask for the help of Mr Charles Pyke, who I am given to understand is a private detective. My name is Rajiv Lohar."

"I am Charlie Pyke. Unfortunately, I have several pressing matters at hand, which means I cannot take on more investigations at present."

Mr Lohar struggled between polite acceptance and desperation. Desperation won. "Please, Mr Pyke. You have a fine reputation, according to the newspapers. If it is a matter of money, I have savings."

Charlie could have cautioned him not to believe everything he read in the newspapers, especially the Dunedin Ladies' Journal, which had printed several wildly inaccurate articles about him in the past year. But the earnestness of the man's plea was undeniable. Charlie wavered, but he could not turn the man away.

"Please, come in Mr Lohar." Charlie showed their guest through to the drawing room, there being nowhere else to receive him properly. He hoped Grace had had time to put the room in order. "I'm afraid you find us in disarray, for which I apologise."

Shrewd eyes took in the closed curtains and rumpled state of his hosts. Mr Lohar's eyes widened before he bowed his head to

72

hide his embarrassment. "Please excuse my intrusion at such an early hour, madam."

Grace gestured towards an armchair. "Take a seat, sir. I am Miss ... I am Mr Pyke's wife. It is past ten o'clock, a perfect reasonable hour to call. You only find us in disarray because I have just returned from attending a birth. Would you like tea?" She saw his hesitation. "I was about to make a pot. I'm parched."

Rajiv Lohar bowed his head. "Thank you for your kindness, madam."

By the time Grace returned, Charlie had opened the curtains and dispensed with the usual opening pleasantries. He introduced Mr Lohar as Grace placed the tea tray on a central table, poured three cups, and gestured to the plate of biscuits. From the speed Grace devoured her tea and two biscuits, Charlie realised she must be famished as well as parched. Fortunately, Mrs Brown's honey and oatmeal creations were nutritious enough to sustain an army on the march.

Mr Lohar pressed on. "I fear I am under suspicion of killing my employer. The police have removed his body and locked up the house. I am a foreigner. Naturally, they will blame me. I have nowhere else to turn."

Charlie exchanged a glance with Grace, acknowledging her slight nod with a slow blink. "You are employed by Mr Arthur Glanville?"

Their would-be client's lips parted. "How did you know? You reputation as a detective is well deserved, I see."

"By unfortunate coincidence, I am aware of the deaths of both your employer and his cook, Mrs Seaton. Are you aware that Mr Glanville's cook died the day before yesterday?"

"The police told me Mrs Seaton died in a fire. A terrible way to lose one's life." Lohar searched Charlie's scorched face. "You were there, Mr Pyke?"

"I was. I regret I could not save her. In fact, Mrs Seaton was dead before the fire was set, which is the reason the police harbour suspicions about her employer's death. Her death was neither natural nor self-inflicted."

A moment passed, while Rajiv Lohar frowned at them, until the implications struck home. "Mrs Seaton was killed? Deliberately? If that is so, the situation is even worse than I thought. Please, I beg of you, help me. Not only for myself, but for Mr Glanville and Mrs Seaton, who were both fine people."

The familiar sensation of becoming entangled in the sticky web of an investigation stole over Charlie. They could not let this man down. Passing the case to Alistair made sense, except that Alistair also wanted to have time to enjoy the rare visit from his wife's family. Marrying a detective did not make for a simple life. To be fair, marrying a doctor was hardly plain sailing either. Between their separate work lives, Charlie feared he may spend the rest of his life communicating with his wife via scribbled notes.

Charlie sipped his tea, wishing he could read Grace's mind. She would have every right to be cross if he plunged them into another murder investigation with the ink barely dry on their marriage certificate. But he doubted that would be Grace's reaction.

Grace refilled her cup. "Please excuse our hesitation, Mr Lohar. We would like to help you, but the timing is difficult for us at present because of other commitments."

Mr Lohar rose. "Of course. I understand. You must have a great many important cases to deal with."

The dignity of the man's countenance cut Charlie to the quick. Mr Lohar thought they were dismissing him as unimportant, perhaps because of the dark hue of his skin. "It's not that, Mr Lohar. Our families have travelled from afar for a wedding."

Grace went to the sideboard to retrieve one of the wedding photographs, which Lily had developed in her laboratory-darkroom yesterday. Charlie's father, Sergeant Thomas Pyke, and Alistair Stewart stood on either end, with Charlie's mother and aunt between them. She showed the photograph to Mr Lohar. "My husband's parents, his aunt, and his aunt's husband."

Lohar glanced politely at the picture. His mouth formed a perfect "O" as he took in the two petite Chinese women in the middle. He looked at Charlie.

Charlie smiled. "As you can see, I take after my father in appearance."

"I apologise for questioning your motives for declining me. I only wish you had been available." Mr Lohar took up his hat and turned to leave. His gaze landed on the sideboard, where a photograph of the bride and groom now sat on the top of the pile. "Oh. I am so very sorry to intrude. How rude you must think me to call upon you so soon after your wedding."

"You could not have known, especially given your own difficult situation." Grace was looking Charlie straight in the eye when she said it.

"Wait." Charlie had the feeling he would regret it, but they couldn't let this man leave if he was in trouble. "We will use our contacts with the police to find out Mr Glanville's cause of death. If his death was suspicious, and the police believe you are a person of interest, I will discuss the case with my business partner, Alistair Stewart. I should warn you, we seek the truth, wherever it may be found."

"I would expect no less, Mr Pyke. I thank you for being willing to help when you have every reason not to."

"Take a seat, Mr Lohar. Since you are here, it would be helpful to understand why you believe you are a suspect in your employer's death. My wife is the medical expert for our investigation team. You may speak freely in front of her."

"Perhaps you could start with the circumstances of Mr Glanville's death," Grace said.

"I am Mr Glanville's valet. Or rather, his general manservant, as he keeps a small household. Kept. Mr Glanville's physician, Doctor Johnstone, believed Mr Glanville's death was caused by food poisoning from eating contaminated shellfish. The doctor was present at the dinner party where the seafood dish was served, as were Mr Glanville's relatives, the Tucker family. Later that night, the doctor attended Mr Glanville on his sickbed. The next morning, Doctor Johnstone called a meeting to inform the family and servants of his death. Mrs Seaton refused to accept the implication that her meal led to Mr Glanville's death. I'm sorry to say, Mrs Seaton had imbibed a great deal of brandy and created a dreadful scene."

"Am I right in thinking the dinner party was on Friday night and the meeting on Saturday morning?" This fitted with what Charlie knew of Mrs Seaton's arrival at Lavender House around half past ten on Saturday morning, shortly before the wedding failed to start at eleven o'clock.

"Yes, that is correct."

"Why did the doctor conclude it was food poisoning if no one else at the dinner party was affected?" Grace asked.

"My employer was the only one to become sick because he was the only one who ate the curried version of the dish. Mr Glanville grew up in India and became accustomed to highly spiced foods. Mrs Tucker, who is Mr Glanville's older sister, always preferred bland English dishes, even as a child. As did the other members of the Tucker family, all of whom were born in New Zealand."

"If the death was accepted as accidental food poisoning, why would anyone kill the cook?" Charlie asked. "It rather suggests she saw something and let the person know she suspected him or her."

"I believe you are correct, Mr Pyke," Mr Lohar replied. "When Doctor Johnstone announced Mr Glanville died of food poisoning, there was rather an unpleasant scene. Mrs Seaton as good as implied that someone in the room was to blame. I understood her refusal to accept that her food could have been at fault. Mrs Seaton took great pride in her craft and was very fond of her employer. At the time, I put the intemperance of her accusations down to the shock of Mr Glanville's death and an excess of brandy. But now, I wonder if she had cause to suspect deliberate poisoning."

"Do you believe Mrs Seaton had somebody in particular in mind?" Grace asked.

Mr Lohar angled his head, as if replaying the scene in his mind. "I am not sure. I was distraught myself and not paying close attention. Regardless, I will be blamed by the family. Probably by the police as well."

"Detective Sergeant Kelly is leading the investigating," Charlie said. "He is a fair man and an excellent policeman. You need not worry about Kelly being prejudiced. I take it Mr Glanville's family is not so inclined to be fair-minded?"

Rajiv Lohar replied with carefully considered words. "Mr Glanville's sister married a man called Jack Tucker. The Tucker family, except for the daughter, Miss Henrietta, consider the English race to be superior, especially relative to those of us born far to the east of the English Channel."

Charlie shifted uneasily, being no stranger to such beliefs. "You believe their views to be so entrenched that they would accuse you of poisoning your employer without evidence?"

Lohar didn't blink. "They refuse to eat if I serve the food. When they come to dine, Mr Glanville gives me the night off and asks the maids to serve. I was out late at my chess club that night. In retrospect, I wish I had stayed home to protect my employer."

"You are very loyal," Grace said.

"I have cared for Mr Arthur Glanville since I helped him learn to walk as a child in Calcutta, almost forty-five years ago. Such was the bond between myself and Mr Arthur, the Glanville family took me with them when the family moved to New Zealand in 1862. Mrs Tucker does not appear to comprehend that the entire family would be long dead if I harboured any murderous resentment against them."

"And you wish us to investigate to protect you against such accusations?"

"Partly, Mr Pyke. If Mr Glanville was murdered, my main motive for hiring you is to catch the person who did it, and make them pay for their crime. Mr Glanville deserves no less."

Lohar's fierce determination reassured Charlie that their client's loyalties lay with Mr Glanville. Charlie stood up. "I suggest you leave us to make preliminary inquiries, Mr Lohar. After that, we will decide whether and how to proceed. Where may I contact you?"

Lohar passed him a note. "I am staying with a friend from the chess club until Mr Glanville's house is re-opened by the police."

Charlie saw their client to the door, while Grace retreated to the kitchen with the tea tray.

She returned to the drawing room with a platter of thickly sliced bread, cold roast beef, cheese and pickle. "Eat up, Charlie. Something tells me it is going to be a long day."

Post-Mortem II

After Mr Lohar left, Grace and Charlie stayed at home only long enough to wash away day-old sweat with a splash of cold water and put on clean clothes. Grace would have preferred a long soak in the old clawfoot bath downstairs, followed by a long sleep, but that would have to wait. Before they left to examine Mr Glanville's body, Grace spared a longing glance at their bed, made up with crisp new bed linen, which Anne Macmillan had given them as a wedding present. A bouquet of roses sat on the pillows, their petals dropping onto the mockingly pristine bedclothes.

Grace hurried out of the house after her husband, cursing the tangle of skirt around her legs restricting her stride. When Charlie got fixated on the scent of a murderer, keeping up with his long legs was nigh on impossible. Indeed, it was positively dangerous rushing headlong down the steep slope of High Street in an ankle-length skirt.

As if he read her mind, Charlie slowed down and took her arm. "I'm reluctant to take this case," he said. To the eye of any passer-by, Charlie's arm was looped through Grace's with appropriate decorum, but his thumb ran circles around the soft underside of her wrist. "I can think of better things to do."

Grace shivered at his touch. "So can I, but taking the case is the right thing to do in the circumstances. With Alistair's help, I'm sure we can resolve it quickly and move on to more pleasurable activities. I want to visit Molly and her baby too. And make the most of our families while they are here."

They walked on in silence. Grace consoled herself with the prospect of uninterrupted time together once the Penrose and Pyke families had returned home. "When we have some savings, perhaps we could take a belated honeymoon to visit your family in Clyde."

"That would be wonderful, Grace. Meanwhile, what could be more romantic than another autopsy? Have I told you that the Glanville name is associated with the opium trade? Declan is excited, because Arthur Glanville's death gives the police the opportunity to investigate the drug trade from the inside."

By the time they'd reached the mortuary, Charlie had told her about his visit to the Tucker family and she'd gone through Kathleen and Fred's evidence of Mrs Seaton's locked room and the mystery man within.

Doctor Cranston-Hartfield was stripping off his surgical apron as they arrived. "Ah, the newlyweds. I didn't expect to see you here again. I seem to recall giving you leave, Grace. But then, your instincts have always been razor sharp."

"Does that mean Arthur Glanville's death is suspicious?" Grace glanced at the corpse on the slab, but its secrets were shrouded under a cover.

The police surgeon held up a ceramic dish stained with a silvery-black deposit. "Positive Marsh test."

Grace groaned. "Arsenic, not food poisoning."

"A sizable dose. Sufficient to cause acute symptoms and death within a few hours, as described by the attending general practitioner."

"Can you tell how the arsenic was administered?" Charlie asked. "Mr Glanville's cook was upset when the food poisoning was put down to the meal she made of curried seafood."

The police surgeon put the telltale dish back on the bench next to the post-mortem report. "Arsenic in the meal is the most plausible scenario to ensure a significant amount of arsenic was ingested. A pea-sized amount would have been enough, but this poisoner did not skimp on the dose. Curry would be the perfect choice for a poisoner to ensure the arsenic was ingested without the victim noticing. Arsenic is colourless and odourless, of course, but the average person would not necessarily know that or wish to take the risk. The local doctor put it down to food poisoning, which was a reasonable mistake to make, especially with shellfish on the menu. Personally, I wouldn't touch shellfish collected anywhere near a city, given the amount of raw sewage flowing into the sea."

Grace flipped through the post-mortem report. "With this quantity of arsenic, there is no chance his death was accidental."

"The circumstances tend to preclude suicide as well," Doctor Cranston-Hartfield said. "Unless Glanville deliberately poisoned his own meal in order to implicate somebody else, we have a murderer on the loose. I should add that the victim was only forty-five years old and in excellent health, and therefore had no physical reason to end his own life."

Charlie leaned over Grace's shoulder. "Have you informed Detective Inspector Wallace yet?"

"I've only just finished the autopsy. Tell Wallace he'll have my report within the hour."

Grace and Charlie stayed only long enough to look at the corpse. Arthur Glanville was a middle-aged man in fine condition, with a neatly trimmed moustache, a narrow nose and thin lips.

"He looks a lot like his father, Horatio Glanville," Charlie said. "And his sister, Ariadne Tucker, too."

Grace drew the cover back over the victim, settling it gently on his body out of respect. "Arthur Wellesley Glanville. Son of Horatio Nelson Glanville. The Glanville family certainly has a penchant for heroic names."

Charlie frowned. "Arthur Wellesley? Why does the name sound familiar?"

"Arthur Wellesley was better known as the Duke of Wellington – hero of many battles, including Waterloo. A Prime Minister too. Come to think it, I think he fought in India as well."

"There was a portrait of Horatio Glanville on the Tucker's wall," Charlie said. "Big gun, dead tiger, majestic conqueror and master of the Empire. Old Horatio must have been spitting mad when his plebeian son-in-law chose the names Bert and Sid for his sons."

Grace and Charlie arrived at the central police station in a state of tense silence. Charlie stopped on the steps. "Are you sure you want to continue, Grace? Murder investigations can drag on for weeks. Our old friend Detective Sergeant Declan Kelly has been assigned the case. We could leave it in his capable hands."

Grace was on the step above, at face height. She leaned close. "I think we both know that is not going to happen, Detective Penrose Pyke."

"Should I start calling you Detective Penrose Pyke too, Grace?"

"Mrs Penrose Pyke will do fine for now. We wouldn't want criminals to become confused."

"That'll be a mouthful when we are announced at upper-class gatherings." Charlie put on a haughty voice. "Announcing Detective and Doctor Penrose Pyke, who have failed to slaughter a single tiger, but have tossed many a murderous scoundrel behind bars."

"And saved a few lives along the way. Let's give Detective Inspector Wallace the bad news."

Grace followed her husband through the familiar corridors of the police station to his former commander's office. She could tell Detective Inspector Wallace was in no mood for ideal chatter. Paperwork swamped his desk to sternum-level, with no fewer than three folders encased in the red covers signalling government inquiries. Wallace's woolly eyebrows and grey eyes were always a reliable indicator of his feelings. Today they said "stormy with a chance of thunder".

"Sorry to disturb you, sir." Charlie had worked for DI Wallace for a short time, and had never been able to drop the "sir". Wallace epitomised authority, but also an uncompromising commitment to justice. "I've come to inform you that we have been hired to investigate the murder of Arthur Glanville."

One woolly eyebrow sprang upward. It took a lot to surprise Wallace. "By all that's holy, Pyke. How did you know the man was murdered? I haven't received the autopsy findings yet." The eyebrow descended. "Good morning, Grace. Please don't tell me you are back to your job assisting the police surgeon. Is this what young people call a honeymoon these days?"

Charlie kept a straight face. "Nothing more romantic than a double murder, sir. The family physician, Doctor Johnstone, called the family together to inform them of Mr Glanville's death from food poisoning. We have just come from the police surgeon. The doctor was right, in a way. The food was poisoned – with a large helping of arsenic. The woman who died in the Lavender House fire was Mr Glanville's cook. According to our client, Mrs Seaton knew something. She all but accused one of the people present at Mr Glanville's house the morning she died."

"Darned bad timing," Wallace growled. "We're up to our whiskers in crime. Who is your client, Pyke?"

Given Mr Lohar's distrust of the police, Charlie was reluctant to share that information. On the other hand, he trusted Wallace with his life and owed his former commanding officer for his unwavering support. "Let's just say that Mr Glanville's manservant, Mr Rajiv Lohar, is uncommonly loyal."

Wallace grunted. "I've promised to assign DS Kelly to lead the murder investigation. I hope that won't be awkward for you, Pyke."

Grace took a moment to register what Wallace meant. The detective sergeant's position would have been Charlie's, had he and the police force not parted ways due to a misunderstanding (if being accused of murder and misconduct could be considered a misunderstanding).

"Not in the least, sir," Charlie replied. "I couldn't be more delighted that Kelly got the promotion."

"Kelly will be glad to have your help," Wallace continued, "especially as this case may involve more than a simple family dispute. You know of the Glanville link to the opium trade?"

"Yes, sir."

"We've only got a single detective constable available to help Kelly and scarcely enough uniformed constables to cope with the usual workload. Those in power fail to understand that criminals don't take a pleasant break at the seaside when police staffing levels are cut."

This was exactly the opening Charlie was waiting for. "We expect to have our entire team at Southern Investigations Agency on the case, sir, so that Grace and I will be free to enjoy our new lives all the sooner."

Wallace perked up at this news. "Alistair Stewart has made quite the name for himself solving fraud cases. We could use his experience to unravel whatever Arthur Glanville has been hiding in his accounts, and those of his father, if he has kept them."

"Alistair would be glad to help." Charlie said. "Lily Stewart has useful links in the Chinese community too. She volunteers for a group lobbying to make the sale of opium illegal, except for medicinal uses."

"Excellent. Tell Alistair I'll have a desk available here if he needs it, and Mr Peters at the ready."

The friendship between Alistair Stewart and Robbie Wallace went back to their school days in Scotland. From the gleam in Wallace's eye, he'd enjoy having Alistair around, probably over a fine bottle of whisky, chewing over old times – rugby games won, criminals foiled, inept constables rebuked. But Wallace was right. If there was illicit activity to be found, Alistair would sniff it out, whisky or no whisky. Access to Mr Peters was a godsend. The senior records clerk was a walking filing cabinet.

"My father, Sergeant Pyke from the Clyde police station, would also be willing to assist. Interviewing, checking alibis, raiding opium dens, putting the fear of God into reluctant suspects. If that is acceptable to you, sir?"

Wallace's granite features remained intact, aside from an upward tilt to one side of his mouth, signalling his delight. "A team of experienced officers, available at no cost? I believe I might be willing to allow that, Pyke." Wallace rocked back in his chair, risking gravity. "Leaving me to sit on my rump?" His lip quirked up further. "I like it. I'll get Kelly to deputise your father for local work. Don't want the killer to get off because his statement wasn't taken in an official capacity. Always comes down to the darned paperwork."

"The police will get the credit, naturally," Charlie said. "I'll leave you to your paperwork, shall I, sir?"

Wallace's bushy eyebrows merged back into one another at the mention of paperwork. Grace and Charlie escaped while they could.

Doctor Johnstone

Charlie and Grace found Detective Sergeant Declan Kelly at his desk. The news that it was now a double-murder investigation had him pulling at the traces to start interviewing witnesses. Doctor Johnstone was first on his list.

Declan allowed them a brief stop at the Stewart's house on the way, but only because Charlie insisted on informing the rest of the Southern Investigations team that he had volunteered their services. They stopped only long enough to outline the case. The Stewart and Pyke families agreed that even a honeymoon came second to solving a double-murder with a link to the opium trade. Lily offered to use her contacts in the Chinese community, while Alistair and Thomas were eager to use their policing skills, starting with background checks on the Glanville and Tucker families.

Charlie, Grace and Declan arrived at the doctor's surgery at quarter past one on Monday afternoon. The surgery had seen better days, with a rusting roof and peeling paint. However, the brass nameplate attached to the door was polished to a shine.

Doctor Clifford Johnstone was taller, thinner, and younger than Charlie expected. Perhaps late twenties or early thirties. His impeccable dress contrasted with the threadbare condition of the waiting room. A framed degree from a prestigious London medical school and the confident tilt of the doctor's chin suggested a privileged upbringing. The question was, what had brought a young man with good prospects to a struggling general practice in a country at the far side of the world?

The doctor ran his hand through thinning hair, which was already standing on end. "I'm sorry, gentlemen. I am not seeing any more patients today, as I have a pressing engagement." Johnstone turned back towards his office.

Kelly held up his badge. "This is an urgent police matter, Doctor Johnstone."

Johnstone glanced at the clock behind the reception desk before ushering Charlie and Declan into his office. Grace had to push in behind them before he shut the door in her face. Despite this, Charlie noted her serene expression didn't falter, suggesting she expected no less.

Declan gestured for the doctor to sit. "This is Detective Penrose Pyke, a private investigator, and Mrs Penrose Pyke, the assistant police surgeon."

Johnstone's head jerked in Grace's direction. She didn't blink.

"I am here regarding the death of Mr Arthur Glanville," Declan continued. "First, can you tell me how long you have known that gentleman?"

Johnstone glanced at his pocket watch, but answered the question readily. "I've been Mr Glanville's doctor since I arrived in New Zealand two years ago. I had a letter of introduction to him. Or rather, to his father, who died last year. Horatio Glanville."

"Who provided the letter of introduction?"

"My father knew Horatio Glanville when he lived overseas."

"In India?" Charlie asked, noting the exotic figurines on the bookshelf and putting this together with the Indian origins of their client, Mr Lohar.

The doctor jerked again. Charlie loved a suspect who couldn't hide his reactions.

"I grew up in Calcutta, in India. My family had a long association with the East India Company, as did the Glanville family." Johnstone picked up a paper knife in the shape of a jewelled dagger and twisted it with quick, nervous fingers. "The Glanville family emigrated to New Zealand before I was born. All except Horatio Glanville's elder son, Raleigh, who stayed to run the export arm of the Glanville company. But the connection was sufficient to remind Mr Glanville of the fact when I came to Dunedin."

Charlie reminded himself this was DS Kelly's case, but, as always, curiosity won out over respectful silence. "Why Dunedin, Doctor Johnstone?"

"I completed my medical training in London and returned to India to work as a doctor. I found I couldn't stand the Indian heat after living in a cool climate for several years." Doctor Johnstone gestured ruefully at his pale face and ginger hair. "The opportunity arose to come to New Zealand, and here I am. It suits me well, I have to say." He put the jewelled dagger down. "Why are you asking these questions?"

"You also have another connection to the family, I believe?" Declan said. "Your nurse is Miss Henrietta Tucker, Arthur Glanville's niece."

Red flared across the doctor's cheeks, highlighting his freckles. "Nurse Tucker is on bereavement leave. One must be considerate of one's employees in such circumstances."

Charlie could not resist. "Miss Henrietta Tucker told us you are a very considerate person."

Johnstone leaned towards the compliment with the eagerness of an awkward schoolboy. "She did? How lovely of her. Such a lovely person herself." He snapped back into his seat. "A selfless nurse, I mean. Very dependable and competent."

Charlie smiled internally at these classic symptoms of a man in love, who hadn't yet informed the object of his passion of his feelings. Charlie hoped he hadn't been this inept in his courtship of Grace. "I believe you recommended Lavender House for Mrs Seaton after her breakdown on Saturday morning?"

"That's correct. I hope she is fully recovered now. I expect she is worried that she will lose her position as a cook after her employer's death, and I look forward to informing her she has no concerns on that score."

"How so?"

Johnstone glanced at his watch again. "I am not at liberty to say. I must cut short this interview, as I am due at Mr Glanville's house for the reading of his will at two o'clock."

"Why? Are you a beneficiary?" Charlie was eager to know the contents of the will himself, given that arsenic was commonly referred to as "inheritance powder".

"I'm not a beneficiary. It's complicated. The solicitor, Mr Fairchild, has asked me to be there to answer any questions the family might have."

"Questions over the cause of death, perhaps?" Declan said. "After Mrs Seaton declared that her cooking was not at fault in her employer's death."

"Oh no, there is no doubt about the cause of death. Food poisoning. Classic symptoms – nausea, stomach cramps and so forth. The shellfish, almost certainly. I was at the dinner party myself. Mr Glanville ate a separate dish to the rest of us. Most tragic. Human waste from our fair city flows directly into the harbour, you know. I caution all my patients never to eat shellfish, but Mr Glanville was fond of them and he trusted his cook to know which ones were tainted."

"How soon did his stomach pains start?" Grace asked.

"Not long after the Tucker family departed the house after dinner, as far as I understood the matter from the maid's garbled story. Mr Glanville's manservant, Mr Lohar, came to fetch me shortly before midnight. Mr Lohar had returned from his chess club late and found his employer in a distressed state. There was nothing I could do at that point, beyond dosing the patient with a strong emetic. He died shortly afterwards. I called the family to a meeting at half-past nine the next morning to give them the dreadful news."

"Mrs Seaton made a fuss at the meeting, we understand," Declan said.

"Frightfully embarrassing. Mrs Seaton has always shown exemplary behaviour in the past, but she was very much the worse for drink on this occasion. I fear she must have turned to brandy after I upset her by getting her up at midnight to question her about the preparation of the meal. She still refused to accept my verdict of food poisoning the next morning Most forcefully, I might add. Fortunately, Miss Tucker was on hand to take the cook to a women's refuge I knew of, to sober her up. I should have gone with her, but I had patients waiting and Miss Tucker is very capable."

"You had no reason to doubt the cause of Arthur Glanville's death?" Declan asked.

"Why would I? Mr Glanville was perfectly healthy the afternoon of his death, when he visited me to have his annual health examination. Very careful of his health, he was. I only wish my other patients could be the same." The doctor glanced at his watch again. "I really must go."

Declan rose with him. "We will walk with you. We still have questions about the events around the death of Mr Glanville."

"Why? I don't understand why you took his body for a post-mortem." Doctor Johnstone paused while reaching for his overcoat, a small frown creasing his forehead. "Has somebody made an allegation, or is it in response to the cook's drunken rant?"

Charlie thought the doctor wasn't very quick off the mark if he was only now wondering why they were asking all these questions. However, his answers seemed straightforward. Perhaps Johnstone had never had a patient die under suspicious circumstances. Certainly, the doctor had an air of unworldly innocence that Grace had never had, but then she had experience of her father's cases and an early introduction to forensic medicine. Charlie, who was only twenty-four years old, felt old and jaded next to the doctor's apparent naivety.

Declan answered. "Mrs Seaton died soon after she was taken to Lavender House, Doctor Johnstone. We are treating her death as suspicious, and therefore we also had to make certain of her employer's cause of death. The results of the post-mortem indicate that Mr Arthur Glanville died of acute arsenic poisoning."

Johnstone came to a dead halt with his hand on the office door. Emotions flashed across his face – shock, mortification, and anguish in quick succession. "Poor Henrietta. She adored her uncle." With that, he sprinted for the front door. He didn't stop running until he reached Arthur Glanville's residence, ten minutes early for the two o'clock reading of the will. Even Charlie's long legs, well-practiced on the steep streets of Dunedin, struggled to keep up.

Charlie paused to wipe his boots at the front door and greet the constable on guard, but the doctor ran right past. Johnstone spared a moment to greet a man waiting in the hall before going through to a room beyond. Looking for Henrietta Tucker, no doubt. Charlie couldn't fail to notice the uncommon degree of familiarity Doctor Johnstone displayed within a patient's house. He wondered just how close Arthur Glanville had been to his doctor and why.

Charlie leaned on the veranda post and watched Declan puff up behind him. "Indulging in too many of your wife's steak and kidney puddings, DS Kelly? Or is it too much of that concoction your brother-in-law passes off as Guinness?"

Declan swept a hand towards the horizon. "Just stopped to admire the view, on account of us Irish having poetry in our souls, unlike your lot."

He had a point. Eglinton Road dropped away before them to the flats of South Dunedin and a wide swept of ocean beyond, with no land to speak of for thousands of miles. Charlie grunted unpoetically and went inside.

The only person to have arrived before them was a middle-aged man with a pleasant smile and deep bags under his eyes, who had taken a seat in the hallway. Charlie's gaze dropped to the stain on the man's waistcoat.

The man rose, quickly buttoning his coat over the stain. He rummaged in his coat pocket, withdrawing a child's tin soldier and a tiny silver rattle before finding his calling card. "Mr Percy Fairchild, Mr Glanville's solicitor. I don't wish to appear rude, gentlemen, but this is a private family meeting."

The rumpled solicitor seemed out of place in such a grand household. The entrance hall was almost as large as the cottage Charlie grew up in, but the air hung still and lifeless. A curved stairway swept up past a row of distinguished gentlemen, looking down from their portraits with the arrogant assurance of their lofty status, and the same pale, narrow faces and thin noses as Arthur Glanville and Ariadne Tucker.

Declan showed his badge to the solicitor. "Detective Sergeant Kelly. I am here to investigate the murder of Mr Arthur Glanville. I would be obliged if you do not disclose that fact until I chose to do so."

Mr Fairchild's extended hand dropped. "Murder? I'm afraid you have been misinformed, Detective Sergeant Kelly. Mr Glanville died of food poisoning."

"His death was confirmed as arsenic poisoning this morning," Declan said. "Were you at the fatal dinner party, Mr Fairchild?"

Fairchild hauled up his gaping lower jaw. "Arthur was murdered?" He flopped back onto the seat, fanning his face with the document folder sitting on the seat beside him. "Excuse me. The shock. Arthur Glanville has been my friend since he arrived in Dunedin thirty years ago. He didn't know a soul when he walked into our high school classroom. My apologies, I'm rambling. What must I do, Detective Sergeant?"

"You must continue to read the will as you would under ordinary circumstances. And it is me who should apologise, Mr Fairchild. Had I realised the close personal attachment between yourself and Mr Glanville, I would have been more cautious in my choice of words."

"Would you like a glass of water, Mr Fairchild?" Grace said. "Or brandy?"

"Yes, yes. Dora will get them." Mr Fairchild pushed himself to his feet and took up his silver-topped walking cane. "Come through to the drawing room."

The solicitor walked ahead of them, leaning on his walking cane. Tap, tap, tap on the polished wooden floor. Grace and Charlie exchange a glance. Tap, tap, tap, just like the sound little Fred Coster overheard in Mrs Seaton's room right before she was stabbed.

Baffling Bequests

...
...
...
...

Four people were already in Arthur Glanville's drawing room when they entered. Doctor Johnstone hovered by the door, fiddling with his cuffs. Their client, Mr Rajiv Lohar, gave the tiniest of nods from the furthest corner of the room. Today, he wore a white cotton tunic with a round collar, which fitted him far better than yesterday's tweed coat.

Two women sat next to the manservant, both wearing maids' uniforms. They held hands, using their free hands to press thin cotton handkerchiefs to swollen eyes. They seemed an unlikely pair of maids. Both were around forty years old, with the taller one as alert and watchful as a guard dog, while the shorter one hunched in her seat with the sorrowful eyes of an abandoned spaniel.

The taller maid rose at Mr Fairchild's entry. She took one look at his pallor and strode to the drinks cabinet to pour him a glass of water and another of brandy. "Should I see to the door, Mr Fairchild? We haven't been allowed back into the house since our dear Mr Glanville died. I don't know what to do."

Charlie stepped up. "I'll see to the door. You take a seat, Miss …"

"Miss Dora Eady." The maid bobbed unfashionably low and returned to her seat.

Charlie went back out to the hallway to wait for the family to arrive.

The grandfather clock in the hall was ticking down to two o'clock when the Tucker family walked in. Their astonishment at seeing Charlie was almost comical. Each remained true to the character they had shown at their own house yesterday. Miss Henrietta Tucker gave him a weak smile, her red eyes evidence of her sorrow at losing her uncle. Mrs Ariadne Tucker's glance passed over Charlie quickly, signalling he was beneath her notice. Mr Jack Tucker and his older son, Bert, glowered, while the younger son, Sid, trailed behind, displaying no reaction at all.

Sensing trouble ahead, Charlie asked the constable by the door to come inside. They followed the Tucker family up the hall to the drawing room. Jack and Bert Tucker both wore their work clothes, including heavy work boots. The metal tips of the boots drummed a thonk, thonk, thonk on the wooden floor as they clomped up the hall. Charlie imagined the same boots, tiptoeing as quietly as they could, might well sound like a tap, tap, tap.

By the time Charlie entered the room, Henrietta had taken the seat next to Doctor Johnstone in the opposite corner from the servants. The doctor reached out to pat her on the arm as tentatively as he might pat a stray kitten. Henrietta beamed at him in response.

The other four members of the Tucker family took the armchairs closest to the table at the front of the room, where Mr Fairchild sat tapping his foot and twitching. Declan Kelly took a seat behind the solicitor and directed the constable to the rear of the room. Charlie stood in front of the exit, feet apart, arms crossed, eyes scanning back and forth.

Mrs Ariadne Tucker sniffed loudly. "We are here. Perhaps you might start, Mr Fairchild?"

The solicitor reached for his folder, fumbling as he opened it. "I have before me the Last Will and Testament of Arthur Wellesley Glanville."

The four Tuckers in the front row leaned forward, their eyes bright with anticipation. Henrietta bit back a sob and took out a fresh handkerchief.

"Stop." Jack Tucker pointed at Declan. "That policeman and his bully boys have no right to be here. This is a private family matter." He finished the sentence with a deep, hacking cough.

The solicitor turned to Declan, who gestured for him to continue.

"Detective Sergeant Kelly has the authority to be here." Mr Fairchild cleared his throat and picked up the document in front of him, which shook so badly, he put it down again. "The will begins with bequests to Mr Glanville's long-serving household staff, as one would expect. The rest of the estate ..."

"Wait," Mrs Tucker commanded. "You haven't stated the amounts of the bequests."

Fairchild glanced at the door, but there was no escape. "Miss Dora Eady and Miss Nellie Eady, who have given many years of exemplary service, are bequeathed £40 ..."

The two maids' hands flew to their mouths simultaneously to hide their surprise at so large a sum.

Mrs Tucker gasped. "£20 each? Outrageous."

"As I was saying, the Eady sisters are bequeathed £40 *each*." The solicitor soldiered on, his expression grim but determined. "Mrs Seaton was to have received £50. As Arthur Glanville predeceased her, this sum will go to her relatives, if any."

Jack Tucker leaped to his feet, red-faced. "I don't earn much more than that for an entire year's work and I'm a qualified gas-fitter with decades of experience."

"I'm sure Mrs Seaton had no relatives to speak of," his wife said. "And what, pray tell, did she do to deserve so much?"

"Mrs Seaton gave devoted service as an experienced cook to the Glanville family for thirty years." The solicitor looked down at the document before him, shielding his face from the onlookers. When he continued, his voice had a distinct shake. "Mr Rajiv Lohar receives £200 for his lifetime of service to Mr Glanville."

The intake of breath from the audience was so palpable that Charlie swore he felt the air move past his cheek. Mr Lohar, his prospective client, had been right to seek his help. The manservant was cowering in the back row, rigid with shock. Clearly, the size of the bequest, probably worth four to five years of wages, had stunned Lohar as much as the rest of the gathering.

This time it was the older brother, Bert Tucker, who leaped to his feet. "But the manservant is …." He spluttered to a furious halt, not finding the right words. "He is not even British."

Fairchild looked away to hide his disgust. "The remaining assets of the estate will be split equally between Mrs Ariadne Tucker née Glanville, and her three children, Albert, Sidney, and Henrietta Tucker."

This announcement met with mixed reactions. Mr Tucker and Henrietta were surprised, but pleased, and Sid nodded his approval. Mrs Tucker was undecided, perhaps expecting to have been the principal heir. Bert Tucker jerked at the mention of equal shares. As the oldest male relative, presumably he felt entitled to the lion's share.

Mrs Ariadne Tucker née Glanville leaned further forward, her nostrils quivering. "How much is the estate worth?"

The solicitor flicked an eye towards the door but, once again, resisted the urge to flee. He cleared his throat and sipped some water before changing his mind and taking a gulp of brandy. "There will have to be a reconciliation of the estate accounts, naturally, so I am not in a position to speculate."

"Give us your best estimate," the older brother growled.

With a further unnecessary shuffling of papers, Mr Fairchild mumbled, "Perhaps somewhere in the order of £1000 in total."

The silence was so complete for a moment that even the air in the room did not dare to stir. Then chaos broke loose.

Jack Tucker advanced on the solicitor with clenched fists. "Don't try to deceive us, you snake in the grass. My father-in-law was worth a small fortune. We know Horatio Glanville left his estate to his son, Arthur Glanville, when he died last year. Even Arthur could not have been so spineless as to have let that much dribble through his fingers in so short a time."

Declan Kelly stepped between Jack Tucker and the terrified solicitor.

Bert pushed past them. "Are you telling us that each of us will get scarcely more than the manservant? That conniving –"

Charlie moved to Mr Fairchild's side. "I advise you to curb your anger, gentlemen, and let Mr Fairchild finish."

Bert would not be silenced. "My grandfather was a great man. A man of power and distinction and wealth. This cannot be right. Horatio Glanville promised me he would make my sacrifice worthwhile and I expected Arthur Glanville to honour that promise. As the oldest grandson of Horatio, with no cousins to contest my rights of inheritance, I assure you that you have not heard the last of this."

Jack Tucker's fury was almost equal to that of his older son. "Bert's right. Arthur said he would do right by my sons. Bert could have been earning a decent wage as a gas-fitter like me, instead of working in a menial job in the Glanville family company. And Sid needs money to expand his tailoring business."

Sid Tucker glanced at his gold watch with exaggerated emphasis. "There's no point shouting at the lackey who is reading this preposterous will, Father. We must take immediate legal advice from the best attorney in Dunedin. Any half-baked judge will see that the will is grossly unfair to Arthur Glanville's blood relatives."

Mrs Tucker finally recovered her power of speech, and she applied it at screeching volume. "Inconceivable! How can Arthur's estate only be worth £1000? I demand an explanation, Fairchild. In fact, I demand an investigation of your competence in the matter."

"A swindle," Bert Tucker muttered. "Plain as the nose of my face."

Mr Fairchild's cheeks may have been the colour of overripe tomatoes, but he retained his dignity in his ramrod posture and raised chin. "Sir, madam, I must ask you to restrain yourselves. I assure you I am telling you the truth."

Mrs Tucker sank back into her chair. "And I am telling you, Mr Fairchild, it is impossible – utterly impossible. Why, this house alone is worth that much. Before my father died, he passed the export business in India to my oldest brother, Raleigh. My younger brother, Arthur, inherited everything else when my father died last year. Arthur had his own money too. His inventions had made him a modest fortune."

Mr Fairchild shuffled his papers again. "The house is not part of the estate, Mrs Tucker. Your brother has sold the property. I assure you, Mr Arthur Glanville sought and received independent legal advice before taking this step. That is all I am at liberty to disclose."

From his position next to the solicitor, Charlie had an excellent view of the beneficiaries of Arthur Glanville's unexpected will. The Tucker family, including Henrietta, were now stunned into silence. But they were not the only people in the room caught unawares by the sale of the house. The colour had drained from the faces of the two middle-aged maids, who had been so pleasantly surprised by their large bequests. And no wonder, as this house was their home. Mr Rajiv Lohar and Doctor Clifford Johnstone were either better at hiding their emotions, or the news did not come as a surprise to them.

Whatever their expectations of the sums involved, every person in the room gained from Arthur Glanville's death, and thus had a motive to see him dead. Especially so if they thought his estate would be worth a fortune. The only question was, which of them wanted him dead badly enough to murder him?

Mrs Tucker recovered her wits first. "My father's house. Our family home. Sold?"

Bert was still unable to form words, but his brother Sid stepped into the breech with ill-disguised anger. "How dare he? Horatio Glanville made a fortune, and his son dares dishonour that success? Uncle Arthur had no right to dispossess his heirs by giving his fortune away."

"I demand to know when this was done," Mrs Tucker said. "And what happened to the proceeds of the sale?"

"I am not at liberty to disclose any further information on the sale of the house, as it does not form part of the estate." Mr Fairchild gathered up the documents and snapped the folder closed. "However, I can disclose that the fortune amassed by Horatio Glanville had dwindled to almost nothing by the time he died. Mr Arthur Glanville inherited very little when his father died last year, aside from this house. Perhaps it is best if we leave the discussion there for the moment. I urge you to reflect upon the matter and consider the fact that Mr Glanville had the right to do as he wished with the house he inherited and the rest of his own estate."

Bert loomed over the front table, slamming his fist onto the wood. "Balderdash! It's family money. You'll be hearing from our attorney, Fairchild. And if I find out you coerced my uncle into this abomination of a will, I'll be suing you, too."

Bert stormed towards the door, but Charlie intercepted him. Bert tried to push him aside. His hand landed on Charlie's burn, sending pain lancing through his injured arm. Meanwhile, Jack, Ariadne and Sid Tucker clustered around Bert, demanding to be let out. Charlie stumbled back against the door, holding it closed.

Declan had had enough. "Everybody sit down. Now," he bellowed. When the startled Tuckers returned to their seats, Declan resumed speaking with quiet authority. "The death of Mr Glanville is the subject of a police inquiry. The estate of Arthur Wellesley Glanville will not proceed to settlement until the investigation is complete."

"But Uncle Arthur died of food poisoning," Henrietta said.

"I regret to inform you, Miss Tucker," Declan said, "that your uncle died of acute arsenic poisoning. You will all remain in Dunedin whilst we conduct a full investigation. Furthermore, you will not leave this room until I conduct preliminary interviews."

"Arsenic? But how ..." Henrietta stammered.

Bert Tucker turned and jabbed a calloused finger towards Rajiv Lohar. "There's no need to interview us. Arrest that man."

What The Maids Saw

In the scuffle following Bert's accusation against Rajiv Lohar, Charlie and the two policemen had their hands full of Tuckers. Grace, who was standing in the shadows at the rear of the room, was more than happy to leave them to that thankless task. Instead, she followed the hasty retreat of the two maids out the rear door. They interested Grace, these two women who must have been around forty years old, still working as maids in a household with no housekeeper. Perhaps their sisterly bond was so close, they ran the household jointly.

Grace followed them to the kitchen, stopping at the door to listen. Her standards of behaviour had slipped since getting into the detection business. One sister was sobbing, while the other was murmuring comforting words, while stoking the stove under the kettle. Grace peeked around the doorframe.

The shorter of the two sisters, Nellie Eady, was the one sobbing. "Arsenic! As if it was not bad enough that our dear Mr Glanville died so suddenly."

Dora left the stove and gathered Nellie against her sturdy shoulder, rubbing her back with tender strokes. "There now, Nellie. Calm yourself, my dear. A nice strong cup of tea is what you need. There'll be time enough for tears at the funeral."

"How can you think of tea when our home is to be sold, Dora? Why would Mr Glanville not have told us?"

"I expect that is why he left us such a large sum of money, so we could make our own home after his death. Right now, the sale of the house is not our main concern. Now is the time to be brave and clever. We must do all we can to find out who did this terrible thing to our Mr Glanville."

Nellie's sobs died away into gurgling hiccoughs. "What do you mean, Dora?"

"Arsenic does not get into a man's food by mistake, my dear." Dora's voice was soft, but edged with cut glass. "He was murdered."

A squeal erupted from Nellie, but she cut it off quickly. "That will be why that other detective was with Detective Sergeant Kelly. I know who he is. Do you recall that article in the Ladies' Journal last year?"

"Nellie, dearest, you know I never read that gossip rag."

"The big man standing by the door was Mr Charles Pyke, Dunedin's most famous detective. I'm sure of it, Dora."

"Is he indeed? I wonder how Mr Pyke came to be involved so quickly, when the announcement of Mr Glanville's murder has only just been made? Mr Lohar went out very early this morning. He must have suspected something when the police took Mr Glanville's body away yesterday evening. The question is, what made the police suspicious in the first place, when Doctor Johnstone certified his death as food poisoning?"

Grace hoped her heartbeat was not audible in the silence that followed. Clever, observant witnesses who wanted to help were gold dust to an investigation.

Nellie spoke again, uncertain this time. "Perhaps I am mistaken. I read in the Ladies' Journal that Mr Pyke married his sweetheart on Saturday. He'll be off on his honeymoon. Somewhere marvellous, I expect. He must be ever so wealthy if he is so clever."

The amused snort passed through Grace's nostrils before she could stop it.

"Who's there?" Dora's voice, sharp and commanding.

Grace showed herself. "My apologies for intruding, ladies. I came to talk to you and overheard your conversation. I am Mrs Charlie Pyke, but do call me Grace. Unfortunately, my husband and I do not have the means to take a honeymoon out of town at present. The reason we have been so quick to take the case is that Mrs Seaton's death was also murder and it occurred during our wedding. Mr Pyke and our team of investigators will find out who did this, you can be assured. We could use your help."

Nellie burst into tears again. "Mrs Seaton? Murdered?"

Dora appraised Grace with shrewd eyes.

Grace appraised Dora right back. The sisters obviously shared a close bond, but were complete opposites in both personality and appearance. Grace wondered if they were two women who had found sanctuary within a kind and unconventional household, rather than sisters, but it was not relevant to the case.

Dora kept up her inspection for another few seconds, before giving a barely noticeable nod. "Time for that cup of tea, Nellie."

Nellie rose on command and wiped away her tears. She bustled about the kitchen, clattering the kettle against the teapot and clinking cups onto a tray in a manner hazardous to fine porcelain. Grace was left in no doubt who was in charge, for all that Dora had issued her instructions in a soft, soothing tone.

A rack of implements hung above the kitchen bench, inches above Nellie's wispy, grey-streaked hair. Several metal skewers of various sizes dangled from it, reminding Grace that long, thin stabbing weapons might be found in any home.

"Take a seat, Mrs Pyke. Grace. You may call us Dora and Nellie." Dora took the seat at the head of the kitchen table, gesturing for Grace to take the seat to her left. "We were told Mrs Seaton died in a fire. Am I to understand the fire was deliberately lit?"

Grace sensed that honesty would work best for an astute woman like Dora, even though Grace ought to keep the details of Mrs Seaton's murder to herself. She compromised with a partial truth. "Mrs Seaton was dead before the fire started. The fire was lit to make her death appear accidental. It makes one wonder. Who would go to such lengths to kill a cook at the risk of causing the death of the other innocents inside the refuge?"

"The lowest scoundrel, to be sure," Dora said. "Her death so soon after Mr Glanville's cannot be a coincidence, especially after Mrs Seaton refused to believe Mr Glanville had been poisoned by her cooking. Do you think she knew who poisoned our employer?"

Nellie rattled up to the table with a tray of tea. She stumbled on a flagstone, but Dora rescued the tray with such practiced hands that Grace would have missed it if she hadn't turned at that moment.

Dora set the tray down and began to pour. "Fruit cake, Nellie. And while you're there, prepare a tea tray for the detectives, please. Men need food in their stomach if they are going to keep their wits about them and arrest the right man."

Grace watched Nellie scurry across the kitchen into the pantry. Was Dora sparing her sister from listening to the details of Mrs Seaton's demise, or did such bossiness come naturally?

Dora answered her question by pouring forth information at a rapid clip in a low voice. "Mrs Seaton was a fine woman. She rarely touched a drop of alcohol. For her to have imbibed an excess of cooking brandy shows she was under overwhelming stress following Mr Glanville's death. I believe she had her suspicions, but she had no time to share them with me."

A voice from the pantry interrupted. "I can't find the cake, Dora."

"Top left, in the coronation tin. You'll need the stool to reach it." Dora's lips tightened, perhaps in anticipation of Nellie balancing on a stool.

Grace hurried on. "Could Mrs Seaton have added arsenic to the food by mistake? Perhaps mistaking arsenic kept for vermin for an ingredient in her cooking?"

"Absolutely not. Mrs Seaton never allowed any dangerous substances in the kitchen. Certainly, nothing as dangerous as arsenic. If any vermin needed seeing to, I got the gardener to use traps. The gardener lives in his own house and stores nothing on Mr Glanville's property. There can be no doubt about the culinary skills or loyalty of Mrs Seaton, who worked for the Glanville family all her life. She was devoted to Mr Glanville. The same is true for Nellie and I, although we have only worked for Mr Arthur Glanville, while the cook worked as a scullery maid for Mr Horatio Glanville first. Our Mr Glanville's father, that is."

The clatter of a dropped cake tin lid in the pantry made Grace wince. "Can you tell me who was in the house the day of the fatal dinner?"

Dora paused while Nellie assembled a tea tray and retreated from the kitchen. The tray, presumably bound for the detectives, could be heard rattling down the corridor before disappearing into another room without an accompanying crash. "Mr Glanville only keeps a small staff. Nellie and I went about our regular duties all day, although we did less dusting upstairs than usual, so we could prepare the dining room and clean the silver. Mr Lohar attended to Mr Glanville in the morning and left at noon for his half day off, not returning until after the dinner was over."

"Did anyone visit on the day leading up to the dinner?" Grace asked.

"Mr Fairchild, Mr Glanville's solicitor, visited around two o'clock in the afternoon. You need not add Mr Fairchild to your list of suspects. He and Mr Glanville have been best friends since they went to Dunedin High School together. As for his visit, I presume it was a business matter, rather than a social matter, but I do not know for certain."

"Why was Mr Fairchild not invited to stay for dinner?"

"It was a family dinner with the Tuckers. Besides, Mr Fairchild has a wife and five children. He prefers to spend his evenings at home with his family." Dora nodded her approval. "Mr Glanville respected that."

"But Doctor Johnstone was invited," Grace said.

"Mr Glanville hoped that the doctor would soon be family. Which reminds me. After Mr Fairchild's visit on Friday afternoon, Mr Glanville went to visit Doctor Johnstone."

Grace's ears pricked. "Was he feeling unwell?"

"Fit as a fiddle," Dora said. "He went for his annual medical examination."

Nellie returned with a plate of fruit cake. "Not that there was anything wrong with him. He said it was always best to ensure that everything was in good working order rather than waiting for it to break down and have to fix it. Our Mr Glanville had a funny way of talking like that, as if he looked on everything as a machine. He was a brilliant engineer, you know. Invented some little whatsit before he was twenty years old. Bought his own house at the age of twenty-two on the back of it. That's when me and Dora started working for him. Our first and only employer."

When Nellie took a seat and reached for a slice of cake, Grace noticed that her hand shook. Nellie saw her looking and dropped her hand to the table to support it. Shaking palsy, probably in its early stages. No wonder Nellie suffered from clumsiness. All the more reason to fear for a future without their generous employer.

Grace looked back at Dora. "Was it this house he bought? The whatsit must have been a great success to purchase such a grand home."

"It was a valve for regulating gas flow," Dora said. "Mr Glanville bought a modest house, just big enough for two maids, a manservant and a cook. We have been together, like a family, ever since. We only moved to this house last year, after Mr Glanville's father died."

Nellie crumbled her cake with the tips of her fingers. "I preferred the old house. Cosy, it was. Our Mr Glanville preferred the old place too. He said this house was built on bones, whatever that meant. This place is too much for Dora and me at our age. Most of it is never used."

Grace wanted to know more about why Mr Glanville chose to live in a house he disliked, but the solicitor would be better informed about Mr Glanville's motives for moving from his own home into the Glanville family house. She wanted to concentrate on what happened here in the hours before the poisoning. "Did anyone else visit the house the day of the dinner?"

"Not that I know of," Dora said. "I went out for an hour or so in the early afternoon on an errand."

Nellie pushed her plate aside, leaving the crumbled cake uneaten. "We did have a visitor while you were out, Dora. I was polishing the silver for dinner. Mrs Seaton answered the door. I didn't see who the visitor was, but I am sure it was Mr Glanville's Chinaman, because the study had that smell about it when I went to take up Mr Glanville's tea."

"What smell, Nellie? Honestly, you smell things where no one else can."

"I tell you, Dora, that Chinaman has a peculiar smell. You know how they all smoke the most disgusting tobacco. He'd been here before, you see, Mrs Pyke."

"Can you describe the Chinese gentleman, please, Nellie?" Grace crossed her fingers that Nellie wouldn't say they all look alike. She would have liked to ask if the distinctive smell was opium, but she doubted Nellie would know opium from bath salts.

"Ever such a pleasant gentleman he is, Mrs Pyke. Sammy, Mr Glanville called him, so they must be close friends. Always polite. His English is quite easy to understand, and he wears normal clothes. A bit on the thin side and quite small. Mr Glanville always received him as he would any other gentleman. If he didn't have that awful scar on his face, he would look entirely respectable."

The scar would be a more useful identifier than the name Sammy. The English settlers of this land had a habit of giving nicknames to "foreigners" whose names they couldn't or wouldn't pronounce. "John" was used as a generic name when they couldn't be bothered to do even that much. Any name was better than many of the crude insults often used instead. Lily had told Grace that many of her friends had chosen an English name for themselves rather than leave it to the whims of the general populace.

108

Grace searched for a delicate way of asking her next question. If Mr Glanville was involved in the opium trade with a Chinese partner, did he also partake of the merchandise? "Did Mr Glanville seem odd in any way when his visitor left?"

"Odd? Not so I noticed, Mrs Pyke. He was distracted and forgetful, but that's not unusual. Mr Glanville had quite forgotten about the family dinner. Now you mention it, he did seem a little out of sorts. Not ill, but worried, as if he had heard news that upset him. Do you think the Chinaman poisoned him?"

Grace was quick to scotch that idea in case unfortunate rumours started involving untrustworthy foreigners. The last thing the Chinese community needed was more strife when even the government disparaged them and taxed them more than other immigrants. "No, not at all, Nellie. We just need to know everything about his day."

"Well, that's a relief, with Sammy being a friend and all. Mr Glanville saw Sammy out himself. Mr Lohar had the afternoon and evening off."

"Did Mr Lohar come home at any time during the afternoon or evening?"

Dora answered. "No, he didn't, and he's not a suspect either. He was devoted to Mr Glanville, as we all were. Mr Lohar went to see a friend in the afternoon and to his chess club all evening. He didn't come home until after everyone was in bed. Mr Lohar never left the house the following day, so Mr Glanville's body would not be left alone as his soul made its way to the afterlife. Henrietta came back here after taking Mrs Seaton to the refuge and can vouch for him. They laid the body out and tended to him together, bless them."

Nellie burst into tears again at this description of devotion. Dora swiped her own tears away and patted her sister's hand absent-mindedly.

Grace admired the close-knit camaraderie of Mr Glanville's household. Unconventional they might be, but obviously also loyal and content. "Perhaps we could move on to how the meal was prepared and served?"

Again, Dora took the lead, forcing the emotion from her voice as she recalled the events of the fateful day. "Mrs Seaton insisted on cooking everything from the freshest ingredients. She always purchased seafood taken from further down the coast, far away from the city sewage. Her food has never once caused an upset stomach in her life. She went to the market in the afternoon and began cooking when she returned. Mrs Seaton was a woman who prided herself on her skills and preferred to cook alone. As far as I know, nobody entered the kitchen until the bell rang for Nellie and I to serve." Dora's lip twisted up. "Need I add that neither Nellie nor I were responsible for our employer's death?"

The obvious devotion of the two maids made them unlikely suspects, Grace conceded, although a bequest of £40 each was a lot of money for women in their position. People had killed for far less. The question remained – if it wasn't someone with access to the kitchen, how did the arsenic get into Mr Glanville's meal? If the killer was not a member of the Glanville household, the murder must have been planned in advance to have had the arsenic ready. But, if it was someone outside this house, how did they know that Mr Glanville would eat a separate dish to the rest of the guests – a spicy curry to disguise any unusual taste?

"I can see what you're thinking, Grace," Dora said, "but there was an opportunity to put the arsenic in the food. I took out the first lot of plates, which included the seafood curry that only Mr Glanville ate. When Nellie went into the kitchen to fetch the other plates, she scalded herself over a boiling pot on the range. I left the plates on the hall table when I heard her scream."

"Miss Henrietta ran in behind Dora," Nellie said, "and Doctor Johnstone arrived a moment later, so they must have been close by. Miss Henrietta cooled my burn under cold water, and then the doctor bandaged it with the medical kit Mrs Seaton keeps in the pantry."

"Any of the guests might have come into the hall in the few minutes we were busy," Dora concluded.

"I admit I am baffled, ladies," Grace said. "The killer must have brought the arsenic to the house, but how would he or she have known that Mr Glanville would eat a separate dish? Specifically, curried seafood, which was perfect to pass off as food poisoning?"

"Oh, lass, is that what's worrying you?" Dora chuckled. "I thought you must be suspecting us. The answer is simple. Mr Glanville always ate spicy food, especially when the Tuckers came to visit. He had a taste for hot curry that none other could stomach. I think it tickled him to be different to the rest of the family, who revelled in their Englishness. Mrs Tucker wouldn't even take hot mustard on her roast beef, let alone let curry pass her lips."

"And seafood was always his favourite," Nellie said. "He always said, 'God's bounty is on our doorstep, Mrs Seaton. Why would I eat anything else?' Mr Glanville loved to walk on the beach and breathe the salt air. 'Nothing but ocean for thousands of miles,' he'd tell me when he got home with sand all in his boots. 'Thousands of miles, Nellie, isn't that astounding?' And he was right."

"I think I would have liked your Mr Glanville," Grace said. "I've stood by the sea and thought exactly the same thing."

The three women sipped tea in companionable silence for a minute or two until Grace felt the pressure of time slipping by. "I'm sorry to have to ask so many questions when you are grieving."

"Time enough to grieve later," Dora said. "Ask anything and we'll do our best to help."

"Where was Mrs Seaton after the doctor and Henrietta came into the kitchen to tend to Nellie's injury?"

"She stayed long enough to get the medical kit and ask if she could help. After that, Mrs Seaton went to inform the family that there would be a slight delay in serving. When I saw Nellie was not badly injured, I went out to take the plates into the dining room. Mrs Seaton was already at the hall table, ready to do the same. She was cross at Mr Tucker, who had come out looking for more wine, as if he was the master of the house, not a guest."

"The father, you mean? Jack Tucker."

Dora nodded. "The polite son, Sid Tucker, was there too. He had come to take the plates through, because he didn't want the dinner to become cold. Very thoughtful of him. Of course, I rushed to take the plates off him and told him he must be waited on or Mr Glanville would be cross."

"And Bert Tucker?"

"That lazy good-for-nothing wouldn't lift a finger to help. I suppose he remained in the dining room with his mother and Mr Glanville, probably guzzling all Mr Glanville's fine wine."

Nellie tutted. "Now, Dora, don't be too harsh on the nephew, just because his manners are a little rough. Cook said Bert was making an effort to be nice to his uncle when she went into the dining room to apologise for the delay. He even poured his uncle a glass of port after dinner."

Port laced with arsenic, perhaps? Grace knew they should not assume the poison was in the curry, when arsenic was so easy to administer in any food or drink. Conceivably, it might even have been put into the food at the table, if the person beside Mr Glanville was adept at sleight-of-hand. The sisters seemed content to talk at length, so Grace made the most of it. "Mr Glanville sat at the head of the table, I imagine."

"Of course," Dora said. "Between his sister and his niece, as always. Both Mrs Tucker and Mr Glanville were encouraging dear Miss Henrietta to converse with Doctor Johnstone, who was sitting next to her. Mr Glanville was keen for his beloved niece to marry the doctor. The doctor is obviously head over heels for her, but needs a boot in the pants to make a move."

Nellie sniffed at her sister's coarse language. "Really, Dora, the poor doctor is simply a little shy, which is no bad thing in my

112

book. And Miss Henrietta is too modest to believe her feelings are reciprocated. The doctor will not find better than Miss Henrietta. She's a qualified nurse, you know, the perfect doctor's wife."

Grace wished all witnesses could be this talkative and observant. "I understand Mr Glanville never married."

Nellie's eyes flooded again. "He lost his one true love when he was young. Terribly tragic. He never loved again. Mr Glanville keeps a lock of her hair in his bedside drawer. After that, he devoted himself to his engineering and charitable work. A brilliant man, he was, and a great loss to the world. Not the most sociable of men, but the few friends he had were friends for life."

Grace handed her another handkerchief from the steadily diminishing supply she kept on hand for grieving families and distraught patients. "Mr Glanville seems to have been on excellent terms with all those who worked in his household. I get the feeling he was particularly close to Mr Lohar."

Nellie sobbed. Her sister looked equally distressed, but held her tears at bay. "Mr Lohar is devastated. They have been together since they were children. Mr Lohar was devoted to his employer and I won't hear a word against him, no matter his origins."

"Mr Glanville was the best of men," Nellie sobbed. When the sobs subsided, she reached into her apron pocket. "Oh, Dora, I almost forgot. Mr Fairchild gave me a letter Mr Glanville wrote for us in the event of his death."

Dora sliced the letter open with a clean knife. The knots of tension in her jaw sagged with relief. "Mr Glanville has arranged for us to stay on in this house for as long as we want, with an increase in our wages as well. He says the solicitor will explain the new terms of our employment and we can choose to stay or not."

Nellie flung her arms around her sister. "I knew he wouldn't have left us with no home. I knew it Dora. He would never do such a thing."

Dora turned to Grace with tear-filled eyes. "It's the Tucker family you ought to be investigating, Mrs Pyke. Henrietta loved her uncle, but the rest were after his wealth. Bert Tucker was here last week, asking his uncle for more money again. Mr Glanville must have refused, because Bert's shouting could be heard throughout the house, no matter that the study door was closed. I thought the door would come off its hinges when he slammed it on the way out. Bert Tucker was given every opportunity a young man could desire, but he never made it past lugging crates in the warehouse. I've heard him call himself the Warehouse Supervisor or some such, but that's all hogwash."

"Mr Glanville didn't refuse Bert," Nellie said. "He told me when I went to take him his tea after Bert left. He apologised about the door-slamming and said he thought he had been accommodating to his nephew, by telling him he would consider a loan if Bert came back with a business plan to prove he knew what he was about."

Dora blew out a huff of breath. "Waste of money giving money to a man who can scarcely remember which fork to use for his fish."

Grace still had more questions than answers, but she saw that the Eady sisters had had enough for now. And Charlie needed to know what she'd found out, sooner rather than later. "Thank you both for being so helpful. I'll leave you to grieve Mr Glanville and Mrs Seaton."

Dora nodded. "Come back again if you have any more questions. We are rather frayed at present, but we will both do anything we can to catch the repulsive beast who did this."

114

After The Will

Out of the corner of his eye, Charlie had caught sight of Grace slipping out after the maids as chaos descended on the rest of the room. Charlie glanced around to see who needed his help the most. At the front of the room, Mrs Tucker accosted Mr Fairchild, accusing him of malpractice. Any sane man would quail at the sight of a steaming mad Mrs Tucker, but at least the solicitor had his walking cane to ward off any physical attack.

Mr Jack Tucker turned on Doctor Johnstone, accusing him of lying about the food poisoning and implying the doctor knew more than he was telling. Miss Henrietta Tucker rose to the defence of her admirer, stepping between him and her father, denying the doctor had any part in the poisoning.

Sid Tucker remained in his chair, stunned by the sudden aggression surging around him.

Meanwhile, Bert Tucker was working up a head of steam. He shouted another accusation of murder at the manservant, Rajiv Lohar, before storming to the rear of the room, fists clenched. Lohar fled, but stumbled and fell. Charlie reached his prospective client just as Bert Tucker grabbed Lohar by the collar. Bert hoisted the manservant off the floor and pushed him up against the wall, gripping him so hard that Lohar turned an alarming shade of blue before his eyes.

Charlie launched himself at the assailant and hauled him off. No mean feat, as Bert's size and musculature rivalled Charlie's, and Bert was driven by rage. When Charlie broke Bert's hold, Mr Lohar dropped to the floor with a thump and a choking groan. Bert whirled and swung a wild roundhouse, which Charlie dodged with ease. A rapid uppercut followed, catching him off-guard with its sudden power. Charlie had just enough time to clench his stomach muscles, or he would have lost his breakfast.

Declan dashed to his aid, grabbing Bert Tucker from behind and hauling him backwards. He had one handcuff clipped on Bert's wrists before he recovered his balance. Declan dragged his captive across the room and clipped the other handcuff around an ornate iron stanchion by the fireplace.

While Declan dealt with Bert Tucker, Charlie helped Mr Lohar off the floor. "Are you hurt?"

Lohar shook his head. "Does this mean you are taking the case, Mr Pyke?" His voice rasped, but he managed a tight smile.

"Looks like it," Charlie replied. "And Bert Tucker will be top of my interview list. Do you wish to have him charged with assault?"

"No. No harm has been done, and I would not wish the Tucker family to have an additional grievance against me."

"Then I suggest you leave now, Mr Lohar. Detective Sergeant Kelly and I will come and take your full statement as soon as we are finished here. I suspect it will be late afternoon by then. Will you be at the address you gave me earlier?"

Lohar nodded and slipped out the back door. Across the room, Mr and Mrs Tucker were conducting a heated argument with Declan Kelly over his decision to arrest Bert rather than the manservant. Charlie pictured Grace sitting in the kitchen with the maids and a nice cup of tea. He sighed and went to Declan's aid.

Sid Tucker recovered his poise and stepped in before Charlie got there. Sid calmed his parents with a drawn-out shush and a wave of his elegantly manicured hands. "Detective Sergeant Kelly, I apologise that tempers have boiled over." He nodded towards the doctor and solicitor, who were standing by the door with Henrietta. "Gentlemen, I extend my family's apologies to you, too, for the way our feelings were expressed."

Sid waited for their nods of acknowledgment. "However, I do not apologise for those feelings of anger and resentment, which are entirely justified by the appalling situation we find ourselves in. Naturally, the Tucker family will assist the police with their inquiries to establish the cause of Arthur Glanville's death. However, we will also contest his will with the full force of the law."

Charlie stepped in. "Mr Lohar has graciously declined to press charges against your brother for assault."

Declan held his hand up for silence. "In that case, and if there is no further trouble, I will consider releasing Mr Bert Tucker. Before I make my decision, I will take preliminary statements from each member of the Tucker family. The constable will remain here to ensure none of you leave. Doctor Johnstone, we will talk to you again later. Mr Fairchild, please wait outside. I'll talk to you first."

The solicitor didn't wait to be asked twice to vacate the room. The doctor was almost as fast, waiting only to exchange a few words with Henrietta Tucker. Declan gestured for Charlie to follow him and for the constable to guard the door.

The doctor was waiting outside. "I insist on being present at the interview of Miss Henrietta Tucker."

"The interviews will be conducted in private, Doctor Johnstone." Declan forestalled the doctor's response with a raised hand. "Miss Tucker is a competent adult. However, you may remain here and escort her back to the surgery if you wish."

Mr Fairchild showed them to the study, a room which reflected Arthur Glanville's interests. The furnishings were made by craftsmen for practical purposes rather than decoration – a sturdy desk, comfortable chairs, and plain, thick curtains. Display cabinets contained Eastern curios, the books on the shelves were well-thumbed, and the table was littered with parts for mechanical devices. Arthur Glanville's desk was neatly piled with papers. The room lacked any sign of self-indulgence – no rows of liquor bottles, no aroma of ingrained cigar smoke, no portraits of Arthur Glanville with his foot on a tiger's head.

Mr Fairchild picked up a metal object from Arthur Glanville's desk. "Mrs Tucker was right about one thing. Arthur Glanville was a brilliant man who made a modest fortune with his inventions. This was the first – a new design of valve to regulate gas flow. That's how Mr and Mrs Tucker met, in fact. Arthur was invited to the gasworks' annual picnic. He took his sister, against their father's wishes, and she fell in love with Jack Tucker. Tucker was a handsome man back then – a real charmer."

"I wonder that Horatio Glanville allowed the marriage of his daughter to a man of Jack Tucker's status," Declan said.

Fairchild put the valve aside and waved them to the cluster of chairs by the window. "Horatio wasn't pleased by the match, but he had little choice. Miss Ariadne Glanville was of age, and she could be just as stubborn and uncompromising as her father. She was determined to marry Jack Tucker, and that was that. I don't mean to imply disapproval. I believe it has been a happy marriage for the most part. In fact, I believe Horatio rather admired his daughter for her strength of character and Jack for refusing to bow to Horatio's will. Jack turned down a hefty bribe to turn his back on Ariadne, according to Arthur."

Charlie pulled up one of a pair of simple rosewood chairs, leaving the two armchairs for Declan and the solicitor. "I take it from Mrs Tucker's tirade in the drawing room that she inherited nothing from her father and felt aggrieved by it."

Fairchild settled into the less-used armchair with the ease of a man who had spent many hours in this very spot. "On the contrary, Horatio Glanville bought his daughter and her husband a house when they married. He also gave her a substantial dowry, which was invested on her behalf, with the income paid as an allowance."

The remaining armchair must have been Glanville's own, as it was worn with use and closest to the table and window. Declan took the other chair out of respect. A knock on the door interrupted them. Charlie perked up at the rattle of cups on a tray. Breakfast suddenly seemed a distant memory.

The shorter of the two maids deposited the tray with a clatter on the table beside the chairs. "I took the liberty of bringing food from the pantry, Mr Fairchild. It seems a shame to waste it if the house is sold."

"We are most grateful, Nellie," Fairchild said. "I am glad you are here. I have a letter for you and Dora from Mr Glanville. It was his express wish that you and your sister be given a legacy that ensured you could choose your manner of living after his death. His hope, and mine, is that you will stay on in this house. That is all I can say at present, but I shall be in touch with further information shortly."

Nellie Eady grasped the letter with a shaking hand. "Thank you, Mr Fairchild. Mr Glanville has always been the kindest and most considerate of employers." She withdrew quickly, tears in her eyes.

Charlie poured each of them a cup of strong tea. Fairchild waved the food away, leaving Charlie to pile plates with thick slices of rich fruit cake and luscious ripe apricots for himself and Declan. If there was a man in Dunedin who liked his food more than Charlie, it was surely Declan Kelly. As Declan had rightly said, many a time, a detective without fuel for the body is a man who risked making crucial errors of judgement.

Charlie resumed his seat and took the opportunity to shovel cake and fruit into his empty belly while he had the chance.

"You were talking of Mrs Tucker's dowry," Declan said, between slurps of tea. "Did she not inherit the money outright at his death?"

"Horatio wanted to keep the money away from Jack Tucker. Not that he distrusted the husband. He admired Jack as an honest, hard-working man, but he was never happy with his daughter's choice and felt she needed a dowry to fall back on if the marriage did not last."

"You appear to know the family well, Mr Fairchild."

"The Glanville family settled in Dunedin just over thirty years ago, when Arthur was fourteen. He was enrolled at the school I attended. We have been best friends ever since. I went on to train as a solicitor and Arthur became my first and most loyal client." Fairchild leaned forward, an iron determination replacing the wistful air of reminiscence. "Whoever murdered my friend must be found and punished, Detective Sergeant Kelly."

"That is our intention, Mr Fairchild." Declan put his cup down and got out his notebook. "First, I need you to explain why the estates of Arthur and Horatio Glanville did not contain the fortunes the Tucker family expected."

"I was not Horatio Glanville's solicitor, so my knowledge of the matter is limited to what Arthur told me. As I understand it, Horatio had already divested the two halves of his business before his death last year. The export business in Calcutta was sold to his older son, Raleigh, for a token £1. Shortly before his death, Horatio sold the New Zealand business, without informing his family beforehand, to a man called Clive Jardine. Before you ask, I know nothing about the man."

"Why didn't Horatio leave the New Zealand importation business to his younger son, Arthur?" Declan said. "Presumably Arthur Glanville had some role within his father's business."

Fairchild let out a bark of astonished laughter. "Good lord, no. Arthur would not have a bar of it. He was a thoroughly decent man, despite his upbringing. Arthur refused to work for his father unless he stopped supplying opium to opium dens. Thus, Horatio sold the business. Although Horatio's will named his younger son, Arthur, as the primary beneficiary of his estate, the only remaining asset of any great value was the house. Arthur tried to find out what happened to his father's fortune, but Horatio had hidden or destroyed his papers before his death. It's possible that Horatio had debts to settle, or perhaps investments that failed. International trade can be a fickle business. Fortunes can be made, but just as easily lost. Maybe this Jardine fellow took the business in payment for a debt. With the documents gone, we will never know."

"So, Arthur never found out for sure what happened to the reputed Glanville fortune?"

The solicitor got up to pace the room. He halted at a small table by the window, where a backgammon board was set up, ready to play. "I thought he didn't care enough to pursue the matter. Arthur was a man of modest needs. A few close friends, a weekly evening of backgammon with me, his dedication to his inventions. He neither wanted nor needed money from his father, as far as I could tell. To be honest, I was surprised he moved into this huge house when he was so happy in his own modest establishment."

Mr Fairchild stopped fiddling with the backgammon pieces and returned to the armchair. He sat in silence for a few moments, his brow etched with sorrow. "However, I believe Arthur did find out something recently. Something that disturbed him. He didn't share his suspicions with me, but he did instruct me to transfer this house and the bulk of his investments into a charitable trust. He retained the right to live here and keep his household staff."

"Thereby putting his assets out of the reach of the Tucker family after his death." Charlie said. "When did this happen?"

"The last of the paperwork was signed a few days ago. Arthur did not inform his family, as you saw for yourselves today. Perhaps he should have."

The flare of Declan's nostrils showed he shared Charlie's suspicions at the proximity of the death to the transfer of assets. "The police will require full disclosure of the details of this charitable trust and any other information you hold, Mr Fairchild."

"Of course, Detective Sergeant Kelly. May I request a brief delay whilst I inform the trustees and take advice? You will understand that the ink was barely dry and thus the legal situation must be reviewed before I proceed."

Declan pulled out his pocket watch. "Twenty-four hours, Mr Fairchild. Starting now. One last question. Where were you on Friday afternoon and evening?"

Fairchild flushed at the implication, but he answered readily enough. "I attended a meeting with Mr Glanville at two o'clock to give him a copy of the signed documentation. I did not stay long. Arthur seemed distracted. More than distracted – worried. But he did not say why. I spent the evening at home with my wife and children, as usual. I have two maids and a cook if you want independent verification. In fact, our elderly neighbour came over in the evening, as I recall. He's been lonely since his wife died."

"And Saturday morning?"

"I choose not to work on a Saturday, so I can spend time with my children. I was not informed of Arthur Glanville's death until about noon, when the doctor sent a note. He wanted to tell the family first, naturally. I received a message from Mrs Tucker later on Saturday, requesting my presence here at two o'clock today to read Arthur's will."

Declan rose to shake his hand. "Thank you, Mr Fairchild. I look forward to hearing from you."

Grace came as soon as Mr Fairchild left, suggesting she had been waiting by the door.

Charlie breathed in her scent and felt the tension in his muscles relax, as if she was his own personal dose of opium. "What news from the Eady sisters, Grace?"

Grace took the vacated armchair beside him, covering his hand with her own. "They are devoted to Arthur Glanville and willing to do anything to help us. Doris Eady is particularly sharp witted. She said there was no arsenic on the premises and believed it was near impossible for the arsenic to have been added prior to the meal being served. The poison was probably added to Mr Glanville's meal during the dinner party, when the two maids, the cook, Henrietta and the doctor were in the kitchen attending to a scalded hand. The plated food had been left in the hall, where it might have been tampered with."

Charlie got up to get Grace a cup of tea. "Did Doris Eady hazard a guess as to the culprit?"

"She made no accusation, but she did say Mrs Seaton suspected someone. Jack and Sid Tucker definitely had the opportunity to put poison in the curry, while Bert could have poisoned the glass of port he served his uncle after the meal. Bert

Tucker was here last week, wanting money from his uncle. He was furious when his uncle refused. Mrs Tucker stayed in the dining room at all times, as far as we know, sitting beside her brother."

"Wonderful news, Grace," Declan said. "If it could only be Bert, Sid, or Jack, that narrows the field admirably."

Charlie took Declan's cup to refill. "I think you're being too hasty, Declan. With so many people trying to help in the kitchen, a moment was all it would take for any of the guests to slip out unnoticed to poison the curry."

"The doctor went into the kitchen slightly after Dora," Grace said. "If he did it, he must have been ready to pounce on the split-second opportunity."

"Or Mrs Tucker could have added the arsenic at the table, if she was sitting beside Arthur," Charlie said. "Who was on the other side of him, Grace?"

"Henrietta."

"So we can add Mrs Tucker and her daughter to the list of those with opportunity," Charlie said.

Declan shook his head. "I don't see it, Charlie. How could they add the arsenic to his meal with Arthur Glanville right beside them?"

Charlie stumbled slightly while giving Declan his cup. Declan poured the spilt tea from the saucer into the cup and took a slurp. "Urgh. How much sugar did you put in this tea, Pyke?"

Charlie grinned. "Didn't you notice, DS Kelly? I slipped in an extra cube right in front of you when I stumbled. You might want to check that slice of cake, too. And be grateful my little sleight-of-hand trick only used sugar, not arsenic."

Declan peered at the white crystals dotting the top of his food. "Very amusing, I'm sure, but you've made your point, Detective Pyke. Any of the Tuckers could be the killer. And anyone else who had access the kitchen where the meal was prepared, although then there is the problem of which plate to poison."

"The maids said the food was prepared fresh from ingredients brought at the market that afternoon and no one else went near the kitchen," Grace said. "What's more, Arthur made a habit of having a hot curry, which nobody else could stomach. The killer must have come prepared with arsenic, needing only a chance to slip it into the food. If Nellie hadn't had her accident, he would have found another way."

"I'd still like a list of all the people who were in the house that day," Charlie said.

"I asked the maids that too," Grace said. "The solicitor attended a meeting here at two o'clock on the day of Arthur's death. Nellie Eady said a Chinese man with a scarred face visited Mr Glanville earlier in the afternoon. Nellie thought Mr Glanville had heard news that upset him. She said the man smelled of a strange smoke. I wondered if the Chinese man Arthur Glanville met had something to do with the opium trade."

Declan was smiling at them. "You two are quite the pair of detectives, even on your honeymoon. Mr Fairchild was adamant Arthur had nothing to do with his father's opium business."

"Maybe Arthur wished to keep his interest in the business secret," Charlie suggested. "We'll have to track down this scarred man and find out what he knows."

"The Tuckers are my highest priority," Declan said. "They were the only people present at the dinner and at the meeting the next morning, when the doctor announced the cause of death and Mrs Seaton made her accusation. Regardless of the large bequests to the servants, it was the Tucker family who expected to gain the most from the death of Arthur Glanville."

"The doctor was also present at both events." Charlie didn't mention that his client was also in the house both days, albeit absent during the afternoon and evening of the fatal dinner party.

"But the doctor had nothing to gain from his death," Declan said.

"Doctor Johnstone is in love with Glanville's niece, Henrietta," Grace said. "That gives him motive, if he expected his future wife to be rich. However, Mr Glanville was in favour of the match according to the Eady sisters."

Charlie was not ready to discount other motives just yet. "Let's not forget that the main beneficiary of Arthur Glanville's fortune is the charitable trust into which he put his assets. The entire financial situation smells fishy to me."

"I agree, Charlie," Grace said. "What's more, it is possible Arthur Glanville's death was not linked to money at all, if he had found out something that implicated the killer. A scandal or illegal enterprise, for example. He was worried about something, that's for sure."

Declan raised a sceptical eyebrow. "Or maybe he poisoned himself to spite the lot of them. Can't say I'd blame him." He rose from the armchair. "Call me an old-fashioned copper, but in my book, money is at the root of most evil. I'm off to talk to the Tucker family."

"I'll join you in a few minutes," Charlie said, "after I've had a rare moment alone with my darling wife."

"In that case, I won't expect you two lovebirds anytime soon." Declan went to punch his friend on the arm, pulling the punch at the last minute, when he remembered the burn.

Chess Moves

Grace waited for her husband to speak his mind, but Charlie seemed more fascinated by the pattern on the Turkish rug than by the allure of his bride. "What's troubling you, Charlie? Is your arm hurting, or is it the case?"

"Apologies, Grace. It's the case." Charlie shifted from the upright chair to the more comfortable armchair, pulling Grace with him.

Grace sank into the warmth of his embrace. "I hope Declan is right that the murders are a simple matter of one of the Tucker family wanting to hasten their inheritance. Even so, any of them might have killed Arthur Glanville, and only Mrs Seaton knew which of them it was."

"I'm not ready to rule out a link to the family opium business, particularly with the mysterious Chinese visitor and the old family friendship in India between the Doctor Johnstone's family and Horatio Glanville. There are still too many unanswered questions. Who is this man, Clive Jardine, who bought the Glanville opium business? Where did the family fortune disappear to? And what was Arthur Glanville so worried about that he disinherited his family?"

Grace closed her eyes, relishing the warmth of his skin against hers and the tickle of his breath against her cheek. "Lily might know the Chinese man, whose name is Sammy. Doris said he had an unmistakable scar, spoke excellent English and appeared to be a well-to-do gentleman. He had visited the house occasionally and was received as a friend. Surely there cannot be many men fitting that description."

"Rajiv Lohar may know his name too. Lohar will also know about the Glanville family history and business." Charlie pulled away from her, so he could look her in the eyes. "Would you be willing to talk to our client on your own, Grace? I would wait until after the Tucker interviews, but this case has me on edge. A killer willing to strike twice in quick succession to protect himself is a dangerous person to have on the loose. Both deaths were carefully arranged to look like accidents, which means the killer must be extremely nervous now he knows the deaths are being treated as murders. I want him – or her – caught as soon as possible. I know it is too much to ask when you're exhausted from being with Molly last night."

Grace interrupted his apology. "Thank you, my love."

"For what, Grace?"

"For trusting me to conduct a crucial interview on my own."

Charlie cupped her chin with his fingers. "Of course I trust you, Grace. I'm just glad you are on my side." He pressed his lips to hers, lingering despite their haste to solve the case. A rap on the door interrupted, which was just as well, or there might have been any number of murders during their distraction.

Grace had enough time to jump from his lap and straighten her clothes, before Nellie came in to collect the tray. Her eyes widened at the sight of Grace's husband, still seated in the armchair, looking attractively rumpled.

"Ooh, sorry to intrude." Nellie grabbed the tray and fled, tripping on a flat section of carpet as she went.

Grace smoothed her favourite detective's hair. "Try not to give any of the womenfolk a fit of the vapours while I'm not here to protect your honour, Detective Penrose Pyke. And don't forget we are invited to a family dinner tonight."

"You be careful too, Grace. I know I don't need to say it, but be cautious with what you tell Rajiv Lohar. Don't forget, he is a significant beneficiary of Glanville's will. Nobody saw him that evening, but it doesn't mean he didn't slip back into the house to put arsenic in his employer's food. I know it doesn't fit with him hiring us to investigate, but still ..."

"I'll be as careful as I always am, Charlie."

"That's what worries me. I'd better go. Declan will have his hands full dealing with the combined wrath of the Tuckers."

Twenty minutes later, Grace stood outside a small cottage in the middle of a long row of identical buildings on the flatter land of Caversham. The cottage was the wild child of an otherwise tidy row. In fact, she wondered if it was inhabited at all, until she noticed smoke curling from the chimney. Grace checked the address on the note Mr Lohar had given them and wished she had a hatchet to help her get to the front door. She pushed through a gate hanging by a single rusted hinge and squeezed through a corridor of overgrown camellias.

Her knock on the door yielded no response. Grace counted to sixty and knocked louder. After another sixty, she heard a shuffling and tapping on a wooden floor.

The man who answered the door would have been a natural for the role of garden gnome. Short, stout, elderly, red-nosed and white-bearded, although lacking a pointy hat and jolly smile. He crossed his arms and thrust his chin out. "What do you want?"

Grace supplied the jolly smile. "I am Grace Penrose Pyke. I wish to speak with Mr Rajiv Lohar."

"Never heard of him."

"Mr Lohar gave us this address." Grace held out the note and Charlie's card.

The gnome considered her with suspicious eyes. "You're not with the police? Or the family?"

"Mr Lohar hired Mr Charles Pyke to investigate the death of his employer. I am Mr Pyke's wife and colleague."

The man moved aside and held the door open enough for her to enter. "You'd better come in, Mrs Pyke. Rajiv has gone for a walk to restore his composure."

128

Grace stepped over the threshold. The dim light in the narrow hall danced with dust motes. "I am not surprised. Mr Glanville's relatives could use a few lessons in politeness, especially in relation to gentlemen hailing from foreign lands."

A rumble of laughter came from behind her as the door closed, leaving the hallway dark. "The Terrible Tuckers I call them. First door on the right, Mrs Pyke."

Grace let herself into a small, cluttered sitting room. Two frayed armchairs filled the space in front of the fire, which was blazing, despite the summer heat outside. Beads of sweat erupted on Grace's face and torso, but the gnome seemed immune to the sweltering atmosphere.

He shuffled into the room, grimacing every time his foot hit the floor. He slumped onto the closest and shabbiest of the armchairs, leaning his walking stick beside it. "Take a seat. I hope the room is not too hot for you. Thirty years as a missionary in Goa did not prepare me for a retirement in the frozen wastes of southern New Zealand."

"Goa?"

"Southern India."

"Is that how you know Mr Lohar? I'm sorry, but I didn't catch your name."

"Can't catch what isn't thrown, eh, Mrs Pyke?" A second rumble of laughter suggested the man was not as dour as he first appeared. "My name is Isaac Upton. I know Rajiv through the chess club, not through our Indian connections. Goa and Calcutta are as far apart as Rome is from London."

Rajiv Lohar's alibi for the poisoning of Mr Glanville depended on his attendance at the chess club. Perhaps the absence of their client was a blessing in disguise, especially as the open sherry bottle and drained glass gave Grace hope that her informant might have imbibed enough alcohol to loosen his lips. "Is there much interest in chess in Dunedin, Mr Upton?"

Mr Upton held up the bottle to her. When she shook her head, he poured another glass for himself. "A spot of sherry after luncheon helps the digestion, I find. Makes the gout tolerable, at any rate."

Grace wanted to tell him that sherry was the worst possible thing he could do for gout, but she was not here as a doctor and Mr Upton did not look like the type of man who cared for unsolicited advice.

Mr Upton took a sip. "Chess? Yes indeed, very popular. We often have more attendees at our meetings than chess boards to accommodate them. We really must find larger premises than the back room of the Workingmen's Club. Not that it matters, as watching a game is always entertaining and informative. Rajiv, now, he's a fine player. You think you have him on the defensive, when the little blighter sneaks up from nowhere and slays your king with a well-placed knight."

"Mr Lohar was at the chess club until late on Friday evening, I believe? Did he win many of his games?"

"Almost certainly." Upton used his walking stick to pull a diary across the table to his side. He opened it to the most recent entry. "I'm the convener, so I keep track of our games. Let's see now. Rajiv played four games on Friday evening, with two byes, two losses, and two wins. Most unusual for Rajiv. He must have been tired that night."

"Two byes?" Grace queried.

"As I said, the number of members means not everyone can play each round. Rajiv sat out a couple of games, as did we all."

The Workingmen's Club was only a couple of blocks from Arthur Glanville's house, which might have left Rajiv Lohar with enough time between games to go home, sneak in, add arsenic to the meal, and return to the chess club. "Did he watch the games he sat out?"

"Probably, but I couldn't swear to it. I would have either been playing or intent on watching the games." Upton put his glass down. "I hope you are not thinking what I suspect you are thinking, Mrs Pyke. Rajiv Lohar had nothing whatsoever to do with the death of Arthur Glanville. He and Arthur may have been master and servant to the world, but they respected and liked each other far more than most brothers. Rajiv was closer to Arthur than the Terrible Tuckers ever were, except for Miss Henrietta."

Grace brushed a dribble of perspiration from her forehead. Another drop slid down her cleavage towards her belly button, tickling on the way down. "They had known each other most of their lives, I believe."

Upton took another slug of his sherry. "Arthur Glanville came to the chess club occasionally. Once, he told me that Rajiv was both a mother and father to him from as far back as he could recall, even though there were only twelve years between them. In fact, Arthur's earliest childhood memory was of Rajiv comforting him after he fell over. Rajiv was his personal servant in a way New Zealanders cannot comprehend, tending to Arthur's every need."

No wonder their bond was close, Grace thought. A child's primary need – aside from food and shelter – was love and attention. How must it have been for Rajiv, not much more than a child himself, given so much responsibility for a young boy's welfare? Did he resent always being the servant, having no life of his own? Taken away from his country to an impossibly distant place and culture?

"I can see you find that life hard to fathom, Mrs Pyke. You want to ask whether Rajiv hated being a lackey all those years, but cannot find a polite way to ask the question."

"You are very perceptive, Mr Upton. I should hasten to say I find Mr Lohar dignified and sympathetic, with no trace of resentment at his situation. Unfortunately, a murder investigation requires the detective to question everyone and everything, no matter how innocent they appear."

Upton nodded his understanding. "Rajiv keeps his feelings to himself with most people, but with me he has found a sympathetic ear. I can assure you, Rajiv Lohar was honoured by the affection

Arthur showed him." Upton leaned forward and prodded the fire into life. Heat surged into the room, just as Grace was beginning to find the atmosphere tolerable.

Upton sat back, basking in the renewed blaze. "Arthur Glanville was a good man, Mrs Pyke. By that, I mean a decent, honest, caring man. He made sure Rajiv had access to an education and home comforts, which is in itself no trivial matter to a boy who would otherwise have been scraping a living on the streets of Calcutta. But, more than that, he treated Rajiv with respect. When Arthur's inventions paid dividends, his first action was to offer Rajiv his freedom and paid passage home to India. When Rajiv declined in favour of remaining as Arthur's valet in his new home, Arthur instead offered him the opportunity to take a wife. An arranged marriage, you understand, is the usual way in India."

Grace couldn't imagine allowing her parents to arrange a marriage for her, let alone allowing an employer to do so. Although, in fairness to her parents, they might have chosen a man with a similar character to Charlie Pyke. But not Charlie. A policeman would not have been a natural choice. Indeed, her parents had expressed doubts about the unknown constable, until they met Charlie for themselves and understood the attraction.

"Mr Glanville's older brother arranged a match," Upton continued. "An orphan girl. Rajiv had been an orphan, too. Nila travelled out to New Zealand with a family of English origin, who did not find India to their taste. Rajiv told me the entire story, you see. Nila became the love of his life. Whatever tiny spark of resentment Rajiv might have had for being in service, Arthur Glanville repaid him tenfold with a life better than he ever imagined. Rajiv Lohar would have stood in front of a charging battalion of angry sepoys rather than risk a hair on the head of his employer."

Grace did not know what a sepoy was, but she did not doubt Mr Upton's sincerity. "What happened to Nila?"

"All good things must pass. Nila died of a fever several years ago. Two of their children still live in Dunedin, but Rajiv was too proud to ask for their help. I was happy to offer him a room here for a few days while the police conducted their inquiry."

With £200 coming his way, Rajiv Lohar would not need the help of his children. Hearing of the lives of Arthur and Rajiv left Grace in no doubt the manservant deserved the bequest for his years of devoted service. In fact, now she knew the family story, she wondered why Mr Glanville's sister wasn't more understanding of the bequest.

"Did you know that Mr Lohar received a bequest in Mr Glanville's will?" Grace asked.

"Rajiv told me years ago that Mr Glanville was leaving him a small sum in recognition of his service. Obviously, being older than Arthur, he did not expect to be alive to benefit. Given how upset he was when he returned here after the reading of the will, I presume even that token of esteem was badly received by the Tuckers."

Grace wasn't about to divulge the size of the bequest without their client's permission, but it was interesting to know he only expected a small sum. "Mrs Ariadne Tucker had the same type of upbringing as her brother, I presume. I'm surprised she wasn't more sympathetic."

Upton choked on his sherry. "Bless your sweet innocence, Mrs Pyke. I fear I have been less that discreet in sharing Rajiv's story with you, but I felt you ought to know so you could understand him. Likewise, it would be terribly indiscreet to hint that Miss Ariadne Glanville was nothing like her brother. From what I've heard, Arthur and Rajiv were terrified of Ariadne as children, as were the rest of the household staff. Rajiv told me she used to beat any of the servants who displeased her. Rajiv still has the scars from her rattan cane on his back. He was covering for Arthur, who had broken a glass ornament Ariadne prized."

The dreadful image of the beating hovered in Grace's mind, making her feel ill. The concept of physical punishment was abhorrent to her, but Grace was not so naïve as to think such violent abuse had fallen out of favour. There were still many men who cited the old rule as gospel – that it was acceptable to beat their wives as long as the rod was no bigger than their thumb. Still, Grace liked to think a woman would not sink so low. Again, her own experience told her otherwise. Grace had seen children at Lavender House who had been whipped black and blue for trying their mother's patience.

A key scrapped in the lock, jolting Grace from the grim thought of a youthful Ariadne Tucker wielding a cane against Rajiv Lohar's back.

Lies Or Alibis

Charlie saw Grace out the door of Arthur Glanville's house on her mission to interview their client. He would far rather have gone with her than stayed here to talk to the Tucker family, but he and Declan together would have a better chance of convincing the Tuckers that the police would not be diverted by threats and excuses.

Doctor Johnstone was waiting outside the drawing room, wearing out the brim of his hat with nervous fingers while he waited for Henrietta.

Charlie took the opportunity to ask a few more questions. He leaned on the wall beside the doctor, as if he too had been instructed to wait. "The maids praised Miss Tucker for her quick actions when Nellie scalded her hand on the night of the dinner party."

The doctor puffed out his chest at the compliment to his nurse. "Rightly so, although the scald was quite minor. Nellie is prone to hysterics."

"It was fortunate Miss Tucker was in the kitchen when it happened."

"She wasn't. Henrietta was in the entrance hall with me. She'd noticed I'd spilled soup on my lapel. Rather than embarrass me in front of her family, she made an excuse to take me out to the hall to see to the stain before the main course was served." The doctor blushed. "It was quite innocent. We weren't alone. Doris, the older maid, was already bringing through the plates."

"Was that when Nellie screamed?" Charlie asked.

"Yes. Doris and Henrietta rushed into the kitchen. I followed as soon as I had put my coat on again. As I said, it was only a minor

135

injury, but the Nellie was comforted by having a nurse and doctor tending to her."

"Very thoughtful of you both. You two took care of Mrs Seaton too, didn't you? The following day, I mean, after she learned of Mr Glanville's death." Charlie watched the doctor closely for signs of a reaction, but he seemed more distracted than wary. The hat brim was already splitting at the edges.

"Er, yes. Henrietta looked after the cook. I only suggested taking her to Lavender House to sober up after her embarrassing outburst. Having Mrs Seaton here in Glanville house would only have added to her hysteria, given her reaction to Mr Glanville's death. I would have accompanied them if I could, but I had patients waiting. What a dreadful twist of fate that Mrs Seaton died in the Lavender House fire. I wish I had never recommended the place."

The doctor's rather distracted manner vanished at the sound of the drawing room door opening. "Ah, here she is now. If you will excuse me, Detective Pyke."

Henrietta emerged with Declan Kelly. Her face was drained of colour and her eyes were glazed, but she lit up on seeing the doctor waiting for her. The doctor had her shawl ready to place gently around her shoulders. He took her arm and guided her to the door, his abused hat lying forgotten on the floor.

Charlie hurried after them to give back the hat. He waited until they closed the front door behind them, leaving him alone with Declan. "According to Johnstone, Henrietta had no opportunity to lace the curry with arsenic. If it was the curry, and not the soup or dessert or wine that was tampered with. The doctor entered the kitchen a few seconds after Henrietta. He could have added the arsenic if he was quick."

"That agrees with what Henrietta told me," Declan said. "I'll check the doctor's alibi for the morning of Mrs Seaton's death when we are finished here."

"He was with his patients, he said, which should be easy to check," Charlie said. "The doctor is either innocent or a fine actor, as he does not appear to have suspicions about Mrs Seaton's death, even now. He assumed she died in the fire and called it a dreadful twist of fate."

"Henrietta also expressed surprise when I questioned her about Mrs Seaton again." Declan drummed his fingers on the door frame. "Are they really such innocents that they have not made the simple leap to a link between the deaths? I find that hard to believe. The two of them could be working together. The doctor could have added arsenic to the meal and been seen by Mrs Seaton, leaving Henrietta to deal with the cook the next day."

Charlie struggled to accept Henrietta and Johnstone as killers, but couldn't rule it out. Each of them would have had to act quickly. The maids said Henrietta returned to the house soon after delivering Mrs Seaton to Lavender House.

"Was Henrietta very upset at not receiving a large inheritance from her beloved uncle?" Charlie asked.

"She was as shocked as the rest of the family at the diminished size of the estate, but was surprised to receive an equal share in his will. Her Uncle Arthur had paid the fees for her nursing training, for which she was grateful, and had promised to give her a dowry when she got married. Unfortunately, Arthur died before Doctor Johnstone made his intentions known in writing."

"Was Henrietta expecting an engagement?"

"She didn't say so in as many words, but it appears that Miss Henrietta Tucker and her Uncle Arthur felt they had the matter firmly in hand, even if the gentleman concerned needed a little prodding to admit his feelings." Declan smiled. "Henrietta is a strong character. I doubt she'll let anything or anyone stand in the way of her getting her man. Now, are you ready to tackle the rest of the Tuckers, Charlie? I'm especially interested in what Jack Tucker has to say. The constable recognised him as one of the protesters outside Lavender House during the fire, but I want to keep that fact to ourselves for the moment. Let's see what he says."

"Lead on, Detective Sergeant Kelly. Perhaps we should tackle Mrs Tucker first, to keep her husband on edge."

"Good idea, but let's focus on hearing their alibis. Mentioning the disappearance of the family fortune again will only create more distress at this point. We still want to keep them on the toes though, to show them who is in charge."

The interviews were taking place in the library, which was accessible through the rear door of the drawing room. Mr Tucker refused to allow his wife to be interviewed on her own and it suited Declan to agree, after a brief show of fake reluctance.

Declan waved the two suspects to the two plain chairs in front of the sturdy writing desk, while he and Charlie sat in comfortable chairs behind the desk. Mr Tucker sat, but his wife cast a pointed look at a nearby armchair. Declan looked at the chair. She sat.

Mrs Tucker refused to be bested by an upstart sergeant. She launched into an extended outburst on the outrageous conduct of the police, bringing the Glanville family name into disrepute by alleging murder and wasting her precious time. Declan was clearly willing to let the tirade continue until Mrs Tucker was blue from lack of oxygen, but Jack Tucker had other ideas. He put his hand on his wife's arm and that was all it took to calm her. She touched her hand to his and subsided into what she probably assumed was dignified silence.

Declan opened his notebook and placed his pencil on a fresh page. "Am I to understand you are refusing to comply with my request for an interview, Mrs Tucker? Do I have to arrest you and take you to the station?"

"Of course I am not refusing to be interviewed. Have I not just told you the relevant points? Must I spell it out, Sergeant Kelly? My brother died of food poisoning. Doctor Johnstone said so. Whoever started the ridiculous rumour that Arthur was murdered should be arrested immediately." Mrs Tucker glared at Declan, as if her statement ought to be enough to halt the investigation.

"You wish me to arrest the police surgeon who conducted the autopsy and found large quantities of arsenic in your brother's body?" Declan raised an eyebrow. "No? Then perhaps you would take us through the events of the dinner party on Friday evening, Mrs Tucker."

Mrs Tucker's lips clenched into a thin line. When Declan was unmoved, she let out an angry puff of air between thin nostrils and began her statement. "There is nothing to tell, Sergeant. We had a perfectly agreeable evening, aside from an unfortunate delay to the serving of the main course. The food was lukewarm by the time it arrived. I've told Arthur a dozen times he should get younger maids and a proper footman to see to the serving."

"My brother-in-law does not care for a crowd of servants getting under his feet," Jack Tucker said mildly, with an approving nod.

"Yes, dear," his wife said, "but there was no reason to countenance such a delay simply because that useless maid hurt her hand."

"Did you leave the dining room when the maid screamed in agony, Mrs Tucker?" Declan inquired.

"No, Sergeant, I did not. Why would I? Henrietta and Doctor Johnstone saw to it. I kept my brother company. Such a fuss over nothing. My husband was forced to retrieve a fresh bottle of wine himself, and Sid offered to bring in the plates. Outrageous. The other maid was perfectly capable of carrying on with her duties. I let my brother know his servants were taking excessive advantage of his slipshod attitude to discipline."

Declan refused to be drawn on the matter, although anyone with an ounce of compassion could have seen he was sorely tempted to comment. "It must have been a shock when Doctor Johnstone called the family to an urgent meeting the following morning."

"At an abominably early hour," Mrs Tucker said. "He sent the note to us shortly after seven o'clock in the morning, before the menfolk left for work. The meeting was at half-past nine. Naturally, we had not the slightest inkling why he demanded our presence."

Charlie found that hard to believe. Arthur's personal physician would hardly call a family meeting early on a Saturday morning if he did not have serious news to impart.

"Well, you can imagine our shock," Mrs Tucker continued, "when the doctor announced my brother had died of food poisoning. I had to partake of smelling salts to revive me. And then that foolish cook started making a dreadful fuss. I felt quite faint. My dear sons escorted me to Sidney's house, which is nearby, to spare me the anguish."

"Who left first, Mrs Tucker?" Declan asked. "You and your sons, or Henrietta and Mrs Seaton?"

Mrs Tucker pouted. "The doctor insisted on seeing to Mrs Seaton first, even though she was disgustingly drunk, whereas I was overcome with the shock of my dear brother's unexpected passing. He asked Henrietta to take the cook to a place for fallen women. I gave up waiting and asked my sons to take me away. If you ask me, the doctor ought to have locked her in her room to sober her up."

Mr Tucker reached over to pat her arm. "Now, my dear, you know the doctor made the correct decision. It would have been dreadful to leave a hysterical woman in a house of mourning. The doctor had patients waiting and Henrietta had enough on her plate, arranging the laying out and undertaker."

Mrs Tucker fluttered a fan in front of her face. "Dear Henrietta. So capable in a crisis."

Having not had a clear answer to his previous question, Declan tried again. "What time did you and your two sons arrive at Sidney's house? And what time did you leave again?"

"How should I know?" Mrs Tucker said. "The doctor's meeting did not last long, what with all the fuss. Half an hour, I suppose. Bert took my arm to steady me and Sidney was ever so kind. My sons had to go to work, so I called on the support of a dear friend who lives nearby. I probably arrived at my friend's house around eleven o'clock."

All conveniently vague, in Charlie's opinion. If true, Ariadne Tucker had an alibi for Mrs Seaton's murder, which must have occurred after eleven o'clock, when Miss Newland left Lavender House, and before eleven twenty, when the fire alarm sounded. Presumably, the cook was murdered just before the fire started, and thus probably around quarter past eleven.

Declan turned to Mrs Tucker's husband. "When did you leave the meeting on Saturday morning, Mr Tucker? And where did you go?"

Mr Tucker answered with neither the reluctance nor the temper of his wife. Indeed, he might have been describing an ordinary day to a casual acquaintance for all the emotion he showed. "I left before everyone else, after Sid said he would look after his mother, because I needed to get back to work. I'm a gas-fitter at the gasworks. I'd been assigned a job at the hospital fixing a faulty gas connector and was expected there around half-past ten. After completing that job, I knocked off, Saturday being a half day."

"What time would that have been?"

Jack Tucker's reply was interrupted by an extended bout of coughing. Then he looked at Declan sideways and slid around the truth. "My shift ends at noon. Might have been little before that when I finished, but I was eager to get home to look after my wife, after the shock of her brother's death."

"What route did you take home?"

"Princes and Stafford Streets. It's the quickest way."

Declan didn't ask if he stopped at Lavender House, which Tucker would probably have denied. Stafford Street was close enough that Jack Tucker must have been aware of the fire. "Thank you. That is all for now. Please send in Sidney Tucker."

Mrs Tucker rose, but did not leave. She leaned over the desk until her face was level with Declan's. "You have the reckless enthusiasm of youth about you, Sergeant Kelly. Perhaps this is your first investigation of a suspicious death? I caution you to put your desire for glory aside. My family had nothing to do with Arthur's death. If you persist in this persecution, I will ensure this is the last investigation you will ever undertake. Do I make myself clear?"

Declan turned to Charlie. "Detective Pyke, remind me of the penalty for threatening a police officer."

Mrs Tucker glared at Declan for long seconds before whirling around and dragging her husband out with her.

An Exotic Past

Soft footsteps padded the length of Isaac Upton's hall. Mr Lohar walked into the room, his head held up in the dignified, expressionless manner Grace had come to expect from him.

Mr Lohar bowed his head. "Mrs Pyke. I was expecting your husband a little later."

Grace wanted to correct her name to Mrs Penrose Pyke, but she suspected it would be a losing battle amongst the clients who knew her husband as Mr Pyke. Besides, now was not the time and place, as the matter was trivial compared to the grief carved into the lines on Mr Lohar's face. She avoided thinking about the lines carved into his back by the rattan cane.

"My husband had to quell the barbarian hordes. He sent me in his stead, as I work for the Southern Investigations Agency too."

Lohar's friend caught her meaning instantly and chuckled. "The Terrible Tuckers. Barbarian hordes, indeed." Mr Upton rose from his chair by pushing himself up with his walking stick. "I will give you some privacy, Rajiv. Mrs Pyke and I were having a lovely chat about chess."

Mr Lohar took the vacated seat. "When I heard voices, I thought it might be policemen coming to arrest me."

"On the contrary, Mr Lohar," Grace replied, "it is the charming Bert Tucker who is most at risk of arrest."

Their client reacted with only a slight arching of his eyebrow. "I am pleased to hear your husband was correct. Detective Sergeant Kelly seems a fair man."

To Grace's relief, Rajiv got up again to put the fire screen in front of the blaze. After thirty years in Dunedin, he was probably acclimatised to cooler weather. He sat down and looked at her expectantly, before rising again to fetch her a cool glass of water from the kitchen. She could have embraced him for his thoughtfulness. Mr Lohar put Grace in mind of their own housekeeper, Mrs Brown, who miraculously anticipated every need.

"I will not detain you for long, Mr Lohar. You must be exhausted after all that has happened over the last three days. However, we do wish to hear what you can tell us about the events leading up to the fatal dinner party." Grace sat back and let their client form his words in his own time, while she sipped the water.

"The morning was much as usual. I expect Mrs Seaton and the Eady sisters were busy with preparations, but I did not enter the kitchen after breakfast. I attended to Mr Glanville's clothes and shoes and other personal matters. Only the grocer's boy and the postman visited the house before I left at noon. Mr Glanville's only appointment was with Mr Fairchild at two o'clock, until the Tucker family arrived for dinner. My afternoon was filled with a walk, a few errands, and a meal with Mr Upton, after which we both attended the chess club all evening."

"Did you leave the chess club at any time during the evening?" Grace asked.

"Not until I returned home shortly after eleven o'clock. I found Mr Glanville suffering from debilitating stomach cramps and nausea, so I hurried to fetch Doctor Johnstone. The doctor did what he could, but it was too late."

Grace gave him a moment to get the tremor in his voice under control, but he gestured for her to continue. "As far as you knew, Mr Glanville had no other visitors that day?"

"A delivery boy might have called without my knowledge. Mr Glanville did not adhere to strict rules about who could answer the door." Lohar sighed. "We all helped each other. We had all been together for so long, it felt more like a family than service."

Grace shifted in her seat to get a better view of his face, not that he allowed much emotion to show. "Nellie Eady said a Chinese man with a facial scar visited in the early afternoon."

Mr Lohar showed neither surprise nor concern. "Sammy Yee Chong? Mr Glanville didn't inform me that he was expected. Not that he would tell me, as it was my half day."

"Is Sammy Yee Chong a social acquaintance or a business associate?"

Lohar paused before answering. "Both, I suppose, in that they were on friendly terms, but met to discuss matters of mutual interest. I cannot speculate on the nature of their discussion."

Can't or won't, Grace wondered. The manservant's lips pressed together, so she didn't push him. Grace wished Charlie was here, as he would know how to extract the maximum amount of information without causing offence.

For lack of a more subtle alternative, Grace dived in with a direct question. "Did Mr Arthur Glanville continue his father's trade in opium?"

Lohar's muscles tensed. He half-rose in the seat, leaning towards her. "How dare you ask such a question?"

Perhaps it was the mind-numbing heat of the room, but Grace had the oddest feeling he might have challenged her to a duel if she was a man. "I apologise for any offence I caused. I only ask because I did not know your employer as well as you do."

The anger vanished in an instant. "It is me who should apologise. You are quite right to ask. I can assure you *Arthur* Glanville is a decent and moral man. His privileged upbringing did not blind him to the truth. He abhorred the sale of opium as an immoral route to wealth. He was appalled at the damage opium does to both the addict and the families who suffer alongside them."

Grace was certain Mr Lohar had emphasised the word "Arthur", subtly implying that the same praise would not be extended to other members of the Glanville family. "Was your employer on good terms with his family, Mr Lohar? Please be frank in your opinions, knowing they will not be shared. Starting with his father, Horatio Glanville."

"My employer and his father were as different as chalk and cheese, as the English say, although a better comparison might be as different as a spanner and a sword. I endeavoured to keep them apart through Mr Arthur's childhood, to their mutual relief. My employer knew his father was disappointed in him, despite his brilliance at engineering. Fortunately, the older brother, Mr Raleigh, was the perfect Glanville heir, so Mr Arthur was allowed more leniency to make his own way in the world."

"We understand Raleigh Glanville took over the Calcutta business, while the New Zealand arm of the business was sold before Horatio Glanville's death."

"That is correct, Mrs Pyke. Mr Arthur was relieved his father sold the business before he died, so he would not be forced to deal with it. If he had inherited the business from Horatio Glanville, he would surely have ceased trading and wound the company up, rather than selling it to somebody else who would continue the opium trade. I expect his father knew that and acted accordingly."

Grace was sure the business dealings of Horatio Glanville warranted further scrutiny. She was less sure whether to fully embrace this lily-white painting of Arthur's character. "Did Arthur Glanville remain in contact with his older brother, Raleigh?"

"I believe they corresponded once or twice a year. The brothers have not seen each other in three decades. There is no animosity, but they were never close. Raleigh is eight years older, which is a large gap when you are a child. Arthur was fourteen when the family came to New Zealand, leaving twenty-two-year-old Raleigh in Calcutta. Of course, they have never had a business relationship either, as Mr Arthur was not part of the family company."

"Do you know the man who bought the New Zealand side of the business before Horatio died?"

"I know nothing about him other than his name – Clive Jardine. A business associate of Mr Horatio Glanville, presumably. Nobody here knew the name, so it is assumed that Mr Jardine runs the business from overseas, using a local manager."

"And how did Arthur Glanville feel about the rest of his family?" Grace asked.

"He was close to Miss Henrietta. They were alike, I think. Capable, decent, honest." Lohar paused at that point, which didn't bode well for his opinions of the rest of the family. "He respected Sidney and his father, Jack Tucker, for making their way in the world through hard work, although I don't think Mr Arthur felt attached to them in the same way he did with Miss Henrietta. Indeed, there was little communication between them, aside from the occasional family dinner out of courtesy."

The pause was longer this time, but Mr Lohar overcame his reluctance and forged on. "His sister, Mrs Ariadne Tucker, hinted she needed a bigger allowance after Horatio died. I believe my employer refused to give her more money, as their father had already made generous provision for her. As far as I know, she did not pursue the matter, but it did chill the relationship between them. Oddly enough, I would say her marriage to Jack Tucker was the making of Ariadne. She learned to value love above status, which is not to say that she didn't want better lives for her husband and sons."

"And the older son, Bert?"

"Bert was pestering Mr Glanville for money to start a business. Bert is … not content with his current position and wishes to advance his prospects. Mr Glanville was not unsympathetic, but he did not wish to throw his money away. He would have supported any of the family if they truly needed it. Indeed, he offered funding on the condition Bert showed him a sound business plan."

Grace recalled Dora's description of Bert slamming the door last week when his plea for money was not immediately granted.

Mr Lohar was warming to his chance to give honest opinions, perhaps for the first time. "The fact is, Horatio Glanville hoped his grandsons would be what his younger son was not – a ruthless businessman to follow in his footsteps. Horatio took the older grandson, Bert, into the business and gave him every encouragement. Alas, Bert was not the heir his grandfather hoped for. He inherited his grandfather's arrogance and ambition, but not his business acumen. Nevertheless, Horatio kept Bert on, and he remains an employee of the business to this day."

"In what role?"

"Bert has a position in the warehouse from which the imported goods are distributed."

"What about Sid?"

"Horatio had hopes for Sid and gave him a loan to get him started in a business of his choosing. Sid has become a well-regarded tailor. I believe Horatio was pleased by Sid's success, but I doubt it was the career choice he had hoped for. Neither grandson can claim they were hard done by."

"And Henrietta?"

Mr Lohar looked at Grace sideways with the beginnings of a smile. "Henrietta was the best of them, but she had one insurmountable failing. Being a woman, she was not worthy of notice. At least, not until she produced male children. In my opinion, Horatio Glanville should have been proud his granddaughter had become a competent nurse, but my feeling is that he considered nursing was not an appropriate calling for a lady."

Grace certainly knew the type. "I understand more than most, having had my fair share of detractors for wanting to study medicine."

"I can imagine, Mrs Pyke. Mr Arthur was extremely proud of his niece. He funded her nursing studies, in fact, and intended to see her married with a generous dowry."

"I wish I could have met him." Grace kept her expression neutral as she asked for the next character assessment. "Ariadne Glanville can't have had an easy childhood if her father had such a low opinion of the merits of women. Perhaps that was why she rebelled and married Jack Tucker? To be honest, I am surprised Horatio allowed the match. Unless he was forced to accept it?"

Her host bit back a smile. "You are very astute, Mrs Pyke. Those of us versed in arithmetic could not fail to notice that Bert was born less than eight months after the wedding. Not Bert's fault, of course, but Horatio never warmed to him. Perhaps that is why Bert is so angry at his lot."

"Bert and Sid. Not exactly heroic names in the Glanville tradition."

Mr Lohar laughed openly this time. "How right you are. Horatio was furious when Jack Tucker refused to name his firstborn after a famous British hero, as was the family tradition. Jack didn't want their lives to be ruled by his wealthy father-in-law, but his wife wasn't too proud to turn down the house and allowance Horatio gave them. I admire Jack. He is an honest working man, making a respectable living as a gas-fitter. He supports his family, rather than drinking and gambling his earnings away as others do, but one got the impression that such admirable qualities were never quite enough for his father-in-law."

"You have known them all for a long time, Mr Lohar."

"I am fifty-seven years old. I was only fourteen when I joined Mr Horatio Glanville's household in Calcutta as one of his many houseboys and servants. Horatio was born into a family who lived and breathed the East India Company. He would have been marked for success and wealth even if he hadn't had the powerful ambition he inherited from his father and grandfather. Do you know about the East India Company, Mrs Pyke?"

"All I know was that it was a trading company formed to import exotic goods into Britain."

"Far more than that, Mrs Pyke. The East India Company effectively ruled large swathes of my country and half the world's trade. At its peak, the Company had an army of nearly a quarter of a million soldiers – twice the size of the entire British Army."

Grace knew the East India Company was reputed to be a major trading company, but this sounded more like a warlord's empire.

149

Mr Lohar shook his head at her doubt. "I am not exaggerating, I assure you. Company men amassed unprecedented wealth from the resources of the East – everything from tea, to silk, to the priceless jewels stolen from conquered Indian rulers. Even minor company clerks sent diamonds home to their families. Those in charge became fabulously wealthy. The Glanville family was relatively low on the rungs, but they still had power over thousands of lives and livelihoods. That is why I smiled when you speculated that Miss Ariadne Glanville must have a difficult childhood. In truth, she was pampered with every luxury and taught she was superior to the darker-skinned people surrounding her."

The image of Ariadne thrashing her servants with a cane sprang to mind. Grace waited for Mr Lohar to continue, but he chose not to elaborate. Grace thanked her lucky stars for Mr Upton's indiscreet frankness.

"How did Horatio Glanville become involved in the opium trade?" Grace asked.

"It is difficult for outsiders to appreciate those years of East India Company dominance," Lohar said. "Opium became part of it because it was a valuable commodity to trade. The East India Company discovered the Chinese people could not get enough of opium to ease their lives after a hard day in the fields. The wealth of China flowed out, while opium flowed in."

Addiction and despair seemed a high price to pay, Grace thought, but then it was not the traders who paid the price. "How did Horatio and his family end up in New Zealand?"

Mr Lohar shot her a cynical smile. "After the people of India rose against their oppressors – an event the British like to call the Indian Mutiny – Glanville saw that the East India Company's stranglehold would fade away. He was correct. Eventually, the British government was shamed into curtailing the power of the Company. Horatio did not wish to go to England, a country he had never visited. He looked instead for a young colony, full of promise and opportunity. Gold had just been discovered in New Zealand. He anticipated that Chinese gold miners would flock to the new find and thus there would be money to be made by importing and selling goods."

"Such as opium?"

"Exactly, Mrs Pyke. Horatio Glanville was an astute businessman. He knew the demand would be there and he would be first on hand to provide what the miners wanted, using his contacts in Calcutta. In fact, he left his oldest son there to oversee the export arm of his business."

"I'm surprised he did not force his younger son, Arthur, to join the family business."

This time, Lohar's smile was proud. "Force has its limits. Arthur Wellesley Glanville was only fourteen when they came to New Zealand, and he was not made in his father's mould despite his grand name. My employer was an engineer from the moment he could stack three wooden blocks to make a tower. He invented a new gas valve, you know. A brilliant man, but not the son Horatio Glanville wanted."

Lohar turned on Grace with an intensity that pinned her to her chair. "Find the person or persons who killed Arthur Glanville, Mrs Pyke, and I will willingly give you all the money I have."

Sid And Bert

When Mr and Mrs Tucker left Arthur Glanville's library, Charlie let out the breath he had been holding. "I've never been more grateful to have a wife like Grace."

"You've only been married for a couple of days, Pyke." Declan gave him a superior smirk, being an old married man of several years' duration. "Awful as Mrs Ariadne Tucker is, I'm sure we've both met worse. At least her husband seems able to calm her temper."

Charlie had to acknowledge there were far worse women than Ariadne, but he still didn't envy Jack Tucker. "Her husband's alibi sounded a little shaky to me. What do you think, Declan?"

"More than a little. Jack Tucker seems a straightforward fellow, but occasionally his eyes slide sideways like a curling stone over uneven ice. The constable who was taking names at the Lavender House fire reckons he saw Jack Tucker there around half-past eleven or shortly thereafter. Too late for him to have murdered Mrs Seaton and started the fire, but you can be sure I will check Jack Tucker's alibi for the preceding half hour. There is something he is not telling us."

Charlie worked through the timeline. Even if Jack Tucker left the Glanville house as early as quarter to ten, it would have been a stretch for him to have gone across town to the hospital, fixed a gas fault, and left the hospital with sufficient time to get back across town to Lavender House in time to kill Mrs Seaton, especially if he had to clock in at the gasworks to pick up his tools on the way.

Mr Tucker's hacking cough worried Charlie. He was not a well man. If Jack had to stop work, his wife's inherited money might be all the family had to live on. Especially as his wife had standards above the aspirations of a working man. The combination of pride and desperation made for a powerful motive.

Sidney Tucker rapped on the door, but did not wait for permission to enter. He took a seat, straightening the already straight seam on his neatly pressed trousers. "Please proceed, Detective Sergeant Kelly. I am a busy man."

Declan took up his pencil and notebook without comment. "Your full name and address, please, Mr Tucker."

Sid answered promptly.

Declan raised an eyebrow. "You have your own house? And yet your older brother lives with your parents. Are you married?"

"I own a modest dwelling. I am twenty-six years old and a successful tailor. Although I have not yet acquired a wife to grace my home, I prefer to live under my own roof."

Charlie didn't blame him after what he'd seen of the rest of the family. Sid paused to size up the men seated before him. Literally, Charlie thought, as Sid let his gaze rest on the points at which Charlie's second-hand set of clothes did not fit as well as a tailor would want. He tucked the darned patch on his cuff under the table.

Sid crossed his legs at the ankle, taking care not to crease the bottom of his trousers. Somehow he made the rigid chair look comfortable, and thus rendered the interview more of a conversation than an interrogation.

"Before you ask, Detective Sergeant Kelly, I freely admit that my grandfather, Horatio Glanville, gave me my start in business as a mercer, selling fabrics imported from India and the Orient by my grandfather's company. I quickly discovered a talent for tailoring and was soon able to pay back the loan my grandfather gave me. I will always be grateful for his trust in me and the support he showed me. Therefore, I had no need of further money from the estate of my uncle."

Declan drew out the silence before speaking again. "And yet, you were angry when the will was read."

153

"Who wouldn't be? My grandfather made a fortune. It ought to have been passed to the next generation, not squandered by Arthur Glanville. I admit I could have used the windfall to expand my business, but it was not essential. I was mainly upset for my mother, knowing how devastated she would be by the unwelcome news."

"Mrs Tucker received a dowry from her father, I believe."

"Of course." Sid shrugged. "However, maintaining a proper lifestyle never comes cheaply."

"I'm interested that you put the blame on Arthur Glanville," Charlie said. "If your grandfather had little of his fortune left when he died, there was nothing Arthur could do."

"I suppose so, if what the solicitor said was true," Sid replied. "Uncle Arthur inherited the house, though, which my mother had expected to inherit as a family home, as Arthur was unmarried and childless."

"In fact, your grandfather sold the importing business before his death, rather than pass it to your Uncle Arthur. Were you aware of that?"

Sid's body didn't move, but tiny creases formed between his brows. "I knew the business had been sold, naturally. My brother made sure everyone knew about it. I assumed my grandfather sold because Uncle Arthur had no interest in it. However, I also assumed the business was sold for a substantial sum, which would have passed to Uncle Arthur when my uncle died."

"Do you have any idea what happened to the proceeds of the sale?" Declan asked.

Sid shook his head. "If Uncle Arthur didn't inherit the family fortune, it must have been lost due to bad luck. Importing goods from far-off lands is a fickle business. A disastrous flood in India, ships caught in a typhoon, debts unpaid. Any number of disasters might have caused a catastrophic loss. That is why I prefer to be a tailor. Gentleman pay well for quality and cannot afford to be delinquent in paying their bills in a town as small as Dunedin."

"Does the name Clive Jardine mean anything to you?" Declan asked.

"No. My grandfather was kind to me, but I was not privy to his business dealings, as you can imagine. Is that all, Sergeant Kelly? My father must return to his employment at the gasworks and I have offered to stay with my mother to ensure she is cared for. Uncle Arthur's death has left her weak with grief."

Neither Charlie nor Declan reacted, but Charlie knew they were both thinking the same. If this was what Mrs Tucker was like in a weakened state, heaven help them if they had to interview her when she was fully recovered. Charlie wondered how Jack Tucker must feel, having to go back to his job at the gasworks, while his son seemed to have no problem taking time off from his own business. One advantage of being your own boss, as Charlie knew, and never stopped appreciating.

"I have a few more questions, Mr Tucker," Declan said. "I need to know where you were on Saturday morning, after Mrs Seaton was taken away. If you could be precise as to the timings, I would be grateful."

Sid took a moment to think. "As I recall, we left here about ten o'clock, except my father, who had left a little earlier. I took my mother to my house, as she was devastated by the news of her brother's unexpected death. My house is closer, being just around the corner from my uncle, whereas our family home is further down the hill. Bert came too. After a soothing cup of tea and a chance to share our grief, Mother calmed down and decided she wished to be consoled by a friend who lives nearby. After they left my house, I went to my business premises in the city. I suppose I must have left about half past ten or thereabouts, as I arrived at my business in the central city around eleven o'clock."

"Do you have a witness to the timing of your arrival?" Charlie asked. The quickest route to the city from here was through the town belt, which meant Sid would have passed close to Lavender House, which was about halfway to the central city from here.

Sid didn't lose his temper, as his brother might have done, but he did not hide his annoyance. "My assistant was out delivering a garment when I arrived. However, he returned shortly after me, when I was busy cutting the fabric for a commission. About a quarter past eleven, I suppose, or a little earlier. I let my assistant go home early, as I had already sent messages to the customers with appointments that I would not be available that morning."

"Do you not have custom from passers-by?"

"I put up the closed sign and worked in the back room of my premises, because I find work soothing when I have had a shock. I confess I had no desire to deal with customers with the death of my uncle weighing so heavily on my mind. I continued to work alone through the rest of the morning and afternoon, doing design work and accounts. And thinking about my uncle, of course. We were not close, but a premature death in the family is always upsetting. I did not poison my uncle or set fire to a bunch of women unwanted by polite society, if that is what you are insinuating."

Declan shut his notebook. "Thank you, Mr Tucker. Could you send your brother in, please?"

Sid stood up, smoothed the near-invisible wrinkles in his suit, and headed for the door without another word.

As soon as he opened the door, Bert pushed past him. "What do you mean by leaving me to last? I have a job to go to, you know."

Declan flicked his eyes in Charlie's direction, given him permission to take over.

Charlie gestured Bert to the chair. "Your sister and mother were naturally distraught, being women, so we felt it was best to talk to them first." Charlie paused. "And your brother Sid is not …" He let the sentence trail, waiting for Bert to fill in the blanks.

"Not as tough as me?" Bert smirked. "Dressing other men is no business for a Tucker, or a Glanville."

I'd bet he makes far more money than you do, Charlie refrained from saying. Sid had built a successful business, dressed

156

well, and owned a house, whereas Bert looked old beyond his years. Grace had passed on the information that Bert lugged boxes for a living, having failed to make good on the opportunity his grandfather had given him. Horatio was clearly a man who believed in giving his grandsons opportunities, but not handouts.

Charlie noted the calloused hands and bent back of the muscular man in front of him. He sat awkwardly, as if the chair had been designed for a purpose other than sitting. Bert was as unlike his brother as a rough-sawn wooden bench was from a Chippendale chair. However, Charlie had no desire to raise Bert's ire at this point in the interview by pointing out this obvious fact. "You are the Warehouse Supervisor at your grandfather's importation business, Mr Tucker. Is that correct?"

Bert sat up a little straighter. "That's right. My grandfather was preparing me to take over the business. If Horatio Glanville hadn't had to sell the business before his death, I would be in charge of the company now."

"Why did your grandfather have to sell, Mr Tucker?"

Bert's smirk vanished. "He didn't tell me. Must have run into some trouble, I suppose."

"I take it you know who owns the business now?"

Bert's eyes narrowed. "The owner prefers to remain private. He runs the business through a manager." Bert continued to glare at Charlie as the silence extended. "I don't know the owner's name. He might not even live in this country. None of my business and none of yours, neither."

Charlie tapped his pencil on his notebook, watching Bert's pout blossom into a full-blown scowl. "A simple matter to find out, I'd have thought, Mr Tucker. In fact, the owner is a Mr Clive Jardine."

"So what?"

Bert Tucker knew the name – Charlie was sure of it – but he disguised it well. "You approached your uncle, Arthur Glanville, for a loan last week, Mr Tucker. What was that for?"

157

"None of your business."

Charlie carefully recorded the response before placing the pencil exactly square on the notebook. "In fact, it is very much my business, as your uncle's refusal gives you a strong motive to get his money by other means."

Bert kept his temper in check, though it caused him obvious physical effort to do so. "You'd better not be accusing me of killing my uncle. Uncle Arthur would have come around. Anyway, he didn't refuse to give me a loan, he just wanted me to write a business plan to prove I could repay him."

Declan cut in. "Where did you go on Saturday morning, after the announcement of your uncle's death?"

"I went with my mother and brother to Sid's cottage. We had to discuss funeral arrangements and such like."

"And to speculate on the inheritance his death might bring?"

"Yeah, sure. Nothing wrong with that. Horatio Glanville ought to have shared his money out to all the family. Leaving his fortune to Arthur was despicable. That solicitor's talk of my grandfather's fortune having dwindled to nothing is claptrap, if you ask me. Arthur probably squandered the money on failed inventions."

"We will look into it," Declan said. "How long was the discussion at Sid's house?"

"Not long. Sid and I had to go back to work. Let's see." Bert scraped thick fingers over a dark rash of afternoon bristles on his chin. "We left Uncle Arthur's house around ten o'clock, more or less. I suppose we spent half an hour or thereabouts talking at Sid's house. I had important deliveries to make in North Dunedin, so I didn't have time to waste on idle chatter."

Both Sid and Bert had given a departure time from Sid's house around half past ten. If they were telling the truth, what was Mrs Tucker doing before she arrived at her friend's house at eleven o'clock? That was still before Mrs Seaton's death and Mrs Tucker had been vague as to times, but it was worth checking.

158

"Did anyone see you pick up the items for delivery at the warehouse?" Declan asked.

More bristle-scraping. "Probably not. I was in and out in a couple of minutes. What's this got to do with Uncle Arthur's death?"

"Routine inquiries," Declan said. "You'll need to supply a list of delivery addresses in North Dunedin, Mr Tucker."

The request ruffled Bert. His lip went out, but he bit it back. "Only one delivery. The Edinburgh Hotel." His eyes slid away. "Stayed for a bite to eat and an ale or two, Saturday being a half day of work."

Charlie was willing to bet the "delivery" was an excuse to leave work early for an afternoon drinking with his friends. "Are you aware that your grandfather made his money selling opium?"

"Perfectly legal," Bert replied. "If you've ever had a toothache or a crook back, you'd be thanking Horatio Glanville for bringing you relief."

"Do you make deliveries to the opium dens in Dunedin?" Declan asked.

"I do what I'm told to do, as every working man must. Beats working in the filthy stench of the gasworks, I can tell you."

"Thank you, Mr Tucker. That will be all." Declan rocked back in his chair, stretching his arms behind his head. "For now."

Declan grimaced as Bert slammed the door behind him. "Bert isn't doing himself any favours."

Charlie glanced at his pocket watch. "I'd better collect Grace, as we have a family dinner tonight. I could pass by the gasworks and Jardine's warehouse to check Jack and Bert Tucker's alibis, if Grace is willing. Sid's shop too, if we've time before it closes for the evening."

"Only if you have time. I wouldn't want you to be late for dinner after the events of the last few days. How are Doctor and Mrs Penrose coping with the transformation of their only daughter's wedding into a murder inquiry?"

"Surprisingly well, Declan, surprisingly well. They are almost as remarkable as their daughter."

Coal Gas And Cravats

With the stultifying heat in Mr Upton's sitting room numbing Grace's senses, and Mr Lohar's extraordinary account of the history of India capturing her full attention, Grace didn't hear the knock on the door. When Charlie entered the room, he seemed almost a stranger to her – a giant looming in the heat haze next to the gnome-like Mr Upton. She shook her head to clear it, wishing she had asked for a second glass of water.

Mr Lohar rose to greet Charlie.

Charlie stripped off his coat and reassured their client that they were making progress on the murder of his employer. "The investigation is still in the early stages of gathering information, Mr Lohar. Our best hope is to narrow down the suspect list by checking the alibis for Mrs Seaton's death, given the short time period in which her murder must have occurred. Speaking of which, do you recall what time Henrietta Tucker came back to the house after leaving Mrs Seaton at the refuge?"

"I'm sorry. I don't recall. She returned when I was deep in prayer."

Grace let her thoughts drift. Suddenly, she realised Charlie was speaking to her. She pushed herself up from the chair. "Yes, I'm ready to leave."

When they were outside again, Grace sucked in fresh, cool air. How odd it seemed to step out into what was still a glorious summer's day and feel refreshed by the ordinary heat. The sun was dropping towards the hills as the afternoon drew on.

Charlie brushed a damp strand of hair from her forehead. "Grace, are you unwell?"

"Better now I am out of the heat of that stuffy sitting room. I was so caught up in tales from Calcutta, I feel quite disoriented stepping back onto the streets of Caversham."

"You've had a long day, after a long night with Molly. I was going to suggest taking a stroll to check alibis, but I think it would be best to take you straight home."

Grace wavered. On one hand, she could feel the effects of the day pushing her to the brink of irascibility. On the other, she wasn't about to admit weakness. "A romantic pre-dinner stroll would be lovely," she said through gritted teeth, "as long as we are not out too late. Lily said to come around early for dinner."

Charlie took her arm and set off at an ambling pace with his coat over his shoulder. "I'm not sure our destinations could be called romantic by any stretch of the imagination. The gasworks, a warehouse near the wharves, and a city shop. The best that can be said of it is that we will be together, which is pleasure enough for me. Shall I recite love sonnets to make up for it?"

Shoot me now, Grace thought. Or, better yet, shoot everyone else and let me tuck up between cool sheets after a long bath. "Perhaps later, Charlie. Tell me what you found out today."

Their route took them past a tannery and the railway workshops, so their noses were well prepared for foul stenches by the time they encountered the nauseating vapours of the gasworks drifting up the street. Grace was thankful there was no looking glass to hand, as she could feel the specks of coal dust gathering on her still-perspiring face. By the time they reached the gasworks – a solid brick building with a tall brick chimney and enormous gas tanks – her white shirt was far from pristine and her innards were roiling. No wonder Jack Tucker had failing lungs, if he had worked here all his life.

As they approached, a straggle of coal-blackened workers were leaving, while cleaner men trudged into the building for the next shift. The households and business of Dunedin used gas every hour of the day and night, and thus the work was never-ending.

"I'm not sure if they'll tell me whether Jack Tucker attended a gas-fitting job at the hospital," Charlie said. "I could use the letter of authorisation Detective Inspector Wallace gave me, but I would prefer to use that only when absolutely necessary."

Grace dug into her satchel for her hospital pass. "I'll try this first." She brushed herself down as best she could and entered the administrative area of the gasworks.

Only one young man was still working, which suited her purposes. Grace took a seat in front of him and flashed the pass under his nose. She smiled tentatively and spoke loudly to overcome the regular thump of the steam engines within the gasworks. The man seemed not to notice the noise, but Grace could feel every vibration making her headache worse.

"I'm Miss Penrose from the hospital. I'm afraid there has been some confusion over a job at the hospital fixing a faulty gas connection. Would you be able to confirm whether a man called Jack Tucker attended a job at the hospital on Saturday morning? Probably between ten and eleven o'clock."

The young man pushed spectacles up on the bridge of his nose, emphasising his protruding eyes. "I'm sorry, Miss. That is confidential information, unless you have a letter of authority from a senior official at the hospital."

Grace screwed up her face as if she was about to cry, which was an easy pretence in her state. "Of course, I understand. It's just that I fear it is my mistake. I cannot afford to lose my position, as I am saving for my wedding trousseau. I would be ever so grateful."

The man took one look at her and judged that making a young lady weep was the lesser crime. He opened a filing drawer and rifled through it. "You are correct. Tucker was at the hospital. Let's see now … apparently there was no problem after all. Probably a minor fault the hospital maintenance team had already attended to. Don't you worry, Miss, you'll not get in trouble. It wasn't clear whether the mistake was at our end or yours, so we have written the job off."

"Oh, thank you so very much. You have no idea how relieved I am by your kindness." Grace rose and left before the man could question her odd request. The success of her subterfuge improved her mood a little, when really she ought to have been feeling all the worse for lying. She didn't care to examine what this said about her character.

Charlie took her arm when they were outside and strode away into the fresher air on the other side of the building, where the odour of coal gas dissipated in favour of the tang of sea air. Even inner harbour sea air, with its salt-laden aftertaste of oil, rotten fish, seaweed and sewage, was better than the gas.

"What would I do without you, Miss Penrose?" Charlie said. "You are worth more to me than any Mrs Beeton housewife with exemplary household management skills."

Grace replied with an unladylike grunt, although his words pleased her. "You wouldn't say that if marriage to me didn't come with the cooking and household skills of the exceptional Mrs Brown."

"Nonsense, woman. I'd have married you even if Mrs Brown wasn't part of the bargain. Probably. Although, now I come to think of it …"

"I suggest you stop there, Pyke, and tell me where we are going next." Grace looked up longingly as a carriage clattered past them, taking its fortunate occupants home.

"Bert Tucker's workplace." Charlie pointed around the curve of the inner harbour to the area of warehouses behind the wharves. "I don't expect to be able to pinpoint Bert's movements around the time of Mrs Seaton's death, because Bert admitted he was in and out in a few minutes, picking up a delivery, and wasn't seen. However, I would like to get a feel for the scale of the place and Bert's role in Jardine's importing business."

"Dora, the maid, thought Bert was a glorified floor hand, lugging boxes and making deliveries, not the Warehouse Supervisor he makes himself out to be."

The walk did not take long, which was just as well, as Grace's reserves of energy were fading fast as the heat of the day slipped away. Jardine's warehouse was on a scale far greater than she had imagined. As they passed the open doors, wide enough for two carts to pass through at once, she reeled and collapsed into Charlie's arms.

"Hey, you there!" Charlie called to the sturdy men unloading crates from a dray. "Can you help us, please? My wife has taken a turn."

The men glanced uncertainly at each other, but Charlie gave them little choice. He lugged his wife's limp body to a crate and set her down, putting his coat on the crate to cushion her delicate posterior. "My apologies, but I cannot let her collapse on the street. Would it be possible to get a glass of water?" Charlie jingled his coin purse encouragingly.

The older man put down his end of the crate they were unloading. "No need for that, sir. We'd be glad to help. It's just that the boss is a bit of a stickler against slacking off."

Charlie callously left his wife and followed the man into the interior of the warehouse. "I'll pass on my gratitude to your boss, if that would help. Or help you unload the crates if you would prefer. I'm sure my wife will be fine in no time after a brief rest."

"No need for that, sir. I have a soft spot for fainting women. The only time my wife ever fainted was when we had a child on the way. Happy days. I hope you are blessed the same as we were."

"Oh, I hope you're right. We haven't been married long, so I never thought ..."

Grace struggled to keep a straight face as Charlie's words were lost when he went behind a towering stack of crates labelled, "Tea – Ceylon". She didn't need to have three years of medical studies behind her to know that she wasn't with child, unless it was the second coming of the saviour. Since their wedding, Grace and her husband had scarcely been in the same room as each other, let alone in the privacy of the bedchamber.

165

She looked around vaguely, spotting crates from exotic destinations across the globe, but mainly from China and India. There appeared to be enough chests of tea to supply the Dunedin population for months, if not years. The younger warehouse worker was gawking at her. She waved a weak hand around the vast warehouse. "Goodness gracious, I feel as if I have stumbled into Aladdin's cave. What is all this?"

"Everything you can imagine from foreign lands," the young man said, with a grin that was half-pride, half-awe. "And plenty more besides. Tea, silk, cotton, porcelain, fancy screens and dishes, and all sorts."

"My father knew a man who imported such things from the East," Grace lied. "Horatio Glanville, his name was."

"Oh, aye, the very man." The young worker leaned on the dray, glad to have a moment's rest. "Mr Glanville sold up to Mr Jardine, the present owner, about a year back."

"Nice fellow, is he, Mr Jardine?"

"Ain't never met him, Missus. Not sure he even lives in the country. Jardine has a manager to run it for him. Runs a tight ship, he does. I'd best be getting back to work."

"We're very grateful for your assistance." Grace smiled sweetly. "I recall my father saying one of the Horatio's grandsons still works here."

"Oh, aye, that'd be Bert Tucker."

Charlie and the older man appeared around the end of a row of crates. Charlie passed her a tin mug, which looked as if it hadn't been cleaned since Eve bit into her apple.

Grace didn't have to fake illness as she looked into the oily slick on the water in the mug. "Thank you, my dear. I'm feeling much better after a little rest. This lovely young man was just saying Bert Tucker works here. You'll recall my father talking of the Glanville and Tucker families, I'm sure. I ought to pass on my condolences to Mr Tucker while I am here, as my father said his uncle passed away recently."

166

"Bert ain't here," the older man muttered. "Never seems to be here when you need him, does Bert." He looked up sharply at them, probably regretting his hasty words to friends of the Tuckers. "That is to say, young Bert is a busy man, always about town, making deliveries. Haven't seen him since last week, he's been that busy."

"I expect he has requested leave to mourn his uncle," Charlie said.

The older man's instant expression of disbelief suggested to Grace that she wasn't the only one who thought Bert Tucker had skived off to the alehouse rather than come back to complete his day's work.

Grace reached her arm up for Charlie to help her up, tipping the mug over as she rose. "Oh dear, how clumsy. I don't know what has come over me today, but I thank you for your kindness."

Charlie supported Grace with one arm around her waist and shook the older man's hand with his free hand, passing him a coin as their palms met. "Again, our thanks for your help.

As they left the warehouse, Charlie fussed over his wife as if he feared she might collapse again at any moment. Until they passed out of sight around the next corner. Then he dropped his arm from her waist and inspected her with a grin. "Are you feeling better now, my fragile little blossom?"

Grace straightened up and rolled her eyes. Charlie need never know just how close Grace was to not having to fake the fainting fit. She bit back a sharp retort and answered more or less truthfully. "Apart from catching goodness knows what diseases from touching that mug, I am miraculously recovered from my convenient moment of weakness."

"Excellent. Then you won't mind a brief stop at Sid's tailoring enterprise on the way home."

Grace glared at her husband, but he failed to notice.

Charlie took her arm and set off at a fast pace for the centre of the city. "Sid Tucker's shop should make a pleasant change from the gasworks and Jardine's warehouse."

167

"We haven't much time," Grace hinted. "The shops will be closing soon."

"Plenty of time, Grace. We won't need long. I managed a quick look at the inventory while the man went in search of that delightful cup of water."

"Delightful indeed. It would seem that the fine porcelain they import is not shared with their workers. What did you find, other than acres of tea?"

"Plenty of opium, that's for sure. The old man has never met the owner, Clive Jardine, and he said nobody else he knew had either. The security at the warehouse is surprisingly slipshod, I thought. Might come in handy if we need more information. But I doubt we'd find out anything useful on either the owner or Bert Tucker. Both seem more remarkable for their absence than their presence."

They took a wrong turn or two looking for Sid's business, which was tucked away down a lane of high-quality shops, next to the most expensive jewellers in town. The phrase *Exclusive Tailoring By Sidney*" scrolled across the upper third of the window in elegant gold cursive. The prices of the items on display took Grace's breath away. Charlie would have to work his burned and knife-scarred shoulders to the grindstone for months before he could afford one of Sid Tucker's suits. Even one of the artistically draped silk cravats would punch a crater in their combined savings.

When Grace stepped away from her perusal of the window display, she caught sight of the bedraggled woman reflected in the pane. She pulled Charlie aside. "I cannot go in like this. Only a select clientele from the upper echelons of society would dare cross Sid's threshold. I look more like a fishwife on a bad day."

Charlie put on his coat again, which was free of the sprinkle of coal dust and smuts that dotted Grace's white shirtwaist. "Perhaps it's for the best. A fiancée wouldn't come to help me buy a morning coat for our wedding. Your disreputable state gives me an idea, though. Whoever set the fire at Lavender House might have traces of ash on his clothes if he stayed long enough to ensure the fire was well alight and sure to spread."

Grace felt unaccountably cheered up at the thought of hard evidence. She held up the cuff of her shirt, where a smudge of grime remained where she had spilled the mug of water. "Or a drop of Mrs Seaton's blood. Now that we have a microscope, even the tiniest remnant might be identifiable. I know from long experience just how hard it is to wash blood out of cotton, no matter how often the shirt is laundered."

"We make a good team, Grace." He looked her up and down. "Perhaps you could come in as my cousin, just off the train from out of town and a little the worse for wear after the journey."

"I have a better idea, if we have ten minutes to spare."

Grace didn't wait for his reply. She headed for the nearby corner of High Street and Rattray Street, where the DIC store stood, waiting to meet their every need. The Drapery and General Importing Company had been open less than a decade, but already it had become an institution in Dunedin. Avid shoppers still expounded at length about the thrill of entering a single emporium, where one could purchase everything from hosiery to napery to ironmongery. One might even buy a piano, if one was so inclined. Grace was not inclined to buy a piano, but she did wish to visit the room set aside for ladies to refresh themselves after the exertions of commerce.

When Grace emerged again a few minutes later, the spring was back in her step. Her face was washed and powdered, her hair was in place, and the eyes of onlookers were drawn away from her grubby white shirt to the beautiful ruby-red silk shawl draped over her shoulders, edged with a gold band and adorned with flowers. She had put it into her satchel this morning in case the perfect summer's day had a cool sting in its tail.

Charlie's expression softened at the sight of it. "I'm glad you still wear the shawl."

169

"It was the first gift you bought me, Charlie. I wore it so often in those years you lived in Wellington, I thought I would wear it out before you returned."

"I wish I had come back to Dunedin sooner. We'd known each other for such a short time. Anything other than friendship seemed an impossible dream to me back then."

Grace took his arm. "We made the right decision. Your time in Wellington with Detective Inspector Stewart was the making of you, and I had my medical studies. It all turned out for the best in the end. Now, my love, I suggest we talk about other matters. With that sentimental glow about your expression, we would never be taken for cousins."

Charlie wiped the smile from his face and headed back to Sid's shop. "While you were titivating yourself in DIC, I was working on the timings. Taking the shortcut through the town belt, it would be only ten minutes at a fast pace from either Sid's house or Arthur Glanville's house to Lavender House. Sid or Bert could have been at their workplaces within a quarter of an hour after leaving the fire, while Jack Tucker would have taken twice that to reach the hospital on foot and not much less if he took the tram."

"Hence your desire to get the precise timing of their movements on that Saturday morning."

Charlie pushed open the door to Sid's shop. Grace left him to talk to the assistant, while she inspected the outrageously priced but exquisite cravats and other gentlemen's accessories.

The assistant appeared from a back room with a pole in his hand. He jerked to attention at seeing Charlie. "Can I help you, sir?" The assistant was perfectly polite, but tiny frown lines appeared between his eyebrows as his eyes took in Charlie's old and ill-fitting suit. "I was just about to close up the shutters for the day."

Charlie rounded his vowels and looked down his nose. "Please excuse the informal attire and lateness of the hour. I had to meet my cousin off the train. One never cares to risk one's best garments at the station. Steam trains may be a technological marvel, but the smuts are the bane of every well-dressed gentleman. As we strolled through town, my cousin reminded me I am in need of an expert tailor."

"Yes, sir." The frown lines vanished. "You have come to the right place."

"I require a morning coat of the very best quality for my upcoming wedding."

Now the eyes sparkled. He put the shutter pole down. "At Sidney's, we guarantee the absolute best quality to be found in the colony. Mr Sidney learned from the best on Savile Row, sir."

This was news to Grace, as it would be to the rest of the Tucker family. As far as Grace knew, none of the Tuckers had ever set foot in Britain, let alone trained in the preeminent tailoring district of London.

"Excellent," Charlie said. "My usual tailor is unwell at present. I need to know that the garment could be completed within a month."

"That would be no problem at all, sir. Let me get our appointment book."

Once the appointment book was open on the counter, Charlie asked if he might see samples of the fabrics. The assistant disappeared into a back room, leaving Charlie to leaf through the pages.

Unfortunately, the assistant was back in seconds with a book of samples. "Might I suggest one of these fabrics, sir?"

Grace put down the tie-pin she was examining. "Perhaps it would be best if I chose the material, cousin. Your fiancée wouldn't thank you for selecting anything but the best." Grace drew the assistant over to the cravat stand. "Naturally, we need a waistcoat and all the accessories as well. These cravats look lovely."

She lingered over each fabric sample, feeling the weight, commenting on the colour, and holding the material against a range of silk cravats. Finally, she heard the scuff of Charlie's boots behind her. She pointed to a fabric swatch, which appeared to be almost identical to all the others. "What do you think, cousin?"

"You have an excellent eye for quality, madam," the assistant said. "The extra expense will be worth it when you see how well the coat hangs."

Grace handed the samples back to the assistant. "I really ought to see what the bride is wearing before we make the final choice. It would be absolutely appalling if I chose a pale cream cravat, if the bride is wearing pearl white."

"Whatever you think," Charlie said. "I suggest we leave this gentleman to close up the shop. Will the tailor will be here tomorrow? The owner of the business is Mr Sidney Tucker, I believe. I know his uncle, who passed away suddenly last Friday night. I'm surprised the shop is open today."

The assistant favoured them with a superior smile. "Mr Sidney trusts me to run the business in his absence. Customers are always our priority, sir."

"But you were closed on the Saturday morning after the death," Charlie said. "I sent my valet down to inspect the quality of the offerings in advance of my visit, and he found nobody here."

"I'm surprised to hear it, sir. Mr Sidney was detained by family matters, but I was here." The assistant paused. "Unless your valet arrived while I was out making a delivery. Unfortunate timing, as Mr Sidney himself was back when I returned."

"Do you know what time you returned? I fear my valet might have gone to the wrong establishment."

"As it happens, I know the time precisely, sir. I looked at the clock, thinking it was later, but it was only a quarter past eleven. Normally, I finish at noon on a Saturday, but Mr Tucker let go early. I expect he wanted to be alone with his grief."

"Ah, that would explain it. I will send a message when I am ready to make an appointment." With that, Charlie took his cousin's arm and left the shop.

Fortunately, they were now close to home, with only the climb up High Street between Grace and a washbasin. She was daydreaming about the crisp new sheets on their bed when Charlie interrupted her thoughts.

"A good day's work, Grace. Sid's account of Saturday morning matches the evidence. If he was at his work premises at quarter past eleven, he could not have killed Mrs Seaton. With Sid Tucker ruled out, the field of likely suspects narrows nicely. Bert is shaping up as a man of dubious character. His father, Jack, is back on the list now we know that his job at the hospital was of short duration, as there was no gas fault to fix."

"Sid had the least compelling motive, too," Grace said, as she struggled up the last few yards to their gate. "He has a successful business and therefore needs the inheritance less than the rest of his family."

"The contrast between Sid Tucker's situation in life and his brother's and father's lives was certainly put into stark contrast by our visits to their work premises." Charlie opened the gate for her. "But everybody needs money, Grace. Sid may charge exorbitant prices, but that doesn't mean he is making a fortune. His appointment book was conspicuously light on appointments."

"At his prices, he doesn't need many clients. Let's have no more talk of murder tonight. I insist on a quick dinner and a long sleep before I think another murderous thought."

A Murderous Meal

Charlie and Grace arrived home to find Mrs Penrose in the drawing room, chuckling over a book.

Mrs Penrose glanced up at their arrival. "Mrs Beeton's advice would bankrupt you before the year is out. Look here. Even an ordinary family dinner runs to three courses. Boiled turbot and oyster sauce with potatoes. Followed by roast leg of pork, apple sauce, broccoli, and potatoes. Finishing with cabinet pudding, and damson tart."

Charlie's stomach growled at the thought of crispy roast pork dripping in apple sauce. He'd hardly had a bite to eat all day.

Grace looked over her mother's shoulder "Charlie found the book amusing too. He recommended I read the medical section."

"You'll particularly enjoy the section on blood-letting." Charlie could see that Grace was having trouble concentrating. He wasn't sure if it was dehydration after the stifling heat of Mr Upton's sitting room, or hunger, or lack of sleep, or a combination of all three.

Mrs Penrose eyed her daughter up. "Grace, dear. I hope you don't mind me saying you appear a little … peaky. Most newlyweds are reputed to be radiant."

"I am tired after being up most of the night, Mama. But the joy of the result was worth it."

On seeing his mother-in-law stunned into red-faced silence, Charlie realised the ambiguity of Grace's explanation. "Molly went into labour last night. Her husband, Doctor Ravenwood, was out on a call, so Grace had the honour of delivering a gorgeous baby girl in the wee hours of this morning."

Mrs Penrose regained her normal colour. "Oh, Grace, you never change. Who else could rebound from a fire during her wedding ceremony, only to deliver a baby the next night and become involved in a murder investigation the day after? I dare not think what tomorrow will bring, or if your long-suffering husband will forgive your absence."

"My long-suffering husband has been equally absent," Grace said. "We both agreed we could not turn this case down, even though we ought to be attending to more important matters, such as thanking our wedding guests and enjoying the company of our long-suffering families."

"In that case," Mrs Penrose said, "you'll be happy to know Jasmine Pyke and I have already attended to the notes of thanks to your guests, and had a delightful chat about our shared joy at your marriage."

Oh, marvellous, Charlie thought, knowing their mothers would have exchanged amusing anecdotes about the respective childhoods of their children. At least the two families appeared to be getting along. There had been talk of taking a tour of the Otago Peninsula together, but the Lavender House fire had scorched that plan. Charlie was about to ask whether they might be excused from the dinner, when Mrs Penrose continued her account of the day.

"We've all been busy too. Lily has been talking to her contacts. Alistair and Thomas spent the day at the police station going through files. Or so they say. I detected a whiff of whisky and a dollop of manly camaraderie when they returned. I gather Detective Inspector Wallace is an old friend. And now I am here to help you dress for dinner, Grace, since you have no maid to help. We're all so looking forward to having a lovely family dinner, after the many distractions that have kept us apart."

Grace bent down to kiss her mother's cheek. "I can manage with Charlie here. Thank you, Mama, for everything. We'll be over in twenty minutes or thereabouts."

Charlie helped Grace up the stairs, noting her wistful glance at the bathroom, where the luxury of a hot soak in the bath beckoned. "It'll have to be a cool washcloth and a quick change of clothes, Grace. I should have told you to come straight home after you worked your magic on the two Glanville maids."

"I'll be fine, Charlie. Just give me a kick under the table if I fall asleep with my face in the soup."

While Grace stripped down to her underclothes and washed, Charlie rummaged through her wardrobe for her favourite midnight-blue evening gown. Once the water in the basin was filthier than her face, Grace tossed the grubby towel down and turned to see what he had laid out on the bed.

"Charlie, dearest, while I appreciate the concept of dressing in fine clothes to bolster my sagging spirits after a gruelling day, don't you think my best evening gown is mite too much for a family dinner?"

Charlie pulled a dark velvet jewellery box from behind his back. "We've been so busy, I haven't had the right moment to give you my wedding gift."

Nestled inside the box, in a bed of satin, was an exquisite sapphire and diamond necklace, made at the same jewellery shop as her engagement ring. The stunned look on Grace's face as she opened the box was worth every penny. He braced himself for a rebuke for buying such an expensive gift, but Grace spoke with her heart.

"Charlie, it's absolutely gorgeous – the most perfect gift imaginable."

Charlie clipped the necklace around her neck. "You look beautiful," he said, as she paraded in front of the looking glass. "In theory, you will look even more beautiful once the gown is on, but I must say I prefer the minimal-clothes look. Remove another couple of layers, and you will look like a goddess."

"Don't tempt me, my love. I fear my mother will come looking for us if we are late, having promised to be over soon." Grace did another twirl in front of the looking glass. "Your present from me is under the pillows on the bed."

Charlie dragged his eyes away from his wife. Under the pillows, he found a pair of silk dressing gowns, deliciously soft to the touch. The larger one was the same jade green as his eyes, while the smaller one was midnight blue. "Grace, these are perfect. I look forward us having the opportunity to wear them. Soon, I hope."

"Very soon," Grace confirmed. "Come here, husband, and take your shirt off."

Charlie stripped his shirt off willingly, wondering just how late they could be to the dinner party. "Are you thinking what I'm thinking? That we could lock the front door and put a sign up to deter intruders?"

"I may be thinking the same, but I also know Lily is planning a celebratory dinner, so you can wipe that smirk off your face, Pyke. I need to tend to your burn, or it will become infected." Grace made quick work of it. "It's unnatural how quickly you heal, Charlie. Now, put a fresh shirt on or we will be so late, questions will be asked."

Five minutes later they were standing in front of the Stewart's house, next door to their own. Grace straightened his tie before they entered. The door stood open. Laughter and loud chatter drifted down the corridor. "Ready, my love?"

Charlie ran his fingers along the necklace. "With you by my side, I am ready for anything." His fingers trailed off over her pale skin. "I'm sure no one will mind if we excuse ourselves early."

Alistair raised his glass as they entered. "I hope you newlyweds had an enjoyable day in each other's company."

Charlie gave his business partner a sardonic grin. "How could it be anything but enjoyable, Alistair? A new client, an autopsy, a violent contretemps at the reading of the will, several hours of interviewing suspects, and a jaunt around the festering corners of Dunedin city, testing alibis. Just your average day on a romantic honeymoon."

Charlie's father, Sergeant Thomas Pyke, pressed glasses into their hands. Charlie would have preferred water, but the family dinner had taken on a festive air. As Grace's mother had said, Alistair and Thomas were already red-cheeked and jovial.

"Mrs Grace Penrose Pyke, may I say how radiant you look this evening?" Thomas said, rolling his r's more than normal. "My son is a fortunate man."

After everyone had admired Grace's necklace, Alistair pulled up an armchair and rolled a few more r's. "Rounded up the murderer yet, Charlie?"

"The good news is that we have a limited number of likely suspects," Charlie said, as he made himself comfortable in the armchair. "Arthur Glanville was poisoned with arsenic at a dinner party, attended by his sister, Mrs Ariadne Tucker, her husband, Jack Tucker, and their adult children, Bert, Sid and Henrietta. Apart from the Tucker family, the only other people present were Arthur's doctor, Clifford Johnstone, the cook who was killed the following day, and two maids. All of them benefitted from Glanville's will, although Johnstone only does so if he marries Henrietta."

Grace propped herself on the arm of his chair. "The maids are unlikely suspects, because they adored their employer and have vowed to bring the killer to justice. Arthur Glanville has been good to them, keeping Nellie on despite her shaking palsy, which makes her clumsy."

"We think Mrs Seaton was killed because she knew who the poisoner was," Charlie said.

"Could the killer have added arsenic to the ingredients earlier in the day?" Doctor Penrose asked. "Or entered the house during the dinner?"

"Unlikely, but not impossible," Charlie said. "Fortunately, our client was absent and has an alibi."

"In fact, Mr Lohar could have left his chess club unobserved between games," Grace said. "However, his loyalty to his employer appears to be beyond doubt."

Charlie frowned at this news, but made no comment.

"Tell us more about who benefits from Glanville's death," Alistair said.

"The servants got substantial bequests and the Tucker family inherited the rest of Arthur Glanville's estate," Charlie replied. "However, it was only a fraction of the fortune they expected. It seems the supposedly wealthy grandfather had sold off his assets prior to his death, and the proceeds appear to have vanished. There is something extremely odd going on with both Horatio and Arthur's financial affairs, but the solicitor, Mr Fairchild, was reluctant to share details. He is hiding something, but he has an alibi for the cook's murder, as he wasn't there when she made her accusation of poisoning."

"The bad news is that it is unlikely we will be able to identify Glanville's killer," Grace said, "as each of the suspects had the opportunity to put arsenic in Mr Glanville food or drink during the dinner party." She paused for dramatic effect. "In contrast, none of them could have killed Mrs Seaton."

That got the family's attention. Six heads leaned in to hear Grace's explanation.

"Mrs Seaton was stabbed by a long, thin weapon in a locked room. Our witnesses say Mrs Seaton herself locked the door. Yet Fred Coster heard what he thought was a man's voice in her room, shortly before the fire started. The window was two storeys up, with no available ladder or other means of ingress. The killing was in response to Mrs Seaton's unexpected accusation shortly before, so the killer cannot have planned the attack in advance."

Alistair's eyes were alight. "A locked room mystery! Nobody could have got in or out, yet we have a murder. No wonder Charlie couldn't turn the case down."

Mrs Penrose, ever practical, offered a solution. "Could the killer have used a spare key?"

Grace shook her head. "All the keys were accounted for. Besides, the outer door to Lavender House was locked. However the killer got in, he or she risked a high chance of being seen."

"What about the woman who took the cook to Lavender House?" Lily asked.

Again, Grace shook her head. "Henrietta Tucker had already left Lavender House when Mrs Seaton locked her bedroom door. If she did get back in, Mrs Seaton might have opened the door to her, but Henrietta couldn't have left the bedroom door locked from the inside. The only thing in favour of Henrietta is that only women are allowed inside the refuge."

"Does Henrietta strike you as a potential killer?" Jasmine Pyke asked. "I've heard it said that poison is a woman's weapon."

Charlie had heard that saying too, but he knew it was only true up to a point. Women were less able to use brute strength to kill a man, which meant poison was a better option for a woman. However, it was not unknown for men to resort to poisoning as well, while women might wield a frying pan or other weapon with devastating effect.

"Anyone can be a killer in the right circumstances," Charlie said, "but I would be surprised if Henrietta did it. She was devoted to her uncle and was the only one of the family who truly grieved his death. I simply cannot see her poisoning Arthur Glanville. I would be shocked if Henrietta killed Mrs Seaton, but she had the medical knowledge to inflict the precise stab through the heart. The only way I can imagine her taking a life is to protect another person. We ought not to forget that Henrietta's admirer, Doctor Clifford Johnstone, is also a suspect. He had the medical skills, and a connection to the Glanville family through his own family in India."

"If a woman did it, Mrs Tucker would be my first pick." Grace's lip curled with distaste. "Mrs Tucker beat her servants with a cane as a child. I have no trouble imagining her using arsenic to hasten her inheritance or protect her family. Did she have an alibi, Charlie?"

"Mrs Tucker says she was with a friend. Jack, Bert and Sid Tucker each went into town around the time of Mrs Seaton's death. The quickest route is through the town belt, passing close to Lavender House. Sid's assistant gave him an alibi, but the other Tuckers' movements are yet to be verified. Alistair, you've spent the day searching the police records. Did you uncover anything useful about our suspects?"

Alistair Stewart's fingers absent-mindedly curled the ends of his handlebar moustache, which he often did when contemplating evidence. "Bert Tucker is the only one with a criminal record. He has received a couple of warnings and a fine for drunk and disorderly behaviour. He was also charged with being part of an illegal gambling ring. He got off due to lack of evidence, but the officer who investigated added a note to the file suggesting Bert might have been the ringleader. The officer suspected Bert of pulling the strings from a distance, but carefully arranging the scheme to make it look as if he was a minor player."

Short-tempered, brawn-before-brain Bert Tucker – the organiser of an illegal gambling ring? Charlie had pegged him as a bash-with-a-brick type of man. "I thought Bert seemed too dim-witted for an audacious poisoning and a cleverly covered-up stabbing. Perhaps I was wrong."

Grace's soft hand touched the nape of his neck. "Never underestimate the intellect of a man just because he is well endowed with muscles."

"I hope you are not comparing me with Bert Tucker?" Charlie said. "Stab me through the heart right now if you think I am foul-tempered and greedy. But I have to agree with you, Grace. If Bert Tucker organised a gambling ring, he had us all fooled. He certainly has a powerful motive, in that he felt he deserved to inherit the family fortune, being the oldest son."

"The ringleader comment was only one officer's impression," Alistair said. "But it seems clear that Bert Tucker is a man who puts money before morals. Apart from Bert, the rest have no police record, which might mean only that they are clever at hiding their crimes."

Charlie inhaled the delicious aroma wafting from the kitchen, detecting the scent of one of Lily's mouth-watering Chinese specialty dishes. His stomach gurgled loudly, to everyone's amusement.

"Dinner will be served soon, Charlie," Lily said. "We're waiting for another guest. Don't ask. It's a surprise." Lily attempted to distract her hungry nephew with more news. "Your father went through all the information held by the police on Horatio Glanville and his business. Did you find anything, Thomas?"

Sergeant Thomas Pyke shifted to his voice of authority out of habit. "The Dunedin police have spent many hours investigating Horatio Glanville over the years, but never found evidence sufficient for a criminal charge. Horatio was scrupulous at paying taxes and import levies, and was a registered importer of opium, as required by the law. Despite the substantial profits to be made from the opium trade and from importing other Oriental and Indian goods, he achieved a virtual monopoly."

"One wonders how he kept competitors at bay," Alistair said.

"Precisely my thought, Alistair." Thomas Pyke flicked through his notes. "The police records contained no convictions for violence or intimidation against anyone associated with Horatio's business, although the police had their suspicions. Horatio was either an exceptionally astute businessman or ruthless, or both. He timed his arrival in Dunedin perfectly, just as the gold rush was creating a boom for importers and a market for opium. Horatio was perfectly placed to profit, having experience of the trade, contacts in India, and plenty of money to fund the business. He was never involved in operating opium dens, which are the more dangerous end of the trade."

"The disappearance of Horatio Glanville's fortune sounds as dubious as a magician's trick, if you ask me," Alistair said. "I would need to look at his accounts to get to the bottom of that. The police files showed nothing untoward, such as failed investments or debts. The trouble is, the Dunedin police would not necessarily have a record of such problems, especially if the trouble stemmed from overseas business dealings."

"Horatio's accounts couldn't be found after he died," Charlie said. "Did you get anywhere with the man who bought the business from Horatio Glanville before he died? Clive Jardine."

"A resounding blank space on that name," Alistair replied. "Mr Peters called in his network of records clerks, but didn't manage to come up with so much as a birth or marriage record. The only appearance of the name is as the new owner of the business sold by Horatio Glanville. He either operates the business from overseas through a manager, or Clive Jardine is a fake identity."

"I read once that people who go by a false name often choose one with the same initials," Doctor Penrose said. "Could the doctor, Clifford Johnstone, be this mysterious Clive Jardine, who took over the Glanville business from Horatio?"

"An excellent suggestion, Doctor Penrose." Charlie ticked off the points on his fingers. "Clifford Johnstone had connections to the Glanville family in India. He arrived less than a year before Horatio's business was sold. His explanation for why a well-qualified young doctor came to Dunedin rang a little hollow. And now, here he is, two years later, a man of means with his feet under the Glanville table, and Glanville's niece all but hooked."

"I had thought the doctor an unlikely suspect," Grace said, "as Arthur Glanville was worth more to him alive – at least until he secures Henrietta's hand in marriage. But, if the doctor is Clive Jardine, Arthur Glanville would have been horrified when he discovered the truth, meaning Johnstone had a powerful motive to silence him."

Alistair tweaked his moustache into an extravagant curl. "Especially if Johnstone used dubious means, such as blackmail or calling in a debt unexpectedly, to get Horatio to hand over the

Glanville business. A business that is still importing opium legally in large quantities and presumably making substantial profits."

"Opium abuse is becoming an epidemic," Grace said, being careful to avoid eye contact with her husband. "Everything from laudanum to children's cough syrup contains opium these days. However, we'd be lost without it for pain relief. Naturally, men like Horatio Glanville claim they are providing a necessary service."

"A dubious claim, at best," Doctor Penrose said, "Frankly, I'd be happier if the government regulated all imports, allowing only enough opium into the country for use in reputable medicines. The medical community has been lobbying government for years for better regulation, and Lily tells me the Chinese community is doing the same in relation to opium smoking."

"Tonight's guest is the expert on such matters. I visited him today to ask for his help." Lily jumped up at the sound of the bell at the front door. "Perfect timing. It seems our guest has arrived."

Whomever Charlie was expecting, it was not the man who entered the room with Lily. The man was of a similar age to Lily and not much taller, with the same slim features, almond eyes, and jet-black hair. He was neatly attired in an English-style suit, with a starched collar stiffer and higher than the current fashion. But these unusual features faded into the background when he turned his head to greet them. A ghastly scar slashed across one side of his face, from his eye to the corner of his mouth. The wound had not been properly stitched, leaving a raised welt, which pulled one side of his lips up into a permanent grimace.

Ghost Man

Grace, being nearest to the new arrival, rose and extended her hand. Close up, the visitor smelled of strong tobacco rather than opium. "Have I the honour of addressing Yee Chong?"

Lily was startled at Grace's use of the stranger's name, but the visitor turned bright inquiring eyes on Grace, before bowing. "Most people call me Sammy."

"Most people call me Mrs Pyke," Grace replied, "although my correct name is Mrs Penrose Pyke. But I prefer to be called Grace. What is your preference, sir?"

Sammy Yee Chong smiled, narrowing his eyes still further. "Sammy is fine by me, especially in the company of friends, but I thank you for your consideration. As long as you don't call me 'Johnnie' or 'Ching-Chong', I am content."

Lily recovered her poise. "Sammy, may I introduce the rest of my family? My sister, Jasmine, and her son, Charlie Pyke."

Sammy bowed to the tiny figure of Jasmine Pyke, who was wearing a flowing dress of bright Oriental silk, which accentuated her Chinese features. His eyes widened as Charlie stepped forward to shake his hand.

"Charlie takes after his father, Sergeant Thomas Pyke," Lily said, "apart from his green eyes."

Sammy looked up at the tall, broad Englishman, who was now standing on Jasmine's other side, and nodded.

"Everyone is in Dunedin for Charlie and Grace's wedding," Lily explained. "Grace's parents, Doctor George Penrose and Mrs Louisa Penrose, are here from Wellington. And last, but not least, my husband, Alistair Stewart."

"A pleasure to meet the family of one of our tireless supporters," Sammy said. "I'm not sure if Lily told you that the group I work for is trying to put an end to the horrors my people suffer through addiction to opium."

"Come through to the dining room," Lily said. "We will talk over our meal."

Sammy bowed to his hostess. "I apologise for being late. I had to attend a meeting to discuss how much I was at liberty to say."

Grace looped her arm through Sammy's, taking him to the dining room. "May I ask who the meeting was with and what the outcome was?" She settled their guest into a seat near the middle of the table, with herself beside him and Charlie opposite. Grace didn't want either of them to miss a word or expression from the unexpected guest.

"The meeting was convened by Mr Percy Fairchild, with Mr Rajiv Lohar, Doctor Clifford Johnstone, and myself in attendance." Sammy smiled at the surprised faces around him. "We are the trustees of a charitable foundation established by Mr Arthur Glanville not long before his tragic death. Mr Fairchild asked me to pass on his apologies for not telling you earlier today, but he felt he should consult with us first, given the circumstances."

Charlie recovered from the surprise revelation first. "Are you aware Mr Glanville was murdered, Sammy?"

"I am. The other trustees and I will do all we can to assist your inquiry. Arthur Glanville was a great man. He abhorred his father's trade in opium and decided to employ his own fortune to right the wrong. The house and money he transferred into the charitable trust will be used to establish a medical clinic to help people addicted to opium and other drugs. Doctor Johnstone has agreed to be the medical superintendent, Mr Fairchild is the executive director, and Mr Lohar will manage the clinic. I will be responsible for supplying the patients."

The stunned silence around the table was not broken until bowls of steaming food arrived from the kitchen.

186

The news that Arthur Glanville had spent his fortune on a medical clinic to help addicts left Grace feeling both overwhelmed and jubilant. His father, Horatio, would be exploding from his grave at the insult to his legacy, if such things were possible. Grace's delight only lasted long enough to realise that Arthur's charity would give the Tuckers an even stronger motive to remove him before the paperwork was signed. Had one of them found out what Arthur intended to do with his fortune and acted, not knowing the trust had already been established? It would explain why Arthur had been worried on his final day. Or perhaps Arthur had found out the doctor he had trusted to run the clinic and marry his niece was not the man he seemed.

Grace turned to Sammy to acknowledge her support for the foundation. "I'm so relieved. Not only to understand the mystery of Arthur Glanville's diminished estate, but because the medical clinic will be very much welcome." She hesitated to ask her next question, but there was still a killer to find. "We know you visited Arthur Glanville the day he died, Sammy. Can you tell us why? It might help us to identify his murderer."

Lily served the noodle soup as Grace spoke, showing her respect for their guest by personally serving him first. Sammy nodded his gratitude and complemented the feast before replying.

"An outstanding matter of trivial paperwork. I did not stay with Arthur long. However, I gained the impression he was distracted. When I asked him why, Arthur said he had recently discovered information about his father's business that disturbed him. How much do you know of Horatio Glanville's business dealings?"

"We know of his East India Company connections and trade in opium," Charlie said. "Also, that Horatio sold the business to a mystery man called Clive Jardine before his death. Horatio was reputed to have a fortune, but it could not be found after his death last year."

"Ah, yes, the mysterious Clive Jardine. The *Guilao*."

Jasmine and Lily smiled, leaving Charlie to explain. "*Guilao* means Ghost Man. It is used as a pejorative term for foreigner in Cantonese."

Sammy nodded. "In the case of Clive Jardine, the word is also literal. He is a ghost. He does not exist, except on paper."

Despite her hunger, Grace's spoon hovered over her plate, untouched. "You think Clive Jardine is a false name, to hide the real person behind the opium business?"

"I am sure of it, Grace. Anyone versed in the history of India and China would be suspicious of such a name. Robert Clive, also known as 'Clive of India', is a famous figure in the East India Company. Famous to those of like mind, I mean. Infamous to the millions of Indian people he subjugated and plundered. His military campaigns made him a fortune and gained him control over Bengal."

Grace recalled the stifling sitting room and their client's soft voice. "Rajiv Lohar told me that even lowly clerks in the East India Company sent diamonds home to their families, while the principals of the company amassed vast fortunes. He said the company accounted for half the world's trade, with an army twice the size of the entire British Army. Opium from India was one of the commodities traded."

"Quite so," Sammy said. "Not so much a business as an empire. And that's where William Jardine enters the story. He started his career as a doctor, but became the leading exporter of opium from India to China, against the express wishes and laws set down by the Chinese. Opium smoking spread like an epidemic in China thanks to men like Jardine, robbing ordinary workers of their lives and stripping China of its wealth. Jardine wouldn't let anything stop him. He lobbied the English government to go to war to protect the trade. William Jardine became one of the richest and most powerful men in Britain. He was even elected as a Member of Parliament."

"The Glanville family has a tradition of naming sons after English heroes," Charlie said. "Horatio Nelson and Arthur

Wellesley, the Duke of Wellington. If a Glanville chose a pseudonym to go by, he could hardly have done better than Clive Jardine."

A doctor with family connections to the East India Company might well have made the same choice, Grace thought.

"Arthur Glanville was certainly suspicious when he discovered his father had sold the company to a man called Clive Jardine," Sammy said. "I have a feeling Arthur found out the man's true identity, but he died before he could pass his suspicions on. Jardine may masquerade under a false name and conduct a legitimate business, but make no mistake – when profits are at risk, such men become dangerous. You must undertake your investigation with extreme caution and a keen awareness of those who walk behind you."

Sammy Yee Chong's hand went unconsciously to the scar on his face, fingering the raised rim where it slashed across the outer portion of his lip. When he realised Grace was watching him, his hand dropped to his spoon. With a twisted smile, he dipped the spoon into his soup. "Enough talk of Jardine. Come, let us enjoy this fine meal before it gets cold."

When the soup was drained to the last slurp, Grace's mother asked the question that had kept her frowning since the start of the meal. "Why did these men continue to ship opium to China when the Chinese had banned it?"

"The answer lies in tea, Mrs Penrose."

"Tea? The beverage?"

Sammy inhaled the aroma of sizzling dumplings, which Lily was spooning onto his plate. "The English love their tea. China had tea to sell, but the English had nothing the Chinese wanted in exchange. Opium was the solution to their problem. The Chinese people could not get enough opium to help them endure long days in the fields and long nights without enough to eat. Thousands of tons of tea, silk and other valuable products were shipped from the harbour of Canton to Britain, in exchange for opium addiction. A poor bargain, I'm sure you'll agree. China was incensed by this disregard for their laws, hence the series of battles known as the Opium Wars."

Mrs Penrose set her fork down, her meal untouched. "I will never look at a simple cup of tea in the same way again. I don't know what to say, except I am sorry for the greed that has ruined the lives of so many Chinese people."

"Arthur Glanville felt the same, Mrs Penrose. His feeling of guilt was very personal, given his family involvement in the opium trade. The irony is that the New Zealand government is starting to share our concerns about the effects of opium abuse. Not because of what the Chinese community is saying, but because the use of opium has started to spread into the wider population."

"I've heard whispers of it," Lily said. "Sad to say, I've heard opium smoking has become the latest amusement for young people with too much time on their hands. Daring young ladies, even, bored with the doom and gloom of the economic depression and eager for women to have the same rights as men."

Grace dropped her fork with a clatter. "How ironic if women were to get the vote this year, only to squander their success by wasting away their lives in opium dens."

"It's only a rumour, Grace," Lily said. "They wouldn't be smoking in opium dens, but in their own salons and drawing rooms, where they are safe from prying eyes and disgrace. It is hardly unprecedented. After all, most of the romantic poets found inspiration from opium. Coleridge, Byron, Keats, Shelley. Foolish romantics see drugs as inspiring, before their lives turn into a downward spiral of addiction."

"Good heavens. Clearly, I have been spending far too much time studying medical texts and not enough time in the real world."

Lily chuckled as she handed Grace a clean fork. "Too much time staring into the eyes of my nephew, I'll be bound, and chasing after murderers."

Grace speared a dumpling. "I can assure you, Lily, I have spent far too little time with my husband. I concede the other point.

Definitely too many murders. We are grateful for the help of everyone here. The sooner this murderer is behind bars, the better."

"Hear, hear," Charlie said. "Now, let us eat this delicious dinner, so I can take my wife home before she falls asleep on her plate. Did Grace tell you she spent last night assisting at Molly Ravenwood's birth?"

Having successfully distracted the family onto the joys of new babies, Grace and Charlie concentrated on restoring their reserves of energy with fragrant dumplings, followed by Lily's specialty dish, beef and black beans.

An hour later, the newlyweds made good on their promise of an early escape from the dinner party. They saw Sammy Yee Chong to the door.

"Thank you for coming to dine with us tonight, Sammy," Grace said. "We may not have put a name to the ghost man's face, but we are much better informed now about his motives and the danger he poses."

"I hope you will take heed of my warning about the ruthlessness of such men, Grace." Sammy took Grace's hand, to her surprise, and raised it to his scarred lips. "I am sorry for what happened to Lavender House. You should be proud of what has been achieved there. If we can emulate even a fraction of that success with Arthur Glanville's legacy, we will be satisfied."

"I'm sure you will," Grace said. "It takes great courage to stand up to the harm caused by men like Clive Jardine. Such courage inspires real change."

Sammy bowed and disappeared into the night.

Roses And Rogues

Grace's legs wobbled alarmingly on the short walk home. The support of Charlie's arm around her waist kept her exhausted body upright, but her mind still reeled with unanswered questions.

Her medical work at Lavender House took her past a Chinese boarding house on Walker Street regularly. It operated as an opium den, but Grace had never been inside. In truth, until now she had viewed opium mainly as an invaluable drug for relieving pain. She knew the toll it took on addicts, but she considered opium a lesser evil than alcohol, which was the drug of choice of the British immigrants. Drunken violence spread visible havoc on innocent victims like a stampede of bulls through a field of flowers. The havoc caused by opium addiction was a quieter, less obvious problem, which the authorities largely ignored, as it mainly affected Chinese immigrants.

"Penny for your thoughts?" Charlie said.

Grace realised she had come to a halt in the middle of the path while Charlie held the gate open. "Have you ever been in an opium den, Charlie?"

"Can't this wait until tomorrow, Grace? It's been a long day." Charlie examined her face in the moonlight. "Shall we sit in the garden for a moment?"

Grace sank onto the bench seat amongst the flowers. In the velvety darkness of a still night, the overwhelming sensations were the scent of roses in full bloom and the touch of the man beside her.

Charlie put an arm around her shoulders and drew her close. "If you wish to know what an opium den is like, I will tell you. But it is not for the faint of heart."

"I want to know, Charlie."

"Close your eyes, Grace. Now, imagine this heady aroma of roses is a choking blend of opium smoke, tobacco, and sweat, only twenty times more intense, making it near impossible to see and breathe. Now imagine tiny rooms, narrow passages, rotten stairways, grimy walls, blackened ceilings – utterly dark and filled with bodies. The only light comes from an inadequate gas lamp and the flicker of a burner, where the opium is heated. Men lie on bunks, inhaling opium smoke from long pipes, and then lying, unmoving, numbed by the effects of the drug. Men who crave oblivion from back-breaking work and the hardship of being alone, working to support wives and families thousands of miles away in China. Imagine craving the release every day, until it becomes difficult to find the energy to work and whatever money you earn goes to opium instead of food, making their return to their loved ones ever more impossible."

At his soft words, Grace felt herself slipping into the scene he conjured, until her skin crawled with the sensations of grime and hopelessness. She shivered. Suddenly, she craved two things – a long, hot bath and the warmth of her husband's embrace. "Enough, Charlie. Let's go inside and forget about the dark side of the world for a while."

Grace closed her eyes again, expecting Charlie to scoop her into his arms and carry her into the house. Instead, she felt him tense beside her. Her senses jolted awake, but the darkness gave no clues beyond the rustle of a creature in the bushes. Was that what Charlie had heard? He had half-risen from the bench, but now he sat back down, giving a tiny shrug. Heightened awareness of danger went with the job.

Charlie bent to lift her, but he was jerked backwards by a hand in the darkness. Fear clutched Grace's heart as she took in the dark figure behind Charlie and the glint of a knife at his throat.

She tried to escape to summon help, but a rough hand shoved her down. A sharp point pricked against her neck, leaving her with the soft, warm, wet sensation of a drop of blood slithering down her back.

"I'm afraid it is far too late to forget about the world," a man's voice said behind her. His voice was harsh, cold, dry – the very antithesis of the dripping blood – but it dribbled into her ear with the same threat of harm. "The real world, that is. The world in which powerful men make profits in lawful businesses, selling to willing customers. Your nauseating concern for the plight of opium addicts tells me you dwell in a world of sentimental make-believe."

"Kindly remove your knife from the lady's neck," Charlie said, in the tone of voice one might use for requesting a clean napkin from a footman. "Let her go and we can talk, man to man."

"I see no lady, Mr Pyke. Only an interfering troublemaker who is foolish enough to believe she can be a man's equal. Although, I must concede your wife has made a rare effort this evening to present herself as a proper woman ought to, in silk and precious jewels."

The knife slashed forwards and downwards, slitting the bodice of Grace's favourite evening gown. A fine line bubbled with red on her skin, where the very tip of the knife had nicked her flesh. Then the knife jerked up, severing her precious sapphire and diamond necklace. The man's other hand slid around her clavicle, neatly catching the necklace as it fell into his black glove.

A caustic mix of anger and terror boiled over inside Grace, but she swallowed it down when she saw the fury pouring silently out of every pore on her husband's body. She knew his muscles were tensing, waiting for the right moment to attack. If Grace showed any sign of panic, Charlie would be the one with yet another scar, if he didn't end up six feet under a marble slab carved with his name. Her hand went automatically to her lips, and then to her heart, a long-used signal to Charlie that all was well, even if circumstances indicated otherwise.

Their attacker was unperturbed. "In the real world, Mr Pyke, the winner takes what he wants, and the loser is fortunate to escape with his or her life and an ugly scar across the face. Is that what you want, Mr Pyke? A wife with a scarred face as hideous as Celestial Sammy?"

Again Grace fought primal instinct for control of her brain. She smoothed her gown, tucking in the severed fabric with careful deliberation as she struggled to remain calm. "I believe you have made your point, sir. Perhaps you would care to tell me whom I have the honour of addressing, and what you want?"

The man behind her chuckled. The knife withdrew from her cheek. "You do not need to know my name, Mrs Pyke. All you need to know is that my employer wishes you and your husband to enjoy your honeymoon and stop interfering with the lawful operation of his business."

"I was under the impression that murder, aggravated assault, and theft are against the law, rather than acceptable business practices in the real world." Since the knife was now at a safe distance, Grace rose from the bench seat and held her hand out to Charlie. "Come, my dear, I think it is time to retire from this investigation and begin our honeymoon, as the gentleman suggests."

The man holding the knife to Charlie's throat looked to his leader for orders at this unexpected development. Both men wore black hoods over their faces, with holes cut for eyes. Grace could make out none of their features, except that both rivalled Charlie for height and breadth.

"Not so fast, Mrs Pyke. We need to ensure your husband has got the message."

Grace replied quickly, before Charlie could share his thoughts. "Gentlemen, you have threatened us with knives to our throats in our own garden. I think it is fair to say we have both received your message loud and clear. What's more, you have ruined my favourite gown, causing me great distress." She fluttered the flap of midnight blue silk, revealing far more of her undergarments and upthrust bosom than good manners dictated.

When both pairs of eyes swivelled to her exposed cleavage, Charlie exploded into action, twisting and punching in one smooth movement. The man behind him crashed backwards into the rose bushes. Anne would be distraught to see her beloved blooms squashed by such a vile lump of humanity, but needs must when the devil drives.

Grace ducked away from her attacker and ran for the house, yelling for help as she went. Charlie lunged for her attacker, but the man jumped backwards out of his reach and dashed around the end of the bench, heading for Grace at a faster pace than she could match in her long gown. She crouched, ready to block his charge with a low, painful blow, but slipped on the grass and went down on her knees. Insanely, her first thought was that the grass stains would be murder to get out of her gown. Her second thought was to huddle in a ball, so the inevitable blow would not slam into her unprotected head.

Charlie reacted in an instant, grabbing the bench and heaving it into the hooded attacker. The man flew backwards into another rose bush with an anguished howl. Charlie stamped on his arm, releasing the precious necklace and another howl.

A lamp appeared behind the hedge separating their house from the Stewarts' house. "Charlie? Grace? What's happening?"

"Two assailants with knives, Alistair," Charlie called. "Take care of Grace for me."

The momentary distraction was enough for the two attackers. They scrambled to their feet and ran, while Alistair Stewart and Thomas Pyke were still clambering over the hedge.

Charlie threw himself at the closest hooded figure, but his feet slipped on the leaf litter and his fingers failed to hold the coat of the fleeing man. By the time Charlie was back on his feet, the man was already halfway over the fence by the street. Seconds later came the sound of two horses being thrashed into a gallop. Charlie disappeared into the darkness, with Thomas close behind him, as a clatter of horseshoes pounded away.

Grace awaited her husband's return, knowing there was no hope of catching the men. Her terror died away in the solid presence of Alistair, with his warm coat over her shaking shoulders. "Jardine's men," she said. "Come to warn us away from his business."

Alistair peered through the gloom. "Which confirms that Jardine has something to hide. Are you hurt, Grace?"

"Only a scratch." Grace tried to match Alistair's composure, but her shrillness betrayed her. "They were responsible for Sammy's scar. We were fortunate to escape so lightly."

Alistair's fingers went to his moustache, twisting the ends while he considered the options. "I don't like bullies," he said at last.

"Nor do I, Alistair." Charlie emerged from the darkness on soft feet. "Those thugs probably followed Sammy to your house. I hope he got home safely."

"We'll see to Sammy, Charlie. Why don't you take Grace inside? Your father and I will keep watch tonight. We'll simply have to be more cautious in future. None of us will be safe until the killer is caught."

Charlie nodded his thanks to his business partner. He scooped his wife into his arms and carried her into the house, sliding the deadbolt behind them. They stood in the hall, glued together, alert for sounds of intruders. Utter silence, apart from the soft whoosh of their breathing close to each other's ears.

"Grace, you were magnificent. How badly are you hurt?"

Grace kept her voice low and light. "Only a small nick. You?"

"Bruised knuckles. That thug had a chin of granite. I'll check the house. I suggest you lock yourself in the bathroom while I do so."

Grace did as Charlie asked. She ran a hot bath, silently thanking Anne Macmillan's late husband, who had been a fanatic in the matter of personal hygiene after the discovery of the role of germs in disease. They not only had a large bath in the house, but a complicated arrangement of pipes to carry hot water to it directly from the stove.

The bath was full by the time Charlie returned. He must have latched every door and window and searched every nook and cranny for unwanted visitors. Grace had never been more grateful for his thoroughness and competence.

Grace met him in the hallway. She knew that look in his eye. If she didn't reassure her husband she was perfectly fine, he would spend the night patrolling the house, when every fibre of her being craved nothing more than to be close to him. "Charlie, it's over. We're safe in here. Safe, and alone at long last."

He examined her, trying to assess her state of mind. Grace could see his determination to stand guard wavering. She wrenched her gaze from the fine line running across his throat where the blade had pressed into his precious flesh. Instead, she focussed on his eyes, while her fingers travelled slowly down his cheek. "Do you know what I feel like?" she whispered.

"I hope I do." Charlie unclipped her hair, allowing her long locks to flow through his fingers and down her back. "Please don't tell me you want to visit an opium den or register a formal complaint with Mr Clive Jardine."

She loosened his tie and collar. "I hadn't thought of that. I was going to say I feel like a long, hot bath after a long, challenging day, but an opium den would certainly be a novel experience."

A slow smile stole across Charlie's face. "*Mrs Beeton's Book of Household Management* recommends cold or tepid baths in the morning, my dear wife. Do you not think a hot bath in the late evening might be viewed as an unnecessary decadence leading to moral decay?"

"I'm not opposed to a smidgeon of decadence and dash of moral decay in the right circumstances." Grace tossed his waistcoat over her shoulder. "Does Mrs Beeton have anything useful to say on the censuring of impertinent husbands?"

"Only that it ought never to be attempted, as the housewife's greatest joy in life should be to ensure the complete happiness of her husband." Charlie eased the remains of her gown off her shoulder, letting out a long sigh as the silky fabric slid to the floor.

"I cannot claim to have read Mrs Beeton's entire book," Grace said, "but I know the first paragraph declares the housewife ought to be the commander of her household, just as a general leads his army. And I command a hot bath, followed by many hours in a comfortable bed with my bodyguard close at hand."

Charlie caressed the soft skin above the ties of her undergarments. "In that case, perhaps you need a devoted servant to wash you?"

"Dearest husband, you read my mind." Grace ran her hands up his torso and pulled his shirt over his head.

And that was the last either of them said on the subject of the management of a traditional household, knife-wielding assailants, or any other topic.

Team Spirit

Charlie woke up the next morning tangled in sheets with the bedcover on the floor, having finally made it to their marital bed by an unexpectedly circuitous and entirely satisfactory route. The experience had left him wondering why married folk ever left the confines of their homes.

Grace came into the bedroom wearing only her new silk dressing gown, loosely tied at the waist, and carrying a tray loaded with breakfast.

Charlie couldn't decide which he wanted first. "Good morning, wife."

Grace racked her gaze over his exposed torso. "A *very* good morning, husband. I hope our activities last night did not aggravate your burn?"

"It was worth it."

"I made coffee. I had the feeling we'd need something stronger than tea today." Grace put the tray down and came over to sit on the edge of the bed. "Did you know that the gold flecks in your eyes sparkle when you are full of the joys of life?"

He ran his fingers through her thoroughly dishevelled hair. "Did you know you still have a blob of soap in your hair?" Charlie reached for the ties of her robe. "I've dreamed of this moment."

Grace brushed his fingers away. "Breakfast, you mean? Or finding a blob of soap?"

"Breakfast, of course. What else could I possibly have been referring to?"

"I'm too hungry to speculate." Grace placed the tray in front of him and slid in beside him. "I cannot believe I have found something you put before food, Charlie Pyke. Not that I'm complaining."

200

After devouring every scrap on his plate, Charlie removed the tray and returned to bed. He leaned back with a contented sigh. If Grace was determined to ignore last night's attack in favour of domestic bliss, he was more than happy to do the same.

Grace nestled into the curve of his body. "Fate has been kind to us, hasn't it, my love?"

"It has. Far more so than I ever dreamed was possible." Charlie kissed the top of her head where it rested on his shoulder. "I really ought to get up. Declan needs to know what Sammy Yee Chong told us." He chose not to mention the other events of the previous evening, but the police would have to know about that too.

"Another few minutes won't hurt. Assuming we believe Sammy, his evidence means Mr Lohar, the solicitor, and Doctor Johnstone are not likely suspects. The charitable foundation was already established before Arthur Glanville's death, and each of them had accepted a role to improve the lives of addicts. They had no motive to kill either victim. Unless Arthur Glanville found out something against one of them."

"I've come to admire Arthur," Charlie said. "I'm sure he wanted his niece, Henrietta Tucker, to be part of the foundation too. He'd already promised her a substantial dowry. I suspect he intended Henrietta and the doctor to marry and live in the house, as medical superintendent and nurse. Rather a neat way of ensuring his niece had a home and vocation, without bequeathing her the property, which the rest of her family would surely have wrested from her control. I only hope my instinct is correct, that Doctor Johnstone is as innocent as he appears."

"Arthur Glanville was a fine man," Grace agreed. "There would have been hell to pay if any of the Tucker family found out their precious family fortune was about to be wasted on Chinese opium addicts."

"Greed combined with righteous anger and thwarted hopes," Charlie said. "Motives for murder don't come much stronger than that, especially if the killer thought he had to act fast to prevent the transfer of assets."

"Not fast enough, as it turned out, since the charitable trust had been signed off just days before."

Charlie breathed in the scent of rosewater, a smell he associated so strongly with Grace that it had the power to revive him no matter the crisis. "Does this feel wrong to you, Grace? Talking about murder when we are meant to be on our honeymoon."

"Logically, it should be unsettling, I suppose. However, I have always enjoyed curling up on your shoulder and talking about our latest investigation." Grace ran her fingers down his body with the attention to detail she brought to all her endeavours. "I am learning that doing so in bed adds entirely new dimensions to the pleasure. In fact, I have to admit that detective work can be most ... stimulating."

Charlie was in no position to deny it. The investigation would have to wait.

The sun had climbed well above the horizon when they finally caught up with Detective Sergeant Declan Kelly by the simple expedient of walking next door to see what their families were planning for the day.

Charlie felt curiously reluctant to let go of his wife, despite ten hours at the closest of close quarters. He hoped his newfound euphoria didn't show on his face, as he released Grace to greet her nearest and dearest. The entire Southern Investigations Agency team was there – the team having expanded from Alistair and Lily to include both sets of parents, as well as Anne Macmillan and her beau, Kenneth Drummond.

Anne kissed his cheek. "You two look as if you had a good sleep, at last."

Anne's eyes twinkled, but Charlie chose not to notice. "Nice to see you, Mrs Macmillan. I take it the temporary Lavender House is ship-shape."

"George and Louisa Penrose have worked miracles alongside my team. Miss Newland and Doctor Ravenwood are in charge today."

Lily moved aside to give Charlie room to sit on the sofa between herself and Charlie's mother, Jasmine. "Detective Sergeant Kelly came by earlier this morning to find you. He said the investigation was under control."

"We did not wish to disturb you." Jasmine Pyke gave her son a meaningful glance and waved towards the group standing behind them. "DS Kelly came back to find you a few minutes ago."

Charlie spotted Declan talking with Alistair Stewart and Thomas Pyke. Declan was downing tea and Mrs Brown's famous ginger cake as he talked. Charlie understood the need to grab the opportunity to eat whenever possible during a busy investigation. He leaned back on the comfortable sofa, his usual urge to join the group of policemen being curiously absent this morning.

Lily nudged him in the side. "You look far too content for a detective in the middle of a double murder investigation."

Declan spotted him and came over. "Good morning, Mr Penrose Pyke." Declan pulled his pocket watch out of his waistcoat with a flourish. "Goodness, is that the time? DI Wallace would have me whipped if I was this late to work."

For once, Charlie didn't give a fig about being late. "Fortunately for me, I don't answer to Wallace. It may have escaped your notice, Detective Sergeant Kelly, but I am on my honeymoon."

"And here's me thinking you were busy with a client to attend to and thugs to beat off." The grin dropped from Declan's cake-crumbed face. "There's been a development. A man came in to the central police station this morning to report seeing an Indian man at Lavender House on Saturday morning. He said he's only now

203

reporting it, because he thought nothing of it until he read about the fatal fire in the newspaper."

Charlie sprang to attention, all remaining thoughts of indolence vanishing. "Did the witness provide a description?"

"An Indian man with greying hair in a white cotton tunic with a round collar. I've walked the streets of Dunedin since I was tall enough to reach the door latch, and I've rarely seen a man matching that description. I searched the Glanville house, Charlie. Mr Lohar had three white cotton tunics and no other clothes aside from an old set of tweeds and Sunday best. It must be him."

Charlie steepled his hands in front of his face. This new evidence did not fit with the client they had come to know – the devoted servant willing to spend his own money to apprehend the man who killed his employer.

"That's not all, Charlie," Declan said. "The witness was coming through the town belt, so he was at the back of the house, unlike all the other witnesses we have talked to. Rajiv Lohar was seen exiting the back door to Lavender House. The witness was in a hurry to get into town, but he recalls thinking it odd to see a man was coming out of a women-only refuge. He also recalls the sound of a fire alarm behind him as he walked away, so the timing fits with the start of the fire."

It seemed a little too convenient that the witness had come forward now, but Charlie conceded his doubts might stem from reluctance to accept evidence against his client. However, everything down to the marrow in his bones told him Rajiv Lohar was not the killer. Logic told him the witness was lying.

"An Indian man in a white tunic is hardly likely to go unnoticed by the residents of Lavender House, Declan. Not exactly the costume one would choose to kill a woman and light a fire. Quite apart from that objection, there is the fact that most people would use the public path to pass through the town belt. The rear of Lavender House is not visible from the public path. One would have to scramble through the trees and undergrowth to see the rear door properly, or take the private path beside Lavender House around to the rear."

"I know, Charlie," Declan said. "But my hands are tied. The witness has signed a sworn statement, which I cannot ignore."

Grace was having none of it. "The two maids said Mr Lohar never left the house that morning, Declan. Mr Lohar was so devoted to Mr Glanville, he wanted to stay with his body. We have Henrietta's word that he was there when she came back to attend to the laying out."

Declan turned his palms upward in a what-can-I-do gesture. "I'm sorry, Grace, but the police have to act. If Lohar was seen coming out of Lavender House just before the fire alarm was raised, I will have to bring him in for questioning. I'm sorry, but it's not appropriate for you to be there."

"I'll go," Kenneth Drummond said. "Mr Lohar will need legal representation."

Charlie thought for a moment before rising from the sofa. "Thank you, Mr Drummond. Our client will be grateful to have the best lawyer in Dunedin in his corner. However, I'm not convinced he will need you." He went over to the table and started sketching. Drawing was much easier on a flat surface, and nothing to do with the plate of moist, delectable ginger cake within reaching distance.

Grace poured him a cup of tea and watched the sketch coming to life. "Who is that unfortunate creature, Charlie?"

"Don't you recognise him, Grace? It's Mr Lohar."

Declan came over to join them. "That looks nothing like your client. Rajiv Lohar is slim and fine-featured. This man is thickset and hook-nosed. You've got the round-necked tunic right, though."

"How right you are." Charlie started a sketch that captured Lohar as he really was. When he was finished, he ripped both out of his notebook. "Declan, I assume you have an address for the witness who saw Mr Lohar?"

Declan flipped his notebook to the right page.

Charlie's doubts receded. "Less than a block from the Edinburgh Hotel, which our friend Bert Tucker likes to frequent. I smell a set-up. I suggest you find the witness and present the first picture to him, asking him if this was the Indian man he saw. If my hunch is correct, he has been paid to provide a fake witness statement and thus may never have seen the real Lohar."

Declan picked up the two drawings. "Bert Tucker trying to put as off his scent, you reckon? Worth a try. It leaves me in a bind. I need to get Lohar in for questioning, and arrange a search of all the houses for arsenic and thin stabbing weapons, as well as checking alibis."

Sergeant Thomas Pyke, now officially deputised to the Dunedin police force, took the drawings from Declan. "I'll track down the witness and check Bert Tucker's alibi at the Edinburgh Hotel while I am in the neighbourhood. If the witness has been set up by Bert Tucker, you won't need to bring Rajiv Lohar in."

"And I've got some documents to track down," Alistair said, "thanks to an idea Kenneth had."

"A way of discovering the identity of the mysterious Clive Jardine," Kenneth Drummond added. "The one piece of evidence we have of his existence is his signature on the sale documents for Horatio Glanville's importation business. Once Alistair finds the documents, we'll know who Jardine's solicitor was. There's a fair chance I will know him."

"Good idea," Charlie said. "But won't the attorney simply claim he cannot disclose his client's name?"

"Client-attorney privilege will keep the attorney from speaking to the police," Drummond agreed, "but we legal professionals are a law unto ourselves. A nod and a wink in the right direction is common enough practice if the stakes are high. No man wishes to stand in the way of justice for a double-murder."

"We'll leave straight away," Alistair said.

"If you can wait a moment, I'll copy these sketches of the chief suspects." Charlie always sketched the key players in any investigation in his notebook. His pencil flashed across the paper, capturing the essence of each suspect with the minimum number of strokes. "Show Jardine's solicitor pictures of the Tucker family and see if he recognises one of them as Clive Jardine. I'll give you pictures of Arthur Glanville's solicitor, the doctor, and Mr Lohar too, just in case. Send word as soon as you have a name."

Jasmine Pyke joined them. "With the team scattered around Dunedin, you'll need me to stay here to coordinate any messages. If you tell me where you are going, Charlie, I can forward the messages to you. I want this killer caught quickly, so we have no repeat of last night's barbarity. I've looked forward to having Grace as a daughter-in-law for so long, I couldn't bear any harm to come to her."

Grace pulled her mother-in-law into a tight embrace. "We'll be careful, Mrs Pyke. I have a nice safe plan for my morning, checking Jack Tucker's alibi at the hospital."

"I sent a constable to the hospital yesterday," Declan said. "Jack Tucker went to the front desk and received a pass for the maintenance area. The maintenance staff don't recall seeing him, but they confirmed the gas was working. I've sent the constable to re-interview the witnesses at the fire to see if we can pin down Jack Tucker's arrival time at the fire."

"Did the constable check that there was ever a problem with the gas in the first place?" Grace asked. "I'm wondering if Jack Tucker really went to the hospital for health reasons. A lifetime in the gasworks inhaling coal dust, tar and noxious gases is dreadful for the lungs. I don't like the sound of Mr Tucker's cough, or his pallor."

"By all means, use your contacts to investigate, Grace," Declan said. "I'm grateful for all the help I can get."

"I have been cultivating a clever young woman in the records office at the hospital," Grace said. "It's amazing what a few kind words and the occasional offer to track down a missing medical file will do to ensure the support of under-appreciated clerical staff. I'd also like to track down those society ladies who are reputed to be smoking opium. Any thoughts, Auntie Anne? We're looking for somebody young, wealthy, daring and bored, with a liberal attitude to moral standards."

Anne Macmillan's vast network of contacts across the highest and lowest corners of Dunedin had earned her the role of the investigation agency's "society spy". Anne closed her eyes and thought for a moment. Charlie imagined a miniature records clerk – dressed in black with just a hint of white lace at collar and cuffs – hunting through that sharp old brain searching for the right match within several decades' worth of contacts.

"Miss Felicity Halbrook springs to mind," Anne said. "A blue-stocking, who fancies herself a poetess and an activist for women's rights, but only if she isn't required to exert herself by traipsing the streets collecting signatures for the suffrage petition. I'll call Johnny Todd and his gang in to act as messenger boys. When I track down an address for Miss Halbrook, I'll have one of the lads take it to the hospital."

Grace nodded her thanks. "I know Miss Halbrook by reputation. Enough to secure a visit, I hope."

Charlie handed Drummond the finished sketches. "I'll go with Grace. Pa, we'll leave word at the front desk of the hospital. If you have the witness statement before we leave, we can meet there."

Declan watched on with his hands on his hips and a grin on his chops. "In that case, I'm free to go to the Tucker's house to execute a search warrant. The killer would have to be thicker than a block of Oamaru stone to have kept the weapon and the arsenic, but it's worth a try."

"I'll meet you there if I can, Declan," Charlie said. "We should search Sid's house too. Is there anything else we've missed?"

Mrs Penrose had watched on with her usual placid composure from an armchair. Her hands were clasped lightly in her lap and her smile remained benign, but her eyes were as lively and all-seeing as her daughter's. Charlie had learned not to underestimate his mother-in-law. Now, her head perked to the side. "Detective Sergeant Kelly, may I make a suggestion?"

"Of course, Mrs Penrose. The more the merrier."

"Assuming the murderer did not take an entire packet of white arsenic powder to the dinner, you may be looking for a small container or twist of paper that would fit into a pocket to be easily deployed at a moment's notice. Or a vial, if he took a solution or paste of the poison. There is a chance that a little of the arsenic might have caught in the seams of the pocket it was carried in. You might want to wear gloves when you examine the clothing."

"An excellent thought, Louisa," Lily said. "Might I suggest I accompany you, Declan? If there is a tiny trace of arsenic, I will be able to detect it in my laboratory. Perhaps Louisa would like to join us?"

"I rather think I would, Lily," Grace's mother said. "After all, the more the merrier. Are you coming on our little excursion too, my dear?"

Doctor Penrose shook his head. "I'll leave the arsenic to you, my love. I have an idea I want to discuss with young Fred Coster."

A more improbable team of investigators could hardly be imagined, Charlie thought, with a burst of pride. Or a better family, for that matter.

Opium Ladies

At Dunedin hospital, Grace and Charlie quickly established that the maintenance department had not reported a gas fault at the hospital the previous Saturday. Nor did they recall a visit from a fitter from the gasworks by the name of Jack Tucker.

Their next stop was the records office of the hospital. In her haste, Grace bumped into a junior doctor coming out.

"Don't waste your time in there, Miss Penrose," he muttered as he pushed past her. "The records clerk is about as much help as a leech on gangrene."

Grace went into the office anyway. "Good morning, Miss Smythe. What have you done to get Doctor Carter's stethoscope in a tangle?"

A bright-eyed young lady looked up from behind neat piles of papers. Even the stationery was filed in an orderly manner, with pens, pencils, notepads and other items perfectly aligned in separate compartments of a tray. "Refused to allow him to alter a patient record after the wound he stitched went septic. Honestly, do they really think I am that gullible?"

"Good for you, Miss Smythe. His forthcoming reprimand might remind Carter to wash his hands properly next time."

Miss Smythe gave Charlie a curious once-over. "I read in the Dunedin Ladies' Journal that you are to be married soon, Miss Penrose."

Grace held out her sapphire and diamond ring for inspection. "Our wedding was on Saturday. May I present my husband, Mr Charles Penrose Pyke. We've combined our names to put our union on an equal footing."

"Good for you, Mrs Penrose Pyke. And congratulations to you, Mr Penrose Pyke. I won't ask why you are here so soon after your wedding, because I know you are always busy investigating something or other. What can I help you with today?"

Grace gave silent thanks for the intelligent young women of the world, but wished more of them could be allowed to work in positions that fitted their intellect. Miss Smythe, for instance, ought to be running the hospital, not filing the records. On the other hand, the hospital would stop functioning if they couldn't find the right patient file in a timely fashion.

She didn't insult Miss Smythe by trying to spin an excuse for their inquiry. "We need to check the alibi of a man whose brother-in-law was murdered. I have reason to believe he visited the hospital on Saturday morning around half past ten. Jack Tucker. An appointment at the respiratory clinic would be my guess."

Miss Smythe had Tucker's card in her hand less than a minute later. "Jack Tucker. Appointment for quarter to eleven on Saturday morning for congested lungs. It's down as a fifteen-minute appointment." Her face screwed up into a classic expression of distressed sympathy as she skimmed the notes. "I shouldn't really tell you his prognosis, as you are not the attending doctor."

"No need, Miss Smythe. I am grateful for your efficiency, as ever. I don't suppose you know if the respiratory clinic ran to time on Saturday morning?"

"Does it ever?" Miss Smythe shuffled through timesheets on her desk. "The physician signed off at twelve-fifteen, only a quarter of an hour late."

Grace spent another minute or two exchanging hospital news before departing. She and Charlie walked in silence through a maze of corridors to the front desk. Sergeant Pyke had not yet left a message, but Anne Macmillan had. Miss Halbrook had agreed to meet Grace this afternoon. Grace glanced at the clock behind the front desk. Not yet one o'clock – a little early for a social call. But then, Felicity Halbrook was not a conventional lady from what Grace had heard.

Charlie gestured to a relatively quiet corner of the bustling entry lobby. "What do you make of Jack Tucker's alibi, Grace?"

"If he was seen right on time, at quarter to eleven, and the examination was quicker than usual, Jack Tucker might have left here around eleven o'clock. But it's highly doubtful, if not impossible, that he could get back to Lavender House in time to kill Mrs Seaton and start the fire. The physician was likely running at least a few minutes behind time, if not more. With the state of Jack Tucker's lungs, I can't see him getting to Lavender House in under fifteen to twenty minutes, which takes the time to at least a quarter past eleven. Given the state of the roads, a hansom cab would have been no quicker. At that point, he would still have had to find a way in, gain access to the right room, and stab the cook – all before the alarm was raised around twenty past eleven."

"I agree, it's highly improbable," Charlie said, "but perhaps not impossible if he switched to an earlier appointment or made an excuse to leave early. Would the physician remember?"

"Probably not. The clinics are always a rush to complete in the allotted time."

"If Jack Tucker has a serious lung condition, he must be worried about his ability to continue working and supporting his family. I don't believe Jack wanted to be supported by Glanville money, but he may have had no choice. A large inheritance from his brother-in-law would be exactly what he needs right now. We'll have to wait and see if Declan can narrow down Jack Tucker's arrival time at Lavender House to an earlier time than half-past eleven."

"I wonder if Mrs Tucker knew her husband was seriously ill?"

"I don't know, Grace. Jack Tucker strikes me as a proud man, who would not admit to infirmity if he could avoid it. But his constant coughing must have his wife worried. Despite their difference in upbringing, my impression is that Mr and Mrs Tucker love each other."

Grace rested her fingertips on his hand. "Love is a powerful motivator. There is nothing a wife wouldn't do for a beloved husband."

Charlie's fingers curled around hers. "And nothing a proud working man wouldn't do for a wife who deserved the best. We shouldn't forget Henrietta either. As a nurse, she must realise her father's health is deteriorating."

Grace released his fingers reluctantly. "I'm going to visit Miss Felicity Halbrook. I'll look forward to seeing you later."

"I'll wait here for my father, even though I'd rather be with you, Grace. In fact, it might be better if I came with you. After the attack last night, it's not safe for you to be alone."

The memory of the knife pressing against her throat was fresh in Grace's mind, but admitting she needed protection was a dangerous precedent. "It's not *my* safety we should worry about, Charlie. Taking you with me to face a den of blue-stocking female opium addicts? My dear husband, they'd eat you alive."

Grace pushed away the image of the knife glinting in the moonlight and hurried out of the hospital before she could be tempted to change her mind. The thought that Charlie would be there at the end of the day, every day, kept her going.

Miss Felicity Halbrook lived in an attractive house of modest size in the hills above and to the north of the hospital. Grace had never met her, but she knew enough of the lady to be intrigued. Anne had been right. If any society lady was rebellious enough to dabble in opium smoking, it would be her. There had been scandalised whispers when Miss Halbrook remained alone in the family home after her parents died, despite being unmarried at the overripe age of thirty or so years. As time passed, she had migrated to the less scandalous and largely ignored category labelled "eccentric spinster".

In many ways, Grace admired Felicity Halbrook and her clique. They attended literary soirées and rode their safety bicycles around the city in the most daring of attire – the so-called "rational dress". Most of the women wore convertible skirts, which could be unfastened at the back to divide safely over the bicycle wheel. Felicity Halbrook raised eyebrows and outrage by wearing knickerbockers. Baggy enough to disguise the shape of her legs, but undeniably trousers rather than a skirt.

In truth, Grace envied these women their freedom of choice. Although she longed for clothing that gave her freedom of movement, Grace could not afford to waste her hard-earned money on new outfits. Besides, she would be thrown out of medical school if she dared attend in anything other than a shape-hiding ankle-length skirt and a high-collared shirtwaist.

A slim boy answered the door. He inspected Grace with an impertinent frankness. "Miss Halbrook is not at home to visitors."

Grace amended her first impression. Despite the slim build and trousers, this was no boy. "I have an appointment. Grace Penrose Pyke."

The boy-girl gave her a second appraisal before leading her down the hall. The pungent, flowery smell of opium drifted towards them from an open doorway. Languid voices and occasional soft chuckles drifted with the smoke. Full marks to Anne Macmillan for knowing her mark.

Before they reached the source of the smoke, Grace was taken into a small sitting room.

Felicity Halbrook joined her a minute later, wearing an article of clothing Grace understood to be called Jodhpurs, which were more normally seen on male equestrians. The shirtwaist she wore on her top half was a startling violet colour and diaphanous. For once in her life, Grace felt boringly conventional.

Miss Halbrook's voice drifted from loose lips as she waved towards an armchair. "Grace Penrose. I have long intended to further our acquaintance. I believe you would find our company stimulating, given your admirable success in breaching the masculine sanctum of medical school."

Although she shared Felicity's views on women's rights, Grace had little desire to seek a deeper level of acquaintance. She preferred to breach boundaries by merit and hard work, not lying on a sofa, puffing opium, and discussing the intellectual prospects of women. However, now was not the time for philosophical debates.

Instead, Grace took a seat. "I'm sure I would, Miss Halbrook, but I'm afraid I have little time to spare between work and medical studies. And marriage. I am Mrs Grace Penrose Pyke now."

"Oh dear, that is a shame."

Grace wasn't sure if the shame referred to her lack of time or her marriage, not that it mattered.

"Do call me Felicity. Mrs Macmillan did not tell me why you wished to see me, Grace, but the new surname reminds me that your name was linked to the private detective called Pyke."

"My new husband. I won't waste your time, Felicity. All I wish to know is the identity of the person who sells you opium. I promise you I won't reveal the source of the information. This inquiry in nothing to do with your perfectly legal activities."

"Then what is it to do with, Grace? You will understand my reluctance to name names."

"Two innocent people have been murdered. The person who sells opium is a person of interest, as a source of information and potentially as a suspect. The opium supplier need never know who divulged the name."

"Murder twice over? A bad business." Felicity drifted around the room, sunk in thought, before dropping into an armchair. "The man who supplies our opium is called Clive Jardine."

Grace tried not to let her excitement show, even though she wanted to leap up and dance a jig. The elusive drug dealer was about to be unmasked. What a fool to become involved by openly selling the opium himself, especially to young ladies such as Felicity. Grace wondered at his sanity for risking his reputation. "What is he like, this Jardine fellow?"

Felicity fluttered a hand dismissively. "He dresses the part of a gentleman and drops hints he would welcome an invitation to our parties, but he is rough around the edges. However wealthy he may be – or pretend to be – he was born to humble origins. I do not entirely trust him, but, as you say, we are doing nothing illegal. He supplies the goods, I pay him, and that is the end of it, as far as I am concerned."

Grace had borrowed Charlie's notebook. He had a knack of capturing a person's character in his drawings, such that even a pencil sketch was instantly recognisable as a real person. She opened the page to Sid Tucker, who best fitted the well-dressed, low origins description. "Is this him?"

Felicity frowned and reached for the notebook. "I don't think so."

Grace flipped back to the first sketch of the Glanville investigation. Felicity shook her head at the manservant, solicitor, and doctor, but she hesitated again at Jack Tucker. The next sketch was Bert Tucker.

"That's him. I'm sure of it. The artist has captured the hint of arrogance in an otherwise uncouth face."

Grace let out a held breath. "Thank you, Felicity. Your assistance may be critical to solving the murders. Might I also suggest that Jardine is not a man to be trusted. If I may take a few additional details, and then I will be on my way."

When they were done, Felicity stood up and reached her hand out for a limp handshake. "And I thank you, Grace. I will be more careful in future from whom I purchase my pleasures. You are welcome to join us if you ever find yourself bored with your husband."

Grace thanked her informant and took her leave, knowing she would have no cause to return.

Terrible Tuckers

Charlie's father arrived at the hospital soon after Grace left. Charlie took him to a quiet park nearby.

"You were right, son," Thomas Pyke said. "The witness agreed the drawing of the hook-nosed man was Rajiv Lohar. He even commented on what a nasty, ugly foreigner he was and what an appalling state of affairs that such people were allowed to roam freely about the city."

"Charming. He sounds like exactly the sort of man Bert Tucker would call a friend. Did he confess?"

"Ratted out his friend Bert without a single qualm when I threatened him with an arrest for making a false statement to the police. He admitted taking money from Bert Tucker, but only because he truly believed the foreigner to be a murderer. Or so he said."

"Nice work, Pa. I was sure of Mr Lohar's innocence, but Declan's visit this morning had me doubting my judgement. I'd better tell Declan the good news straight away, unless you want to."

"I still need to follow up Bert Tucker's alibi at the Edinburgh Hotel." Thomas half rose and then sat down again on the park bench. "Charlie, we were talking this morning about how much you and Grace are sacrificing for this case. Alistair wants you to know that he is willing to take over with the help of the rest of the family. We wouldn't want your dedication to your work to come between you and your wife so soon after the wedding. Both Alistair and I know all too well the toll police work takes on loved ones."

Charlie's thoughts jumped back to the stimulating morning he had spent with Grace. "Having the support of family means the world to us, Pa, but I can assure you that detective work is not a wedge between Grace and me, but a shared passion that binds us together. I know it seems odd to outsiders, but we want to work together to see this murderer brought to justice."

His father put an arm around his shoulder. "We thought you would say that, but be assured we are here if you need us. Grace is one in a million, but then so are you, Charlie. Your mother and I couldn't be prouder of you both."

His father's words touched Charlie more than he could express. "Thanks, Pa. Grace suggested we visit you in Clyde when we've saved enough for a proper honeymoon."

"We'd like that very much." His father looked as if he was about to say more, but instead he said he'd best be off if the case was to be solved by dinner time. Sergeant Thomas Pyke strode off, whistling a merry ditty.

The whole lot of us are quite mad, Charlie thought. Mad, but happy.

Charlie found Detective Sergeant Declan Kelly at the Tucker house, writing up his notes on the search.

Declan took Charlie out into the garden, away from the flapping ears of Mrs Tucker and her lady's maid. "Your Aunt Lily and Grace's mother have already left," Declan said. "They've taken two coats and a pair of gloves for testing. I didn't find any arsenic, but I did find several sets of expensive clothes hidden behind Bert Tucker's work overalls. Bert is either being paid exceptionally well for a warehouse worker, or he has a profitable side-line."

"Interesting," Charlie said. "My father confirmed Bert paid the witness to make a false statement implicating Mr Lohar. He's checking Bert's alibi for Mrs Seaton's murder now."

"Mrs Tucker's whereabouts are still unaccounted for as well. Her maid says she came home around noon on Saturday. Mrs

Tucker claimed she had been upset by her brother's death and visited a friend, who brought her home in her carriage. I was about to pay a visit to the friend."

Charlie and Declan exchanged news of their investigations on the way. Declan and his constable had talked to witnesses willing to swear that the solicitor, Percy Fairchild, was seeing clients at the time of Mrs Seaton's death, while Doctor Johnstone had patient appointments. Fairchild was definitely ruled out, as he also had a solid alibi for the night of the fatal dinner. The same was true for Sammy Yee Chong.

"However, Doctor Johnstone's alibi is not as tight as I first thought," Declan said. "After he informed the Tucker family of Arthur Glanville's death, the doctor returned to his surgery. According to his assistant, he arrived shortly after ten o'clock on Saturday morning. The doctor cancelled all non-urgent patients and dealt with the rest promptly, before making three house calls between eleven and twelve o'clock. The first patient was not at home, having got better and forgotten to cancel the appointment. The second patient denied the doctor came to see her, but she was a woman of such advanced years that she spent ten minutes telling me about Queen Victoria's coronation as if it was yesterday. The third patient said the doctor arrived between half-past eleven and noon."

"Ruling our Lohar, Fairchild, and Sammy is good progress," Charlie said. "Sid Tucker's alibi held up too. His assistant is certain Sid was in the shop at quarter past eleven on Saturday morning, which means he cannot have murdered the cook."

"Excellent news. Anything on the other Tucker men?"

"Jack Tucker attended a hospital appointment rather than a gas fault on Saturday morning. It's highly unlikely, but not impossible, for him to have got to Lavender House in time to kill Mrs Seaton. Bert Tucker is not the warehouse supervisor he claims to be. He seems to spend most of his time making deliveries, which leaves him firmly in our sights."

"Henrietta Tucker is probably in the clear too," Declan said. "One of the protesters admitted leaving the vicinity of Lavender House around eleven o'clock and following a woman matching Henrietta's description towards the path through the town belt. He particularly recalled her as she turned and told him to leave her alone, thinking he meant her harm. He was a scrawny runt of a man. Frankly, he seemed more frightened of her than she of him. He turned and went the other way, while she continued up the path. Henrietta could have doubled back, I suppose, but it seems unlikely."

They reached stone gateposts topped with rampant lions, which formed the entrance to the house Mrs Tucker visited on Saturday morning. Mrs Tucker's friend was far from pleased to have policemen at her door during afternoon visiting hours, but she allowed them to be hustled into a dingy back room, where she left them waiting for ten minutes while she attended to the more genteel callers.

Eventually, she pushed open the door, shutting it quickly behind her. "What is it you want?" She brought the calling card close to her face, squinting at it. "Detective Sergeant Kelly."

Declan stood up politely while she took a seat. "We need to know if Mrs Ariadne Tucker visited you on Saturday."

"Indeed she did. Poor Ariadne was so frightfully distraught at the passing of her brother, I felt compelled to forgive her for the ungodly hour of her arrival."

Declan frowned. "She arrived very early on Saturday morning?"

Charlie perked up. Had Mrs Tucker known of her brother's death before the doctor announced it at half-past nine on Saturday morning?

The friend fluttered her hands, as if unable to believe it herself. "Before noon! My maid was still attending to my coiffure."

Declan pursed his lips to suppress his amusement. "We need to know the time of her visit more precisely."

"I haven't the least idea, Sergeant Kelly. She must have left around noon, as I had a luncheon engagement to prepare for. I told Ariadne she needed to go home and take a strong sedative and a long rest. In my experience, sedatives are the only cure for such a terrible shock. Poor Ariadne was beside herself. I sent her home in my carriage."

Charlie tried to imagine Grace responding to a crisis by sedating herself and leaving others, like Henrietta, to cope with the practicalities. Inconceivable.

"How long would Mrs Tucker have been here, approximately?"

"Perhaps an hour? I'm cannot be certain, the situation being so distressing."

A visit of an hour between eleven and twelve o'clock would eliminate Mrs Tucker from direct involvement in Mrs Seaton's death. However, Charlie could see that Declan was just as dubious about the alibi as Charlie was. This woman was either naturally vague, truly distraught at her friend's plight, or actively covering for her friend. It was impossible to tell which. They would have to leave it for now, as the friend had already risen and pointedly opened the door for them to exit.

"Flamin' heck," Declan said when they were walking away. "I can't imagine what my wife would say about a woman who was still getting dressed at eleven in the morning. Or rather, I know exactly what she'd say. Fortunately, the increase in salary that came with the promotion has me in her good books."

"You deserved it, Declan. You'll be in everyone's good books when you arrest a double-murderer within days of the crime."

"I hope so, even if it will be thanks to you and your family, rather than my own devilishly clever investigation."

"It works both ways, my friend," Charlie said. "You help us, we help you. Are we off to Sid Tucker's house now?"

"Might as well. I fancy we're snapping at the heels of Bert Tucker, but it won't stand up in a court of law if we don't find direct evidence of his involvement in the murders."

Sid's house looked like a modest two or three bedrooms from the outside. Smaller than the Tucker's house, but a cut above a worker's cottage. Grace sat on the stone wall outside, swinging her legs. Charlie could tell by looking at her that she was bursting with news, unless she was just delighted to see him. Either option was fine by him.

She tossed Charlie's notebook to him as he hurried to greet her. "Care to guess the name of the person supplying opium to the wilder fringes of Dunedin high society?"

"Tell me it's Bert Tucker and I'll ..." Declan glanced at Charlie. "Tell me it's Bert Tucker and I'll let my ill-favoured friend kiss you."

"My source identified the man as Clive Jardine," Grace said, "and I'll take whatever kisses are going from your extremely attractive friend."

"Clive Jardine himself." Declan bounced on the spot gleefully. "I don't suppose your witness could describe him?"

"You suppose wrong, Detective Sergeant Kelly. Miss Felicity Halbrook did better than merely describe him – she picked him out of Charlie's sketches with no hesitation." Grace hopped off the wall. "Would you care to guess which person she picked?"

"If it was Bert Tucker, I'll kiss you myself," Declan declared.

Grace held out her cheek for Declan to kiss. "Got it in one guess. Bert Tucker is selling opium to society ladies under the name Clive Jardine."

Declan picked Grace up and swung her around. "Hallelujah. Fantastic news, Grace."

"Kindly unhand my wife, so I can have my turn." Charlie hugged and twirled Grace in one graceful movement. "Selling opium, eh? That explains where Bert Tucker got the money to buy the expensive clothes Declan found in his house. Bert also paid a man to lie about seeing Rajiv Lohar at the Lavender House fire."

Grace slipped from her husband's embrace to the ground. "Did you find a blood-stained meat skewer and packet of arsenic tucked under Bert's pillow?"

Declan sighed. "I wish it were so, but even Bert isn't that stupid. Let's see if Sid Tucker's servants can tell us exactly when Bert left after meeting with his brother and mother at Sid's house on Saturday morning. With luck, we'll find a loose-lipped maid with big ears."

Unfortunately, Sid's maid had normal sized ears and lips, and the good sense to be suspicious of strangers knocking at her employer's door. Even the sight of DS Kelly's police badge left her hesitant. "Mr Tucker instructed me never to let anyone into his house when he is not present."

Declan showed her the search warrant. "I'm afraid you have no choice, Miss." He spoke softly and politely, and had one foot over the threshold before she had made up her mind. "Shall we go to the sitting room?"

The house was surprisingly spacious on the inside and beautifully furnished. Sid Tucker's flair for design showed in the elegant décor, which flirted with garish and came down on the side of tastefully luxurious. Sid favoured Eastern motifs. His grandfather would have been right at home here.

Declan ushered the reluctant maid in and waved at a silk-covered armchair embroidered with peacocks on a leafy green background. "Please, take a seat."

The maid stared at him as if he'd asked her to take her clothes off. "I can't sit in Mr Tucker's sitting room, sir."

"And I have had a busy day, Miss." Declan lilted the words in his most charming Irish accent. "I would dearly love to take the weight off my feet, but it would be impolite to sit while you stand. Can you tell me your name, Miss?"

She perched on the very edge of the seat, after brushing off the rear of her skirt. "My name is Rachel York."

Declan leaned towards her with a conspiratorial smile. "You work in a beautifully kept house, Miss York. Mr Sidney Tucker's tailoring business must be doing well."

"Oh, yes, sir. His clientele is very exclusive." She intoned the words as if parroting a learned phrase.

"Does Mr Tucker employ other help?"

"He is a very modern gentleman, Detective Kelly. He sees to his own dressing, visits a barber and shoe-shiner in town, and dines at his club, so he has no call for a valet or cook. I make his breakfast and see to the cleaning and the laying of the fires." Rachel York crossed her hands in her lap demurely, but could not stop her cheeks reddening. "Naturally, I live out, with Mr Tucker being a single gentleman. A gardener comes by once a week to see to the outdoor work."

Declan nodded. "Of course. We are making inquiries on a matter to do with Mr Tucker's uncle."

"Oh, that'd be Mr Arthur Glanville, who died so suddenly. Very sad, and him so young."

"Mr Tucker must have been upset by the death, I imagine."

The maid blushed again as she struggled to phrase an appropriate answer. Charlie loved a witness who couldn't disguise her emotions. Miss York was perfect.

Declan gave her a kindly smile. "You need have no fear that what you say will reach Mr Tucker's ears. Perhaps he and his uncle were not close?"

"I wouldn't care to imply that there was any ill will between them," Miss York said.

"But perhaps not on especially friendly terms?"

"Just so, Detective Kelly. I thought it a shame, as the uncle seemed such a nice man."

"And Mr Tucker?" Declan inquired.

"He is a fair employer, who pays well and doesn't lose his temper over every little thing. I'll not say a word against him, sir." The maid clearly felt she had not been glowing enough in her praise, because she paused for a moment, before adding, "Mr Tucker was on excellent terms with his grandfather, which might explain his rather cool attitude to his uncle."

"The grandfather being Mr Horatio Glanville?"

"Exactly, sir. He and Mr Tucker would often dine together before his death. Lovely to see such family devotion. His grandfather thought so well of Mr Tucker, he left him his special collection."

Declan smiled encouragingly. "Well, now, Miss York, that is a fine thing, is it not? What type of collection was it?"

"Things he'd collected from across the other side of the world. Figurines, porcelain, weapons and such like."

Declan's ears all but took flight, so hard were they flapping. "Weapons?"

The maid grimaced. "Quite creepy they are, if you ask me, but Mr Tucker takes a great deal of pride in them, as his grandfather did. Makes me dust them once a week on Saturday morning, before I have my afternoon off."

"Last Saturday morning was when Mr Tucker found out about his Uncle Arthur's death," Declan said, with disarming nonchalance. "I believe his mother and brother returned with him to this house afterwards."

"Yes, sir. Mr Tucker received a note from Mr Glanville's doctor shortly after I arrived at eight o'clock on Saturday morning. The doctor had called the family to meet him at half-past nine. They returned here shortly after ten o'clock and stayed for about half an hour."

"You seem quite certain of the times, Miss York."

"I was keen to finish my work on time, you see, because I was walking out with my young man in the afternoon. I had to stop my

225

dusting when they arrived, to see if they wanted tea, and I kept an eye on the clock, not wanting to be late."

Declan had moved to the edge of his seat. "This is very important evidence, Miss York. Please don't be offended if I ask you whether you overheard what they discussed. I imagine you could hardly avoid hearing if you went in to offer tea."

The pink returned to the maid's pale cheekbones. "I heard them talking about how dreadful it was that Mr Tucker's uncle had died so unexpectedly. He's Mrs Tucker's brother, so naturally my employer was comforting his mother. I withdrew to leave them to their grief and make the tea."

An exemplary maid, Charlie thought, and an excellent witness. A pity she wasn't a little nosier, like some maids he'd encountered, who made a habit of being in the right place to overhear what they shouldn't.

Declan let the silence hang for a moment, but she sat still, with her hands crossed in her lap. He tried again. "Was it only grief?"

Miss York's fingers twitched. "Grief and shock at the suddenness of his passing. I gathered that one of Mr Glanville's servants disgraced herself by making a scene."

"You have an excellent memory, Miss York. Just between you and me, the cook was rather distressed by her employer's passing. Can you recall what they said specifically?"

Miss York's head lowered until all they could see of her face was a wrinkled brow and uncertain eyes. "I can't recall the exact words, but I gained the impression the cook was the worse for drink and making foolish accusations. Mrs Tucker was very cross at her, as you can imagine."

"You're right about that," Declan said. "I don't suppose any of the Tuckers mentioned anything about inheriting money?"

The maid's arms wrapped around her waist as if to physically restrain herself. Charlie felt sorry for the poor lass, who was so clearly uncomfortable balancing her duty to keep her employer's confidences against her duty to talk to the police.

"It's a serious police matter, Miss York. You are obliged to disclose the full truth."

"Grief can come out in strange ways, Detective Kelly. Words can be said that would have been better left unsaid."

"The exact words you heard, please, Miss York."

"When I was bringing in the tea, Mrs Tucker said, 'thank the Lord we'll get the money at last'. Mr Bert Tucker replied, 'about blooming time.' Mr Sidney Tucker gestured for them to hush up in front of me. I put the tea tray down and hurried out."

Charlie could see from her face that the word Bert used was far coarser than "blooming", but the intent was clear.

"Anything else?" Declan said.

"No, sir."

"We would like to see the weapon collection, Miss York." Declan anticipated her flicker of doubt. "We have a warrant to conduct a search."

Miss York led them back down the hall to a room near the front door. The collection occupied the entirety of the small room, complete with a copy of the painting that hung over the Tucker mantelpiece. When Charlie looked closer, he realised this was the original. Horatio Glanville with a hunting rifle and his boot on a tiger's head. Probably the same beast whose striped skin took up much of the floor of the room.

The collection featured unusual and rather gruesome weapons of foreign origin, presumably from India and the far east. Amongst the old rifles and pistols, Charlie spotted a curved sabre, a sword with a jewel-encrusted hilt, a many-bladed dagger, and a cat-o'-nine-tails whip. No wonder Miss York did not care to enter the room.

Within the display of lethal weapons, a few rattan canes had pride of place. Charlie recalled Grace's retelling of Mrs Tucker's favourite means of punishing the servants in her Indian youth, by having them beaten with rattan canes.

One cane in particular caught his eye. When young Fred Coster looked through the keyhole of Mrs Seaton's room in Lavender House, he saw a hard and knobbly object of a pale cream colour being held in a black glove. His description matched the ivory handle of the cane. A cane would explain the tap-tap sound on the floor that Fred overheard, too.

"Miss York," Charlie said. "I don't suppose you have noticed this cane missing at all?"

The maid stepped gingerly around the tiger skin, completely avoiding the head end, which had realistic glass eyes and vicious teeth. "Odd you should say that, sir. I had just begun dusting in here when the Tucker family arrived on Saturday morning. When I came back after they left, I noticed this space was empty. Mr Tucker is very particular about nobody touching his collection. I think it had been there earlier, but I could be mistaken. This room does fair play tricks on the mind, as you can imagine, sir."

"I can well believe it." Charlie did not care at all for the type of man who would keep such weapons, let alone the type of man who would keep instruments of inhumane punishment. "Did you see any of the Tucker family enter this room on Saturday morning?"

"No, sir. After I took the tea in, I retreated to the end of the house near the sitting room to attend to my other chores, in case my employer needed me."

"Did they all leave together?"

"I heard Mr Sidney Tucker saying goodbye to his mother and brother. He left a few minutes after them. I didn't see him, as I was in the kitchen washing up the teacups, but I heard the door close and the key turn in the lock."

"Did Mr Sidney Tucker return to the house before you left for your afternoon out?"

"No, sir. He said he was going to his tailoring business, as he usually did on a Saturday. Mrs Tucker came back though, with the other brother, when I had just finished clearing up. She had forgotten her gloves. They stayed in the hall while I fetched the gloves. Took me a fair while, as the gloves had slipped down behind a cushion."

Charlie tried not to look too interested as he sought to phrase his next question in neutral terms. "Did you see if they were carrying anything when you returned?"

Rachel York contemplated Charlie with lively eyes. "Such as a cane, perhaps? No, I didn't, but Mrs Tucker was wearing a cape that covered her body and I didn't see Mr Bert Tucker, because he had gone outside to smoke by the time I returned the gloves to Mrs Tucker. I returned to the far end of the house to complete my work for another twenty minutes or so after that. You may also wish to know that the Tucker household holds a spare set of keys to this house, as Miss Henrietta likes to drop by occasionally with flowers and meals for her brother. A very thoughtful sister, she is. Now, sir, you won't be telling Mr Sidney Tucker that I spoke of such things?"

Charlie smiled back. "Not if we can avoid it. If the situation arises, he will be made aware that you spoke only after being threatened with arrest. Thank you for your candour, Miss York. That will be all for now. Detective Sergeant Kelly and I will conduct a search of the house and let you know when we leave."

Grace handed the maid her card. "If you ever find yourself in need of a new position, let me know."

The maid bobbed politely and retreated to the far end of the house.

Grace saw Charlie's raised eyebrow and shrugged. "We could use another maid now that our household has expanded. Especially an efficient and discreet one like Rachel York. Even more so because Sadie has been walking out with the same man for over three months. Now, would you care to explain why you are so interested in this cane? Mrs Seaton wasn't beaten to death."

Charlie refrained from commenting on Grace's expertise in household management, which Mrs Beeton would have been proud of. "This cane matches what the lad saw through the keyhole at Lavender House."

Declan took out a clean handkerchief and removed the cane from the wall, touching only the end of the ivory handle. "I've seen a similar one before."

He twisted the top and pulled. The handle came free of the shaft. A thin, round core of metal, with a lethally sharp tip, projected from the handle. "Not a meat skewer, but very like it. A sword-cane." Declan examined it. "It's been thoroughly cleaned, using turpentine by the smell of it."

Grace gestured him to the window. "Can I have your magnifying glass, Charlie?" She bent to inspect the top of the cane at close range. "There is a tiny amount of brownish residue. Blood, presumably, but I can't be sure."

"Can you tell if it's recent, Grace?" Charlie asked.

"Impossible to say. It could be tiger blood from decades ago or the remnants of last night's roast beef."

"Chances are, it's Mrs Seaton's blood from Saturday." Declan punched the air in triumph, jerking the vicious spike perilously close to Grace. "Looks like we have the weapon that killed Mrs Seaton and a tight timeframe for it to have been taken. Given the fact that Henrietta and Jack Tucker were elsewhere, and assuming nobody else had access to the spare key, that narrows our suspects to three. Bert and Sid Tucker and their mother. No prizes for guessing which one I favour. We definitely have enough to pull Bert Tucker in for questioning. DI Wallace will have to decide whether we have enough for an arrest."

Charlie had the rising sense of euphoria he got when an investigation starts to come together, but he was not convinced that they had enough for an arrest – or even that Bert Tucker was the killer. "Let's search the rest of Sid's house while we have the chance."

"I'll examine Sid's clothes for arsenic." Grace pulled an old pair of gloves out of her satchel and headed for the door, stepping gingerly around the tiger's head as she went.

"After that," Declan called after her, "you two can go home and take a well-deserved night off from investigating. We'll be making an arrest tomorrow morning. I feel it in my bones."

Locked Room

That evening, Grace lifted her glass, admiring the sparkle of cut crystal in the gaslight. "I want to propose a toast, as this is the last dinner our families will have together for who knows how long. Every one of you has made our wedding a celebration to remember, both in the moments of joy and in coming together to help us solve two murders." She raised her glass. "To our wonderful families, with love."

"To family!" the company chorused.

"Let's have no more talk of crime tonight," Alistair said. "I hope –"

Alistair's hopes were interrupted by a loud knocking on the front door.

"Don't answer it!" Charlie and Grace said together.

The sound of the door opening was followed by a tentative, "Anyone home?"

"Come in, Detective Sergeant Kelly," Lily called. "We're in the dining room."

Declan came in, hat in hands. "Please excuse the interruption during your dinner. Can I have a quick word with Charlie, please?"

Charlie pulled out a chair. "You may as well tell the entire team, Declan."

Declan leaned on the back of the chair rather than sitting. "I only came to say that Detective Inspector Wallace is calling a meeting of the suspects at the Glanville house tomorrow morning at half past ten. He'd like you there, Charlie. Grace too, if that is acceptable. The solicitor, Mr Fairchild, wants a word with us first, so arrive by ten o'clock if you can manage it."

"Of course," Grace replied. "But why?"

"Wallace doesn't think we have enough to arrest Bert Tucker. He wants evidence that Bert had the opportunity to slip Arthur Glanville the arsenic, especially as there is no proof that Bert was at Lavender House. In fact, as we now know, Sergeant Pyke was unable to get Bert's drinking companions or the other patrons to divert from their testimony that Bert Tucker was at the Edinburgh Hotel when Mrs Seaton was murdered."

"He paid them, like as not," Thomas Pyke said. "I'd bet you could get one of them to crack if you took them in to the police station for questioning."

"Maybe," Declan said. "Wallace intends to reenact the events on the night of the dinner party, hoping that somebody will recall a vital detail. If that doesn't work, Wallace plans to put pressure on the Tuckers by emphasising they are all suspects. One or more of them knows more than they are telling. They won't want to risk their own hides to keep somebody else's secret."

"But Bert did have the opportunity to poison Arthur Glanville," Grace protested. "He poured his uncle a glass of port at the end of the meal."

"Unfortunately, Mrs Ariadne Tucker has made a sworn statement that her brother Arthur never drank the port, as he was already feeling unwell." Declan held up his hands when Charlie opened his mouth to protest. "I know, I know. Mrs Tucker is hardly unbiased. She and Bert could have plotted this together. But she is so unshakeable on the point, a jury will believe her. The maid who works for Mrs Tucker's friend has made a statement that Mrs Tucker arrived at eleven o'clock on Saturday morning, which gives her an alibi too. I took the statement myself. The poor girl was terrified, so it's hard to tell if she was saying what she was ordered to say or telling the truth."

Charlie rang rings around the top of his glass until the crystal hummed. "Mrs Tucker's maternal devotion to her son might be shaken if Wallace tells her Bert is selling opium under the name Clive Jardine."

"We can only hope so," Declan agreed. "I'd hate the killer to get away with it for lack of evidence. There is one small piece of good news. The constable who searched Mrs Seaton's room found correspondence with a second cousin in the North Island, who has a football team's worth of children. The cook's £50 inheritance will go to a worthy cause."

Declan shuffled his feet. "Another reason Wallace is calling the meeting tomorrow is to get Sid and Bert away from their places of business so the police can execute a search warrant. Even if the reenactment is a waste of time, Wallace wants to draw it out, so the police team has plenty of time to search. And now, I'll bid you goodnight."

After Declan's departure, the celebratory mood of the dinner party had gone as flat as day-old champagne.

"We're back to the same old problem," Alistair said. "Any of them might have killed Arthur Glanville."

Charlie stared at his empty plate. "Whereas all of them had an alibi for Mrs Seaton's murder. And we still don't know how Mrs Seaton's killer entered Lavender House."

Grace passed around serving dishes, trying to get the dinner back on track while the food was still hot. "None of the alibis for Mrs Seaton's murder are unbreakable. We don't know for sure when Henrietta returned from Lavender House. Mrs Tucker's friend might be covering for her. Mr Tucker might have left his hospital appointment early. Bert Tucker is relying on the word of drinking companions and bribery. And Sid Tucker's assistant could have been wrong about the time, although he seemed certain. However, only Mrs Tucker and her two sons were known to have access to the sword-cane, unless Henrietta had already passed her key to someone else before she took Mrs Seaton to Lavender House."

Charlie spilled the gravy as Grace's words sparked a memory that had been nagging at the back of his brain. He mopped up the drops, hoping no one had noticed. "Alistair, did you find anything on the identity of Clive Jardine? Is that where Mr Drummond and Mrs Macmillan are tonight?"

"Kenneth and Anne are dining out this evening amongst higher society than ours," Alistair replied. "I believe they are using their formidable web of contacts to highlight the plight of Lavender House and gather donations for rebuilding."

"Well, that's good news. Jardine remains a *Guilao*, then?"

"The ghost man is real enough," Alistair said. "Mr Peters and I tracked down the registration documents for the company transfer. Kenneth Drummond knows the attorney who witnessed Jardine's signature, but he is out of town today. Kenneth has an appointment with him tomorrow morning at nine o'clock."

"Does it matter," Lily asked, "now that we know Bert Tucker is Clive Jardine?"

"We need documentary proof of Jardine's identity," Grace replied. "I agree with Charlie about the importance of Jardine to the investigation. The Tucker family was furious at Horatio Glanville for selling the business to an outsider. If we can show Horatio jumped the usual path of succession to hand the business in secret to Bert Tucker, the other members of the Tucker family might be angry enough to admit what they know about the murders. It also gives Bert an even stronger motive to want to stop Arthur Glanville's investigation into Horatio Glanville's business dealings."

"I'm still cross at myself for writing off Bert Tucker as too dim-witted to be our man," Charlie grumbled.

"A recent marriage can have a severely detrimental effect on a man's ability to use his brain," Lily teased. "It's a medically established fact."

"Quick, pass my husband some more food," Grace said. "Nothing will revive his spirits quicker than a lavish serving of roast potatoes."

Amid the laughter, Jasmine Pyke laughed the hardest. "Did I ever tell you Charlie was the smallest, skinniest child at school? His nickname was Bones, because he was skin and bones."

Doctor Penrose stared at Charlie in disbelief. "Grace's nickname was Bones too, because she took a skeleton to school when the children were asked to bring in their favourite pastimes."

"It seems our children were fated to be together."

Thomas Pyke raised his glass. "Now, there's a toast worth making. To Grace and Charlie, the perfect couple. Bones and all."

After that, there was no more talk of murder. Grace couldn't help feeling murder might have been a safer topic, given the number of anecdotes of their childhoods being shared, but their parents had a marvellous time for their last dinner together.

Three hours later, Charlie settled into bed with a deeply contented sigh.

Grace slid in beside him. "How long do you think this state of bliss will last?"

"Until my dying breath." His hand drifted down her back to her buttocks. He sighed again.

Grace poked him in the ribs. "You're hardly likely to feel so contented on your deathbed."

"On the contrary. My last breath will be the most contented of all. I will be surrounded by our children and grandchildren and you will be sitting beside me, holding my hand and saying 'toughen up, Pyke, it's only a sniffle'. And, for once in your life, I'll prove you wrong."

"Idiot man. Is it too late for an annulment?"

Charlie pulled her closer and whispered in her ear. "Way, way too late."

Grace woke up the next morning feeling reinvigorated. She rolled over. The space beside her was empty, causing her a stab of disappointment, followed by a sharper stab of worry at her husband's absence. Visions of knife-wielding assassins raised her blood pressure, until the rattle of a tray brought relief. A handsome man bearing breakfast to one's bed was a fine way to start the day. Enough to make a woman feel smug.

Charlie settled the tray onto her lap, with a kiss for garnish.

Grace tucked in. "These scrambled eggs are delicious. Is Mrs Brown back? I wanted to tidy up before she arrived."

"I cooked the eggs," Charlie said, "but the bread is fresh from Mrs Brown. She's coming back this afternoon. I'm not sure if it's because she misses her own kitchen or she is worried we will create chaos without her here as our housekeeper."

"Both probably. Did you go over to Mr Drummond's house just to get fresh bread for me, Charlie? You are kind. I might have to cancel my plans to seek an annulment."

Charlie wriggled under the covers beside her. "Actually, I went over to make a few inquiries."

"Oh?" Grace said, through a mouthful. Delicious. She'd missed Mrs Brown's fresh bread.

"I woke up early and began fretting over the case. It's unsettling to rush through an investigation this fast. We have to establish how Mrs Seaton's murder was done. I still worry that a woman was more likely to be able to get into Lavender House."

"I don't see the connection with your early visit to Mr Drummond's house."

"Because Mrs Brown knows the serving classes of Dunedin as well as your Great-aunt Anne knows the people above stairs." Charlie wiped a smear of butter off her face. "I've sent Mrs Brown on a mission to find out whatever she can from various servants by ten o'clock."

"Good thinking, Charlie. I take it you're hoping Mrs Brown will get the truth out of the friend's maid, who gave Mrs Tucker her alibi. Perhaps we could get her to speak to Rachel York, too. I felt there was something slightly off about her reaction when she found out we were taking away Sid's clothes for inspection."

"I noticed too, Grace. Luckily, Mrs Brown knows Rachel York's mother. Your father has had a clever idea too, and my father is tracking down a potential witness. I also had another talk to your great-aunt about how it might be possible to get into Lavender House unnoticed, but she is as perplexed as I am. It has been driving me mad."

"You have been busy." Grace brushed the crumbs from her chest to her plate. "Shall we go back to the site of the fire and talk through the layout of Lavender House? There must be something we are missing, unless a trained parrot flew in the window and stabbed the cook. Do we have time before Wallace's meeting of suspects?"

Charlie glanced at his watch. "Plenty of time if we don't get distracted."

"I'll be ready in ten minutes."

Grace hadn't been able to bring herself to return to Lavender House since the day after the fire. It wasn't only the loss of the women's refuge and medical clinic, which had played a central role in the past three years of her life. It was the horror of seeing the charred skeleton of the upstairs corridor, knowing that Charlie might not have made it out alive if the fire had spread through the structure faster than he had expected. The burn scar on his arm would be a constant reminder of how precarious life could be. Ironically, no reminder was needed, as the knife scar on the opposite arm still haunted her from their first investigation together. At this rate, Charlie would have run out of unscarred limbs before she finished medical school.

Charlie stopped her on the doorstep of Lavender House. "You stay outside, my love. I know the damage is hard for you to bear."

Grace went to sit in the shade of a tree in the town belt behind Lavender House, opposite the last window Mrs Seaton looked out before her life was cruelly taken. Grace hoped the devoted cook

238

hadn't suffered the terror of seeing her killer and watching that wicked spike descend into her chest. She shivered, despite the warm morning. Clouds were gathering ominously to the south. Grace hoped it wasn't an omen.

Charlie waved from the window. He looked down at the drop from the second storey and shook his head. Grace racked her brain. As the room was locked with the key still inside, there were only two logical possibilities. The killer either had another key or access to a ladder. Surely the killer could not have carried their own a ladder to the refuge without being noticed? None of the neighbours had a ladder long enough – the volunteer firemen had checked when they needed another ladder to assist their firefighting.

None of the spare keys were missing, but Grace conceded a key might have been stolen and returned after the deed was done, but only by somebody familiar with the Lavender House and confident enough to pass unremarked. A woman, and one who had been there before. On a day when all the regular staff were absent, it would not be impossible. Grace was so deep in her musing, she did not hear Charlie approaching until he was upon her.

"What a beautiful sight." Charlie sat down beside her. "The view is delightful too."

From their vantage point on the slope above Lavender House, they had a lovely view over the houses, down to the harbour. When this case was over, Grace vowed she would make more time to enjoy the pleasures of life. A distant sail zig-zagged across the harbour. Perhaps they could afford to take a few days on the Otago Peninsula? Somewhere peaceful and crime-free. A secluded little cottage perhaps …

A gasp from her husband jerked Grace from her reverie. "What is it, Charlie?"

Charlie pointed to a house two doors down, where a man was up a ladder with a pot of paint. "Declan said none of the neighbours had a ladder long enough to reach the window."

As they watched, the man heaved the ladder up and moved it further down the façade. The ladder wobbled alarmingly for a few seconds before he got it under control.

"Let's find out where the painter got his ladder from," Charlie said. "He might have borrowed it."

The man came down reluctantly. "See those clouds gathering? Reckon there's rain coming."

"We'll only take a moment of your time." Charlie explained about their search for a ladder.

"Oh, aye, the ladder's mine, right enough. I was painting on the morning of the fire. Ran out of paint and had to go for more. By the time I got back, the fire had started and my ladder was gone, so I assumed the firemen had taken it. When a man knocked on my door to see if I had a ladder they could borrow, I said no. Why would I have two ladders, I ask you? I suppose the man didn't know mine had already been taken. I didn't wait around to ask. Me and the missus was bundling up the children and valuables, as you can imagine. Fire spreads between these old wooden homes faster than a thirsty man can knock back a pint of ale."

"But you got your ladder back?"

"I got a bone to pick about that an' all," the man grumbled. "The firemen didn't bring it back. They just chucked it up into the trees behind Lavender House. Took me ages to find it again. I didn't complain, mind you, given the circumstances. 'Tis a terrible thing, seeing a house full of women and children on fire. I'm just glad it wasn't worse."

The man picked up a bottle of turpentine. "If that's all, I'd better be getting back to my painting before the heavens open."

Grace watched the painter douse a rag with turpentine to wipe splodges of buff-coloured paint off his hands. The ladder was splattered with the same paint. She wondered why he didn't wear gloves.

Charlie was watching him too. "I don't suppose you were missing a bottle of turpentine when you got back?"

240

"Odd you should say that. I thought I had another bottle, but darned if I could find it. I like to keep track of it because of the children. Turpentine is poisonous, you know, and wicked dangerous around fire. There's talk of them protesters setting light to Lavender House. Do you reckon one of them nicked my turpentine to start the fire? The fuss and noise that mob was creating around the front of the houses, I was glad to be around the back in the quiet."

Charlie thanked the man distractedly and headed back through the town belt at a trot, dragging Grace with him.

"Charlie, wait."

"What is it Grace? I want to arrive before the meeting starts."

"I have an idea. Can you stall Wallace until I get there? Let him run through the reenactment, but don't let him make any arrests."

Grace didn't wait for Charlie's agreement. She picked up her skirts and sprinted down the hill.

A Gathering Of Suspects

Charlie slowed to a walk as he turned onto the road to Arthur Glanville's house, knowing he had time to spare and not wanting to arrive soaked in sweat.

A scrawny pair of legs poked out between the Glanville gateposts. In front of the legs, an even scrawnier kitten danced at the frayed end of a long flax leaf. The legs stood up at his arrival. "Mornin', Copper Charlie." The voice was muffled by a mouthful of sausage.

"And a fine morning to you too, Johnny Todd." Charlie had given up trying to get Johnny and his band of messenger boys to recognise that he was no longer a policeman. Besides, he didn't mind being called Copper Charlie. With Johnny and his gang, his nickname could have been a lot worse. "Do you have a message for me from Mrs Brown?"

Mrs Brown, their housekeeper, had a wide circle of friends amongst the serving classes, and had proved a valuable addition to the Southern Investigations team in the past. Young maids in particular were often too scared to talk to the police or an investigator, but would freely share information amongst their own.

Johnny chucked an end of sausage to the kitten and swallowed his own mouthful. "Grubber went to the Stewart's house to tell your mam to tell you that Mrs Brown went to the Tucker house to talk to the kitchen maid who knows the lady's maid."

Charlie worked his way through this tangle of relationships to the relevant point. "What did Mrs Tucker's lady's maid say?"

"That Mrs Tucker has been as sour as a crabapple for weeks. Crying and flying into a temper over nothing, according to the lady's maid. She's thought about leaving her position, only she feels sorry for Mrs Tucker because her husband is so ill. Reckons Mrs T is at her wit's end worrying about what will happen when her husband has to give up work. The lady's maid said Mrs Tucker was planning to swallow her pride and ask her brother for help, only the brother died and now everything is even worse."

"Did the lady's maid confirm what time Mrs Tucker arrived home on Saturday morning?"

"Around noon, in her friend's carriage." Johnny yanked up his loose trousers, which only made their short length more obvious. "Mrs Brown and Mrs Macmillan have gone to see the friend's maid. I'll go there now to bring back word of what they found, while they continue on to Sid Tucker's maid. They'll meet you back here."

Charlie extracted a larger than usual coin from his pocket and tossed it to the lad. "Time for some new trousers, Johnny."

"You sure, Copper Charlie?" Johnny cast a glance at the darned patch on Charlie's coat.

Charlie cuffed him lightly on the cap. "Be off with you, lad. I've work to do."

Johnny grinned back, doffing his cap and bowing. Both coin and lad vanished, with the kitten hot on his heels. Johnny had a sharp eye to notice the darn, which had been done by Lily's expert fingers. It was past time to buy a new coat, but the necklace Charlie had bought as a wedding gift for Grace had set his savings back.

Charlie went into the house. Declan and Wallace were setting up the drawing room for the meeting, so he went to find his client. Mr Lohar was upstairs with the doctor and solicitor, discussing the refurbishment of the house for its new life as a medical clinic for drug addicts. Dora was busy taking an inventory of furniture, while Nellie worked in a frenzy with duster and polish. This huge, half-empty house would soon bustle with new purpose, and the world would be a marginally better place. Charlie hoped their mission wouldn't be derailed by the murders.

Mr Lohar excused himself to talk to Charlie. "Can you tell me what this meeting is about, Mr Pyke? I had a constable here yesterday, accusing me of being at Lavender House when the fire started."

"You've nothing to worry about, Mr Lohar. You are no longer a suspect. The meeting has been called because the officer in charge of the case wants to clarify a couple of points before taking a suspect in for questioning." The other trustees had edged towards them, within eavesdropping distance. Charlie raised his voice to include them. "You are proceeding with the plan for the clinic, I take it."

Mr Fairchild answered. "We decided Arthur Glanville would want us to be helping people as soon as possible, rather than delaying to mourn his passing. Doctor Johnstone is moving into the house after Arthur's funeral to take charge of the medical side, while Mr Lohar will remain here to manage the clinic. We have been very fortunate that Dora has agreed to be matron of the clinic, while Nellie will be the head housekeeper."

Nellie must have had the hearing of a cat, because she piped up from the far side of the room. "We are honoured. The clinic is to be named Arthur Glanville House. Isn't that simply perfect?"

"We'll need to hire other staff, such as maids and orderlies," Mr Lohar said. He dropped his voice to a whisper. "Nellie will be in charge of the new maids, which means her shaking condition won't be a problem anymore. You wouldn't think to look at her, but Nellie has a sharp mind and is a dab hand at household accounts. My employer always swore he would be lost without her." He raised his voice to a normal volume. "And we'll need a new cook. Preferably one who can prepare more than mutton stew and stodgy puddings."

"I'll ask my Aunt Lily, who has contacts in the hotel kitchens and Chinese communities," Charlie said. "If you have any need for practical advice on the running of a medical clinic, I'm sure Mrs Macmillan, who has managed Lavender House for several decades, would be happy to oblige."

"I would be most grateful," Doctor Johnstone said.

"I expect Miss Tucker would be interested to talk to her too," Fairchild said. "That is, if she agrees to join us as a nurse."

Henrietta Tucker appeared in the doorway behind him, carrying a tall stepladder with apparent ease. "Of course I will join you, if you'll have me."

Doctor Johnstone hurried over to take the ladder off Henrietta. He swung it upright and set it up under a chandelier that was dangling at an odd angle. Making full use of his height, he had the chandelier hanging straight in no time, with Henrietta supporting the base.

"They make a good team, don't they?" Mr Fairchild said. "Determined and capable. I wish Arthur had lived to see this house reborn."

Charlie murmured his agreement, but his mind was distracted. He had seen how difficult the painter's long ladder had been to shift into place and doubted a woman could have managed it alone. Perhaps he had been hasty in his assumptions.

Henrietta's eyes were fixed on the doctor. "Clifford? You will keep me on as a nurse, won't you?"

The doctor backed down the ladder without looking at her. "The circumstances … your uncle's tragic death … this house … I couldn't possibly expect …"

Henrietta stomped her foot to force him to pay attention. "Doctor Johnstone, do you want me or not?"

The doctor flushed to the roots of his ginger hair. "Miss Tucker … Henrietta … of course, the clinic could not function without you." He glanced at the expectant eyes around him, which urged him on. Johnstone went down on one knee and fumbled a ring box out of his pocket, the velvet covering so worn down by nervous fingers, he must have been carrying the box for weeks. "The truth is, I cannot function without you. Henrietta Tucker, would you do me the honour of –"

"Yes!" Henrietta flung herself at her fiancé to a round of applause and a mumbled "about time" from Dora.

Charlie added his congratulations to the babble of well wishes, although he knew their joy would be short-lived. In his own mind, he was now sure of the killer's identity. All he needed was the hard evidence to prove the case. With the rest of the investigation team still scattered around Dunedin, assembling the last pieces of evidence, he could only hope the arrest would be made today. If not, every member of the Southern Investigations team was in danger – Grace and himself most of all. Seeing the knife at Grace's throat two nights ago had been one of the worst moments of his life. He shut down that dreadful memory before it smothered his ability to concentrate on the task at hand.

Charlie took a beaming Mr Fairchild aside. "You wished to see us? The police team is waiting downstairs."

Wallace looked up from reading through the case notes when Fairchild entered the drawing room. Charlie beckoned the solicitor to the chair in front of the desk and introduced him to Wallace.

The solicitor sat on the edge of the seat, twisting his folder of papers. "I wished to see you about a delicate matter, Detective Inspector Wallace. Along with the establishment of the charitable trust, Mr Glanville intended to set funds aside for Henrietta Glanville's dowry, as he had promised her he would. However, the documentation was not completed before he died, because Miss Henrietta was trying to convince her uncle to put the money into a trust for her father instead. She is a nurse, you see, so she knew Jack Tucker's health was deteriorating."

"I'm not sure I see how the police can assist," Wallace said.

"The trustees have discussed the matter – in the absence of Doctor Johnstone, naturally, as he has a personal conflict of interest. We wish to honour Arthur's commitment to the dowry. My opinion is that Jack Tucker would be too proud to accept financial help, so the trustees have agreed to offer him a position here with a generous salary. Light maintenance work and management of the rights to use the patented gas-valve, that being

246

more Jack's area of expertise than any of ours. The income stream from the valve is sufficient to fund the clinic if it is well managed, so it is a critical job. Jack Tucker would have access to free medical care here too. However, we do not wish to make this offer if there is any suspicion that Jack Tucker was involved in the death of Arthur Glanville. Are you in a position to confirm that, Detective Inspector Wallace?"

Wallace rocked back in his chair. "That's what we're here to find out. Is the matter urgent?"

Mr Fairchild attempted a poker face, but his left eye twitched repeatedly. "I have been informed there will be a legal challenge to Arthur Glanville's will. Making the Tuckers aware of Arthur Glanville's intention to help the family might prevent unpleasant and expensive legal proceedings."

Charlie added his news. "I've just had confirmation that Mrs Tucker's major concern seems to be their financial position if her husband is unable to work. I'm sure she and her husband would be relieved to know as soon as possible."

The grandfather clock in the hall struck the half hour. Right on cue, the front door banged open. The Tuckers had arrived.

When everyone was settled, Detective Sergeant Declan Kelly introduced Detective Inspector Wallace and explained why he had called the Tucker family and Glanville household together.

The suspects in the front row made slight gestures of annoyance – unsubtle glances at watches, mumbled words, sour pouts – but there were no eruptions of overt anger. As before, Mr Lohar and the Eady sisters sat in the back corner, while Mr Fairchild sat at the front and side, nearest the door. Henrietta Tucker and Doctor Johnstone sat halfway back, close together. Unlike everyone else in the room, they looked happy. They tried to hide it, but every few seconds, Henrietta and the doctor would glance at each other and smile.

Declan finished his introduction with a request to reenact the dinner party, starting with the scalded hand in the kitchen. "Can I have everyone to their places please?"

The suspects filed out, heading to the kitchen and dining room. Charlie took the chance to brief Wallace and Kelly about how the killer got into Lavender House with the ladder. As Grace had requested, he asked them to hold off on making an arrest until she arrived.

The three detectives started in the dining room. Wallace sat at the head of the table in Arthur Glanville's place. Mrs Tucker and Henrietta took their places on either side of him, with the doctor next to Henrietta, Mr Tucker next to his wife, and Sid and Bert at the far end. A jolly dinner party it was not.

Mrs Tucker grumbled about this being a waste of time, but she took the lead as narrator when asked. "Dora and Nellie brought the soup in first. After they cleared, there was a long delay, during which we heard a scream. Doctor Johnstone and Henrietta went to help. Eventually, the food was brought in, rather cold. There, you see, none of us did anything. If you ask me, the cook poisoned the food to get her bequest from Arthur, and then killed herself out of remorse."

"Mrs Tucker, we are aiming for a full reenactment, rather than brevity," Declan said. "The doctor and your daughter were not in the room when Nellie screamed, were they?"

"I had spilled soup on my lapel," Doctor Johnstone said. "Miss Tucker kindly took me out to the hall to remove it. Dora was bringing the food out, but put the plates on the hall table when her sister screamed. Dora, Henrietta and I rushed into the kitchen."

"That's not right either," Jack Tucker said. "When I came out to see what was happening and get another bottle of wine, Dora and Henrietta weren't there, but you were by the plates, putting your coat back on, Doctor."

"Why did you come out for more wine?" Declan asked.

"Because the previous bottle was empty, and the maid hadn't put out another on the sideboard in the dining room. All I did was take the bottle from the hall table. I didn't touch the food."

248

"Did you fill the glasses in the dining room, in the absence of the maids, Mr Tucker?"

"No need. Bert had already filled the glasses to the brim, which is why we needed another bottle."

Declan exchanged the briefest of glances with his commanding officer. "Did Bert pour at the table?"

"Really, Sergeant Kelly," Mrs Tucker snapped, "is all this ridiculous detail necessary?"

Declan ignored her. "Please answer the question, Mr Tucker."

"The maids forgot to pour wine for the first course," Jack said, in the deliberate voice of one explaining something blatantly obvious to a dullard. "Bert opened the bottle and poured at the serving table, before bringing the glasses to each of us."

"For heaven's sake, we all drank from the same bottle, Sergeant," Mrs Tucker added.

Charlie saw the spark of triumph in Declan's eye, now that he knew Bert Tucker could have slipped arsenic in his uncle's wine while his back was turned to the table.

"Arthur really ought to have engaged a footman," Mrs Tucker said, "to save his guests the embarrassment of waiting at the table. When my family lived here, my father employed a dozen servants at least. Whereas on that Friday evening, we had to wait so long for our main course that my Sid was obliged to go in search of the food, while my husband went for the wine. Appalling."

"Did Sid bring the plates in from the hall table?" Declan asked.

"The fuss was over by then," Sid said. "The taller maid and the cook brought the plates through and I returned to my seat."

Declan had what he wanted, but he made them continue the reenactment to the end of the meal to draw out the time. Even so, Grace had not arrived by the time everyone returned to the drawing room. Charlie took Declan and Wallace aside. "Can we wait a little longer for Grace?"

"Why don't you stall them with a summary of the investigation?" Declan replied. "After all, your team has done much of the work. I'd like to watch their faces while you talk. Is that acceptable to you, sir?"

"By all means," Wallace said. "Draw it out and watch them squirm. I'd like to take their measure, too."

Charlie leaned casually against the wall, scanning the faces, which were all turned to DS Kelly, waiting for him to release them. Charlie let them wait for a few more drawn-out seconds, before lobbing a single, forceful statement into the silence. "At least one of you in this room knows the identity of the person who murdered Arthur Glanville and Mrs Seaton."

Every single body in the room jerked at the accusation. Every face turned in Charlie's direction, revealing a slew of emotions. Charlie pushed himself off the wall with slow deliberation, as if he had all the time in the world to make his case. Inside, he was churning with the fear they would never have enough evidence to prove the identity of the murderer. He forced himself not to glance at the door, hoping Grace would come to his rescue.

Charlie moved to the centre of the room, scanning the faces again. "One of you added arsenic to Arthur Glanville's meal. Fearing you had been seen by Mrs Seaton, you callously stabbed her through the heart and set fire to a building housing vulnerable women and children to hide the cause of her death."

He let the appalling nature of the crime sink in, before adding a polite apology to put them off-balance. "Forgive me if I use Christian names, given the number of Mr Tuckers in the room."

Mrs Tucker pursed her lips. Her husband was a rigid presence beside her, moving only to take his wife's hand. Henrietta and the maids brushed away tears with handkerchiefs, while Sid radiated outrage and Bert scowled. Doctor Johnstone gawked at Charlie with an open mouth. Mr Lohar flicked his eyes around the room and tried to appear small. Mr Fairchild, the solicitor, watched on with nervous eyes and a rigid jaw.

Bert Tucker jerked his head towards Mr Lohar, who was sitting as far away from Bert as possible. "It's obvious the manservant did it," Bert said. "He had the most to gain from his master's death. £200! I bet he'd do it for two shillings after all those years of menial servitude."

Rajiv Lohar cast a nervous glance at Declan Kelly, but Declan was looking at Bert.

Charlie ignored his client and concentrated on Bert too. "Mr Lohar had left the house at noon and did not return until late that night. He was playing chess at the local chess club."

"He could have snuck back in," Bert said. "I bet if you asked around you'd find the manservant could have killed the cook too."

"As a matter of fact, you are quite correct, Bert," Charlie said. "A man arrived at the police station yesterday morning to swear he saw an Indian man coming out the back door of Lavender House shortly after the fire started."

All eyes turned to Mr Lohar, who shrank further into his seat.

"There! Didn't I tell you it was that sly foreigner right from the start?" Bert gathered up his coat and hat. "Well, get on with it. Arrest the vermin and stop wasting our valuable time."

Charlie motioned Bert to resume his seat. "When the witness was asked to identify the man, he failed to do so. On further questioning, the so-called witness admitted he had been paid ten shillings to report a sighting of an Indian man to the police. Paid by you, Mr Bert Tucker."

Lohar glared at Bert, who let loose an expletive. "The witness is lying," Bert growled, unconvincingly.

"He is," Charlie agreed. "Lying about Mr Lohar, who was actually tending to the laying out of his beloved employer at the time of the fire. Which means our suspects are restricted to the people present at both the dinner party and the announcement of Arthur Glanville's death. The Tucker family and Doctor Johnstone."

Jack Tucker stood up and crossed his muscular arms. "It wasn't one of my family." Unlike Bert, Jack spoke calmly, with the absolute certainty of a man loyal to his family. "The doctor could have slipped arsenic in the food before he went to tend to the scalded hand. I saw him. He was right by the plate."

Mrs Tucker clutched her husband's accusation like a lifeline. "Don't you find it suspicious that a doctor would fail to identify the true cause of death? If Mrs Seaton's death hadn't been suspicious, Doctor Johnstone's verdict of food poisoning would have been accepted, with none of us any the wiser at his infamy."

Doctor Johnstone opened his mouth to protest, but Charlie cut him off. "Food poisoning was the most likely cause of death, given the symptoms. The doctor had no reason to suspect murder at the time."

"That doesn't prove he didn't add the arsenic," Mrs Tucker said. "Has anyone thought to check where he was when Mrs Seaton died?"

"Mother!" Henrietta's normally placid countenance contorted with rage. "How dare you suggest my fiancé murdered Uncle Arthur! He is a doctor, for heaven's sake. He was tending to his patients when Mrs Seaton died."

Charlie was distracted by the arrival of his father and Johnny Todd, so Declan answered. "In fact, Miss Tucker, Doctor Johnstone said he was visiting an elderly patient at the critical hour. However, the patient was unable to recall his visit."

Doctor Johnstone leapt from his chair so fast he knocked it backwards. "I was with her, I swear it. The old dear cannot even recall her own children's names or the day of the week, let alone my visit."

Charlie finished his whispered discussion with his informants. "Sit down please, Doctor Johnstone. Sergeant Pyke has just informed me that the elderly patient's neighbour was in his garden. The neighbour remembers seeing you at the patient's house. He recalls the time precisely, as his wife had just called him in for elevenses when the doctor entered and he returned to his garden twenty minutes later, when the doctor was leaving."

Henrietta flung her arms around her man protectively, while Charlie turned back to Jack Tucker.

"You have defended your family, Mr Tucker, but the truth is that each of you had the opportunity to add arsenic to the food or drink. Your alibi for the death of Mrs Seaton has also been called into question, Mr Tucker."

"What do you mean?" Jack Tucker demanded. "I can prove I was called to the hospital to fix a gas fault."

"We know why you were at the hospital, Mr Tucker." Charlie noted the flare of alarm in Jack Tucker's eyes. "You were also seen at the Lavender House fire after you left the hospital."

Charlie was interested to note that the alarm dropped away. Jack Tucker was more worried his family would find out he was at the hospital for a medical problem than he was about being seen at the fire.

Jack looked Charlie in the eye defiantly. "I passed by the women's refuge on the way home from the hospital, that being the shortest route home. Naturally, seeing the building already ablaze, I stopped to assist. There seemed to be plenty of helpers on the pumps and bucket lines, so I went about my business."

"My Jack had nothing to do with it," Mrs Tucker declared. She stepped in front of her husband and glared at the police contingent.

Charlie had the strong sense that if he had wanted to arrest her husband, Mrs Tucker would have fought like a tiger to prevent it. Charlie gave a noncommittal nod and moved on. He had no intention of arresting Jack. It would have been near impossible for him to have killed Mrs Seaton, especially as Declan's second round of eyewitness interviews corroborated Jack's statement that he arrived after the fire started.

Jack sat down, pulling his wife down too. The door remained closed. Charlie prayed Grace would hurry. He wasn't sure how much longer he could draw this out.

"Every person in the Tucker family had a motive to end Arthur Glanville's life. You hoped to inherit what you perceived to be his wealth. Family wealth you felt entitled to."

"As you well know," Mrs Tucker snapped, "there was nothing worth inheriting beyond a few scraps."

"But you didn't know that at the time, did you, Mrs Tucker?" Charlie said. "It must have been frustrating when your brother refused to increase the allowance your father left you. And then Arthur refused to give money to your son just a few days before his death."

"All I asked for was a small loan to start my own business," Bert said. "I am made for better things than working in Jardine's warehouse. As the eldest son, the business should have been mine. I don't know what my grandfather was thinking when he sold it to Jardine rather than passing it on to family."

"Ah, now that is interesting, isn't it, Bert? Did your grandfather sell the business to a stranger? Or did he pass it to his chosen heir indirectly, using the fake Jardine name as a cover?"

Mrs Tucker interrupted. "What do you mean?"

Charlie was pleased to elaborate at length, as Grace was still absent. "Mr Horatio Glanville had secretly chosen his grandson as his successor. Knowing that passing over his son and daughter would create unwanted family tensions, he passed it on to the grandson via an alias. They must have enjoyed choosing the name for the false identity, in keeping with the Glanville tradition of naming sons after heroes. Clive Jardine, for Robert Clive, conqueror of India, and William Jardine, opium trader. Not that I would call either of those persons a hero, but the glove fits in this case."

"I don't understand what you are talking about," Mrs Tucker said. "We don't have the least idea who this Jardine fellow is."

Charlie went for the jugular. "Your son is Clive Jardine, Mrs Tucker. We have a witness who can attest that Bert Tucker uses the name Clive Jardine to sell opium directly to the fashionable young folk of Dunedin."

Gloves Off

Jack, Ariadne, and Henrietta Tucker let out horrified yelps and gasps on hearing Charlie reveal Bert Tucker as the mysterious Clive Jardine, who had taken over the family business under their noses.

Sid snarled at his older brother. "*You* are Clive Jardine? *You* are selling opium? Selling drugs to rich white people is akin to waving a red flag under the noses of the police force. Are you mad, Bert, or just impossibly stupid?"

Bert Tucker was too stunned to say anything. He didn't even bother to deny the accusation. Beside him, his mother flung icicles from her eyes at Charlie, who ignored them and continued.

"Naturally, we were suspicious of the unusual sale of Horatio Glanville's importing business before his death. So was Arthur Glanville. We suspect he found out the real identity of Clive Jardine and threatened to expose the man who was expanding the opium trade so blatantly."

"Don't be absurd," Mrs Tucker said. "What evidence have you to implicate my son? Bert was with me and Sid when Mrs Seaton was taken to Lavender House. My dear sons were supporting me after receiving the distressing news of my brother's death."

"Indeed, Mrs Tucker. The three of you went to Sid's house the morning after your uncle's death, but not to mourn. In fact, you were gleefully discussing your impending inheritance while your brother's body lay, newly cold, being tended by his devoted servants."

"An outrageous lie!" Mrs Tucker shrieked, but she did not turn to meet the eyes of Dora, Nellie and Mr Lohar, who were on their feet, glaring at the back of her head.

Charlie flipped open his notebook. "Your actual words were, 'thank the Lord we'll get the money at last', to which Bert replied, 'about blooming time' or words to that effect. Your meeting did not last long. Any of you could have left Sid's house in time to kill Mrs Seaton."

"We were nowhere near Lavender House," Mrs Tucker snapped. "Why on earth would we kill the cook, anyway?"

"Because one of you three murdered Arthur Glanville, and Mrs Seaton knew it."

Sid put his arm around his mother to prevent her from throwing herself at Charlie's throat. Sid's response was calm, but firm. "Where's your evidence we had anything to do with either death?"

"Mrs Seaton was stabbed to death using a sharp spike." Charlie gestured to Declan, who produced the cane.

Gasps rippled around the room. Henrietta had to be supported by the doctor, while Dora applied smelling salts to revive Nellie, and Mr Lohar reeled backwards.

Charlie took the cane and twisted the top with a flourish, revealing the wickedly sharp weapon inside. "Your sword-cane, Sid. Given to you by your grandfather."

Sid blanched. "Nonsense. That cane never left my house. If Mrs Seaton was stabbed, it could have been any sharp instrument. An accident. If she was caught in a blaze, she might have panicked and fallen on a sharp object. My brother Bert had nothing to do with her death."

"The killer failed to clean all the blood off. Your maid has testified that the cane was present when the three of you arrived at your house, but missing when she dusted after you left the house. Right before Mrs Seaton was brutally murdered for what she had seen."

Mrs Tucker interrupted. "How can you believe anything that drunk cook said? My Bert is innocent, and I will take you to court if you try to slander him in this preposterous way."

Charlie ached for Grace to rescue him. Still, offence was always the best defence. "Why is it you are so sure of your son's innocence, Mrs Tucker? Is it because you know who the actual killer is? A guilty conscience, perhaps? You were at Sid's house when the sword-cane disappeared. You, more than any other suspect, had the most hope of receiving a large and much-desired inheritance. We have heard stories of your childhood, Mrs Tucker. A rattan cane was always your weapon of choice, was it not?"

All five Tuckers leapt from their chairs at this accusation. Mrs Tucker gave full vent to her astonishingly powerful lungs. Mr Jack Tucker and Bert had to be forcibly restrained by the two policemen, using the full extent of their formidable strength. Sid Tucker yelled that he would have his lawyer eviscerate Charlie, his detective business, and all of Charlie's relations, past, present, and future.

Charlie stood, unmoving, in the face of the uproar. He removed a non-existent speck of dirt from under his nails. Then, Henrietta silenced her family, and almost gave Charlie heart failure, by emitting a piercing shriek.

Doctor Johnstone, who was standing beside her, grabbed her to prevent her collapsing. Henrietta struggled out of his grasp. She pushed through the group around Charlie until she faced her mother.

"Mother, did you poison Uncle Arthur?"

Behind him, Charlie heard the door open. Grace, at last. But it was Charlie's mother and his Aunt Lily, looking pleased with themselves.

Mrs Tucker stood with her mouth agape, staring at her daughter.

"Mother, did you poison Uncle Arthur?" Henrietta repeated.

"Me? Of course not. Henrietta, how could you make such a vile accusation against your own mother?"

Henrietta glared at her mother, unrepentant. "The last thing Mrs Seaton said to me was a drunken slur. I thought she said, 'should wore gloves', which I took to mean she should have worn gloves to come to Lavender House. It puzzled me, because her expression was so intense, as if she wanted to convey an important message to me. But perhaps I heard incorrectly. Mrs Seaton might well have said, '*she* wore gloves'."

Her mother stared at her with saucer eyes. "You're not making sense, Henrietta."

Grace pushed through the melee to stand by Charlie's side, having slipped into the room without him noticing. Anne Macmillan and Mrs Brown had come in with her. Charlie searched his wife's face to see if her mission had been a success, but Grace was focussed on Mrs Tucker.

"Henrietta means that the person who poisoned her uncle must have worn gloves to avoid touching the arsenic," Grace explained. "Mrs Seaton came out from the kitchen first, to serve the meal while Nellie Eady's scald was attended to. The cook saw the killer, but didn't realise it until later, when she found out her employer had been poisoned. After she got over her horror at believing herself responsible for his last meal, she recalled the oddity of the person wearing gloves inside and began to wonder if the poisoning was not caused by the shellfish after all."

"I didn't kill my brother," Mrs Tucker said. "I was in the dining room the whole time. Dora and Cook brought in the food. They had far more opportunity to add the poison than any of us."

Dora sprang to her feet, her face a mask of fury. "I did no such thing! I cared for your brother far more than you ever did."

Mrs Tucker was not about to give way to a mere serving woman. "Oh, did you indeed? And how was it you and your sister manipulated my foolish brother into leaving you so much money in his will?"

"Let me finish, Mrs Tucker," Grace ordered. "I was about to say, what Henrietta heard was not a slurred '*should* wore gloves', nor '*she* wore gloves', but '*Sid* wore gloves.' These gloves, in fact." Grace used forceps to extract a pair of fine kid gloves from a wrapped parcel.

Nellie and Dora sucked in simultaneous breaths. Then silence reigned. Every head turned to Sidney Tucker. Sid's face was the only one not to register shock. Instead, his expression veered towards bemusement.

Sid turned to Detective Inspector Wallace. "Sir, I must protest. Mr Pyke has become bloated with his sense of importance. He has accused each member of my dear family in turn, with not a shred of substantive evidence. Indeed, with little more than drunken hearsay, fevered speculation and an excessive reliance on the dramatic. Where is the evidence that these are the gloves that stirred arsenic into my uncle's curry? They look perfectly clean to me."

Grace nodded at Lily and Jasmine. "My associates have tested the gloves and found traces of arsenic. The gloves were brushed off, but there are always traces left behind."

Charlie's pulse hammered, but Sid Tucker was as cunning as a rat on a sinking ship.

"That proves nothing," Sid said. "I left my gloves on the same hall table the plates were put on when the maid was scalded. No doubt the actual killer spilled a little arsenic on them while sprinkling it on Uncle Arthur's food."

Charlie's heart sank again. Under other circumstances, the evidence might be enough to sway a jury, but Sid spoke with calm assurance and he was wealthy enough to engage a shrewd barrister.

The door opened again. This time it was Alistair Stewart and Kenneth Drummond, followed by George and Louisa Penrose. The boy who witnessed the fire, Fred Coster, clung to Mrs Penrose's hand. Charlie had not the least idea whether all of them – or indeed any of them – had actual evidence, but he couldn't fault the team spirit.

The previous arrivals shuffled further along the wall to make space for the newcomers. The room was becoming crowded with Southern Investigations operatives. Charlie had never been prouder of the Penrose, Pyke and Stewart clans.

"What is the meaning of this?" Sid Tucker asked. "Who are all these people?"

Fred Coster wrenched his hand out of Mrs Penrose's grasp. He pointed at Sid Tucker. "That's him. The man whose voice I heard at Lavender House in the drunk lady's room."

Sid Tucker blanched. "This boy is barely old enough to be at school. He has made a mistake."

"Is that so?" Alistair held up a folder stuffed with documents. "As you know, the man who bought the importing company from Horatio Glanville is called Clive Jardine. He is also the person who had the most to lose from Arthur Glanville's campaign to stop the opium trade."

Kenneth Drummond took over. "Mr Clive Jardine has led us on a merry dance of documents to uncover his real identity. Indeed, his thorough attention to secrecy is suspicious. However, Jardine had to sign legal documents to take ownership of Horatio Glanville's business. The attorney who acted on his behalf has identified the man behind the Clive Jardine pseudonym. That man is in this room."

The attention of every person in the room hung on Drummond's dramatic pause.

"Mr Sidney Tucker, we have irrefutable evidence that you are the owner of your grandfather's importing business. The real man known as Clive Jardine. Your grandfather sidestepped the usual path of inheritance to transfer his opium importing business to his favourite younger grandson. The grandson who had proven he had the business acumen to succeed."

Charlie couldn't resist plunging the knife deeper. "How infuriating it must be, Sid, to hear that your older brother stole your fake name and your opium for his own sordid little dealings on the side."

Bert Tucker risked a cerebral haemorrhage as his blood pressure surged. "Sid, is that true? You slimy, stinking swine.

You'll swing for this. Grandfather's business should have been mine."

Sid rounded on his older brother. "You got your chance, Bert, but you were as much use as a ship without a rudder. If it wasn't for me, you would have lost your job long ago. If I'd known you were stealing opium from me, and risking my reputation by using my name to sell it to rich white people, you'd be wearing the mark of my boot on your rear end for the rest of your worthless life."

"Who's the bigger thief, Sid? Me, for making a few quid on the side? Or my brother, going behind my back to steal my inheritance?"

Sid gave his brother a pitying glance before turning away. "I deserved to be given the family business. It is hardly my fault that grandfather favoured me, when I worked so hard to make something of myself, earning his praise and trust. I only used the Clive Jardine name so as not to rouse your pathetic jealousy. And because the heir of the Glanville fortune deserved to be known by a more illustrious name than dirt-common Sid Tucker."

Jack Tucker stared at his younger son as if he was a piece of muck on the end of his boot. "You ungrateful little guttersnipe. My name not good enough for you? I should have cut ties with the Glanville family as soon as I saw what they were. All airs and graces, but nothing more than blackguards and drug dealers. And now a murderer as well."

Sid backed away into open space. "I admit to being Clive Jardine, an honest businessman who values his privacy. You can scorn my success if you wish, but selling opium is not illegal. I didn't see any of you refusing to accept the allowances and house Horatio Glanville gave you. Uncle Arthur was a disgrace to the Glanville name, but at least he acted true to his beliefs in ridding himself of what he considered tainted money. I loathed his actions in squandering our inheritance, but I did not kill Uncle Arthur. Nor did I kill his cook."

Sid walked towards the door, his chin elevated to effect a dignified withdrawal from the room. "And if any of you repeat the slander that I am a murderer, you will find yourself torn apart by a pack of vicious lawyers before you can take another breath."

Charlie stepped in front of Sid. "I'm not finished yet, Sidney Tucker. Of the three people who had access to the sword-cane, only you could have stabbed Mrs Seaton."

Sid glared at him under hooded eyelids. "And why is that, Mr Pyke?"

"Because the killer got into Mrs Seaton's second storey room at Lavender House using a ladder stolen from a neighbouring house. Mrs Tucker is not strong enough to lift a long ladder and her alibi has now been confirmed by her friend's servants. Your brother Bert was in North Dunedin at the time of her death. That leaves you, Sid."

"Is that all you have? My lawyers will laugh in your face. My assistant has vouched for my presence at my work premises. He is vastly more trustworthy than Bert's drinking pals, even on the rare occasions they are sober."

"I don't doubt it, but Bert was seen by witnesses other than friends."

"And my assistant has sworn I was at my business premises at quarter past eleven." Sid didn't so much as blink.

"I believe him," Charlie said. "That is, I believe your assistant saw the hands on the clock pointing to quarter past eleven. However, putting the hands back by as little as a quarter of an hour would give you an alibi, wouldn't it, Sid? A simple trick. Little more than a moment's work to change the time."

"A fanciful assertion, Mr Pyke. Where's your proof?"

Charlie held Sid's gaze. "I visited your shop late on Monday afternoon and wondered why your assistant was closing early. We had just come from the DIC store and they were not preparing to close."

Sid remained unmoved. "If there are no customers, we often close a few minutes early. What of it?"

"Ah, but it wasn't early, according to the clock in your shop. I checked the time on it myself, worried that I would be late for a family dinner. However, I thought little of it at the time, as I was busy contemplating the discrepancy between the small number of customers in your appointment book and the obvious wealth you display. A minor oversight on your part, Sid, but you really ought to have put the clock hands back to the correct time."

A hint of triumph sparked in Sid's eyes. "I assure you, Mr Pyke, if the police go to my business premises, they will find the clock is set to the correct time. Now, kindly get out of my way. I am leaving."

The certainty with which Sid met his challenge convinced Charlie that Sid had remembered to set the clock back, belatedly. It would be Charlie's impression that the time seemed wrong against Sid's assertion that he hadn't altered the clock. The weight of evidence against Sid was compelling, but not entirely beyond reasonable doubt.

Charlie turned to Grace to see if she could pull any more rabbits out of her hat. Her lips curved into a slow smile. Grace tipped her head at her great-aunt.

"Hold your horses, Mr Tucker." Anne Macmillan's voice might have the quiver of age about it, but the force of her tone could have stopped a cavalry charge. Anne dangled an old pair of black gloves in her arthritic fingers. "We found these at your house, Mr Sidney Tucker. I see from your expression that you thought you had disposed of them. Unfortunately for you, your highly efficient maid found them before the pile of rubbish was thrown onto the refuse cart."

"Being a poor lass, she thought she could clean them and use them," Mrs Brown said. "Lovely soft leather. I don't blame her. She felt a little guilty about taking them, but I told her it was not stealing when her employer had gone to such lengths to discard them."

Anne turned the gloves over. "All it would take is a bit of elbow-grease to get rid of these paint marks."

Grace reached for the incriminating gloves. "Well, well, look at that. The same colour as the paint slopped on the ladder used in the murder of Mrs Seaton. The gloves reek of turpentine too. Look, you can even see traces of a bloodstain, right across the embroidered label with your name on it, Sidney."

Sid tried to make a break for the exit, but he might sooner have fought against a regiment of the East India Company. Charlie stood in front of the door, flanked by his father, Alistair Stewart and Detective Inspector Wallace, forming a wall of constabulary muscle. The rest of the Southern Investigations team fanned out alongside them, their expressions triumphant.

Meanwhile, Detective Sergeant Declan Kelly had his hands full, preventing a furious Bert Tucker from attacking his brother. Despite Bert's flailing fists, Declan Kelly wore an ear-to-ear grin, as well he might after the successful conclusion of his first murder case. A double murder at that.

An Unexpected Journey

Grace and Charlie exited the police station to an exhilarating sense of freedom, now that their part in the investigation was over. They had deposited the evidence and provided written statements with swift efficiency. Sidney Tucker, also known as Clive Jardine, would be charged with both murders, and dealt with accordingly.

The police search team had discovered the records of Clive Jardine's business in the back room of Sidney's tailoring shop. Wallace was as happy as a bloodhound in a butchery. He even cracked a smile as he issued orders for all available men to round up everyone associated with the Jardine enterprise. Declan Kelly assured Charlie and Grace that he would have the police keep an eye out for men with puncture wounds in the shape of rose thorns.

They celebrated their freedom by calling on Molly and Rory Ravenwood on the way home. Grace had tears in her eyes by the time they left. She told herself it was the joy of seeing the proud parents and the honour of being asked to be godparents, and nothing to do with the way Charlie had looked when the adorable little bundle named Jessica Grace Ravenwood was cradled in his arms.

By the time they reached their own home, Grace felt as if the weight of the world had lifted from her shoulders.

Charlie opened the gate for her. "Home, sweet home, at last. I was worried you and the rest of the team hadn't found enough to convict Sid. You certainly know how to keep a man on his toes, Grace."

Grace didn't bother to conceal her smirk. "Now that the investigation is over, I'm more concerned with keeping a certain man on his back."

Charlie swept her off her feet and made haste for the door. He tripped over an unexpected pile of trunks in the hallway, almost sending his beloved sprawling. Another trip to the hospital was the last thing they needed right now. "Hello? Anyone home?"

"In here."

The Southern Investigations team was in the drawing room, sipping champagne despite the early hour. Mrs Brown, miracle worker that she was, had rustled up cheese rolls and other delicacies to stave off the hunger pangs forged by the combination of stress and excitement. Charlie was pleased to see that Mrs Brown had a glass in her hand, celebrating the case she had helped to solve with the rest of the team.

Sergeant Pyke poured champagne for his son and daughter-in-law.

Charlie raised his glass. "One killer and drug dealer safely behind bars in record time, thanks to a brilliant team of investigators."

The team let out a cheer and raised their glasses.

Grace tipped the bubbles back in a single gulp and held her glass out for more. "I'm relieved it's over. Charlie and I could use a break from investigating. In fact, I'm sure we all could."

"I'll drink to that, Grace," Anne said. "And to the success of Arthur Glanville's charitable foundation. Goodness knows the need is there, human nature being what it is. It'll be a fine day when we can replace opium and morphine with an effective painkiller that does not cause addiction."

"I've heard a wonderful new drug has been developed," Doctor Penrose said. "Better than morphine, but not at all addictive. They're calling it Heroin."

Anne pursed her lips. "Hmph. I'll believe that when I see it with my own sceptical old eyes."

"Did anyone have a chance to talk to Henrietta Tucker?" Grace asked.

"I did," Lily said. "The poor girl was in a state of collapse when she found out her brother Sid was responsible for her uncle's death. Doctor Johnstone, I am pleased to say, stood by her. Nothing like the challenge of a murderous relation to either destroy or strengthen a relationship."

Charlie was eager to draw the conversation away from crime. "Are they your trunks in the hall, Doctor and Mrs Penrose? I'm sorry you have to leave so soon, and most grateful you came all the way from Wellington for our wedding. I'm afraid I haven't been able to give your daughter the wedding of her dreams, or you the holiday you deserved."

Mrs Penrose chuckled. "I suspect Grace got exactly the wedding she wanted. Dull convention has never been my darling daughter's forte. As for us, we have had a marvellous break from our usual routine. This detective lark is really quite fascinating."

"As for the trunks, they are your wedding present," Doctor Penrose said. "Come and see."

Mrs Penrose pointed to the trunk with a curly GPP monogram on the lid. "This is yours, Grace. We took the liberty of filling it with new clothes and other necessities, fitting your new station as a respectable married woman. Fortunately, we had your measurements for the wedding gown, so everything is tailor made."

Grace eyed the trunk nervously. Had her mother brought her pretty, ladylike gowns with horrible ruffles and itchy lace? Or the sombre clothes of a married woman who no longer needs to impress eligible young men? Grace could hardly blame her mother for the latter, as her own choice rarely deviated from functional but boring grey skirts and white shirtwaists. With luck, her mother had purchased a new evening gown, since Grace's favourite gown was beyond repair.

Mrs Penrose gestured for her to open the trunk. "Honestly, Grace, your alarm is uncalled for. Do you think I don't know my own daughter by now?"

Grace opened the trunk and gasped. The first thing to strike her was the array of beautiful rich colours in exactly the shades and fabrics she loved, but couldn't afford. She delved through the contents, admiring the quality and simplicity of the designs. Not an inch of scratchy lace nor a ruffle in sight. Not only gowns, but soft gloves, a smart but practical hat, silky underclothes, and a garment Grace has been longing for – one of the new ladies' outfits intended for cycling or riding, which looked like a normal skirt, but which cleverly unhooked to form wide-legged trousers.

Grace's mother looked on with satisfaction at her daughter's delight. "I suspect you will need clothes suitable for riding soon enough. You won't want to slow your husband down by needing a carriage."

Grace drew her mother and father into a tight embrace. "I cannot express how grateful I am. Everything is absolutely perfect. I won't know myself when I look in the mirror. My acquaintances will walk past me in the street."

"Your turn, Charlie." Lily nudged her nephew. "Alistair insisted you should have proper clothes of your own after all these years of raiding Gordon Macmillan's wardrobe."

"Which he has been more than welcome to do," Anne said. "My Gordon doted on Grace. He'd have been proud of what you two have achieved."

Charlie knelt by the trunk.

"Go on, Charlie. Open it." Alistair draped an arm around Lily's shoulders. "As the more famous partner of our detective agency, you have a standard to keep up."

"Infamous, more like." Charlie opened his trunk, emitting a whimper of delight as he rifled through the stack of neatly pressed shirts and trousers, and a tailor-made coat. "I don't know what to say, except thank you." He pulled Lily and Alister into a bear hug, squashing the air from their lungs.

Jasmine Pyke looked on with a mischievous glint in her eyes. "I suggest you leave your trunk packed, Charlie. You and Grace are leaving first thing tomorrow morning, coming with us back to Central Otago. Your father and I have hired you a pretty cottage in Clyde, so you can have a chance to enjoy the start of your married life in peace."

"Out of all possible reach of villainy," Thomas Pyke said. "You can see why we were all in such a hurry to solve the case."

"I will be here to take over any investigations," Alistair said, "and Grace has two weeks before she starts medical school again. It's about time you two had a break away from murder and mayhem after a busy year."

Jasmine Pyke looked at Charlie and Grace uncertainly. "You are pleased, I hope?"

Charlie exchanged a glance with Grace. "Pleased? Ma, we're completely overwhelmed, but also overjoyed. A break away is exactly what the doctor ordered."

Grace mumbled her agreement through a blur of tears as she embraced her parents-in-law.

Doctor Penrose smiled. "You won't know what to do with yourselves with two weeks away from medicine and crime."

"I suspect they will, George," Jasmine said. "But if they do get bored, the countryside is beautiful and we would welcome the opportunity to get to know Grace better. Thomas has a lifetime of tales to tell."

"I'm looking forward to finding out about the mysteries of Charlie's family history," Grace flicked her eyes at Charlie and gave him a ghost of a smile. "Just what every honeymoon needs, a little mystery to stimulate the mind."

Charlie nodded, but his thoughts drifted to the delightfully stimulating effects of their shared passion for detection. He put his arm around his wife, thanking his lucky stars that fate had brought them together. "After all, we cannot get into any trouble recalling old family stories, can we, my love?"

Read On

In Book 7 of the Penrose and Pyke Mystery series, **Murder Over Gold**, Penrose and Pyke cannot resist the lure of an unsolved mystery while on their honeymoon.

With a fortune in gold still missing from the most infamous robbery in Central Otago history, the stakes are high. Watchful eyes follow their every move, convinced the Pyke family know more than they are telling about the missing gold. The town is filled with men desperate for the riches that have eluded them after years of toil on the goldfields. And, most dangerous of all, men desperate to prevent the truth being revealed. The serenity of Grace and Charlie's honeymoon is about to be shattered.

Thank You

Thank you for reading this story. If you enjoyed it, I would be very grateful if you would leave a rating or review to help other readers discover it.

Find out about other books and sign up for notifications of new releases at https://RosePascoe.com.

Historical Notes

This story and the characters in it are fictional. However, elements of the story are based on historical fact.

Chinese gold miners flocked to Central Otago and other parts of New Zealand during the gold rush of the 1860s, hoping to make a fortune to send home to their families in China. The addiction to opium smoking travelled with these men from their homeland, thanks to the flooding of China (and Canton in particular) with opium by British and other foreign traders in the preceding decades.

Much of the opium came via Calcutta, in Bengal, which was a stronghold of the East India Company. The traders exchanged opium for valuable commodities like tea, porcelain, and silk in Canton. British traders like William Jardine made fortunes from the opium trade, despite the opposition of the Chinese authorities. The escalating dispute led to the Opium Wars of the mid-nineteenth century. Hong Kong was born from the conflict as a base for the traders.

The astonishing might of the East India Company is not exaggerated in the story. Established in 1600, it gradually developed a stranglehold on global trade to the East Indies (India and Southeast Asia) and beyond, until the company was finally brought to heel in 1874. With an army of soldiers and a horde of administrators and traders, the East India Company effectively ruled parts of India and accounted for half the world's trade. Company men became rich, while stockholders became fabulously wealthy.

Robert Clive ("Clive of India") got his start in the East India Company and found his calling under arms, effectively becoming the ruler of Bengal after his military successes. He made a colossal fortune for himself and the East India Company, gained a knighthood, and fended off accusations of corruption. The local population was not so lucky, as his administrative failures were said to have contributed to the catastrophic Bengal famine of 1769–1773, with the loss of millions of lives.

Opium, derived from the opium poppy, has a history dating back millennia. As a painkiller, opium was unmatched for centuries. Unfortunately, opium use became so normalised it was added to patent medicines for innumerable ailments, including cough syrups for children. Morphine and, later, heroin were derived from opium. Modern synthetic opioids are at the heart of the current crisis in opioid abuse. As always, there are two sides to the coin. A drug that did enormous good also caused terrible harm.

The story of opium is brilliantly told by Lucy Inglis in *Milk of Paradise: A History of Opium* (Macmillan, 2018). I cannot recommend this book highly enough for its insight into how opium influenced the history of the world through trade, politics, medicine, and addiction.

Peter Butler's *Opium and Gold: A History of the Chinese Goldminers in New Zealand* (Alister Taylor, 1977) provided background on Chinese immigrants and the description of an opium den in Dunedin.

Acknowledgements

A huge thank you to my fabulous beta readers – Mary, Jenny, Kathy and Ross – whose enthusiasm is very much appreciated, as always.

About the author

Rose Pascoe writes historical mysteries with a dash of romance, when she isn't plotting real-life adventures. She lives in beautiful New Zealand, land of beaches and mountains, where long walks provide the perfect conditions for dreaming up plots and fickle weather provides the incentive to sit down and write. After a career in health, justice and social research, her passion is for stories set against a backdrop of social justice. Her heroines are ordinary women, who meet the challenges thrown at them with determination, ingenuity, courage, and humour.

Visit her at: https://RosePascoe.com

9 781991 181398